Born and brough
now live in Swinc
two children were
when she returned to work where she eventually became a
head teacher. She now teaches Creative Writing plus Tai Chi
and Yoga.

For more information, see

www.judithcranswick.co.uk

Also by Judith Cranswick

ALL IN THE MIND
WATCHER IN THE SHADOWS

BLOOD ON THE BULB FIELDS

To Sandra

Judith Cranswick

Best wishes

Judith Cranswick

ANTONY ROWE
PUBLISHING

© Judith Cranswick 2009

Printed and bound by CPI Antony Rowe, Eastbourne

The Bulb Fields in Bloom Tour

Join us for a week of colour and culture and enjoy a magical discovery of Dutch delights. Admire the spectacular displays of spring bulbs in the renowned horticultural extravaganza that is Keukenhof Park. Explore the picturesque town of Delft celebrated for its pottery; The Hague, Holland's seat of government and vibrant Amsterdam, city of canals, cobbled streets, famous for its diamonds, floating flower market and home to over fifty museums.

Throughout your holiday, your Tour Manager will enhance your appreciation of the area with talks and guided walks and be on hand to deal with any difficulties.

Super Sun Executive Travel
Voted Britain's most popular luxury coach company

The Bulb Fields in Bloom Passenger List *

Tour Manager .... Mrs Fiona Mason
Driver .... Mr Winston Taylor

Mr	Tim	Brooke	30s Small, weedy, bit intense
Mrs	Jane	Brooke	Bit subdued, defers to husband much of time
Mr	Edward	Collins	Mr Grumpy – could be real pain keen photographer
Mrs	Joyce	Collins	Large lady, tight curls, friendly
Mr	Kevin	Dobson	} late 40s Friends with Smiths – don't really mix
Mrs	Tricia	Dobson	
Miss	Vera	Palmer	dotty – one to watch, - might get lost
Ms	Eileen	Finch	blonde – v self-assured and capable - teacher
Miss	Nesta	Griffin	quiet - 40s? wears long peasant skirts - Librarian
Miss	Phyllis	Harvey	} elderly pleasant , friendly
Miss	Cynthia	Harvey	sisters the quiet one - blue rinse perm
Mr	Felix	Karpinski	Small, ferity, Brummie accent
Mrs	Rozalia	Karpinska	doesn't seem to understand much English
Mr	Andrew	Killigan	Attractive and knows it! A real charmer
Mr	Gerald	Lee	50s dark hair, grey beard
Mrs	Yvonne	Lee	Ghastly Overhennaed hair – always on her mobile!
Mrs	Elizabeth	Oppenheimer	American – never stops complaining!!!
Miss	Deirdre	Oppenheimer	loud hee-haw laugh
Mrs	Margery	Pettigrew	80s Lovely old dear – friendly, always smiling
Major	Cyril	Rawlings	bald, moustache
Mrs	Lavinia	Rawlings	Plumy voice but friendly
Mr	Gordon	Shuttleworth	nice couple - full of Yorkshire friendliness
Mrs	Barbara	Shuttleworth	- motherly
Mr	Ian	Smith	} Friends with Dobsons
Mrs	Sue	Smith	
Mr	Henry	Unsworth	
Mr	Simon	Wick	Pony tail! Real know-it-all
Mrs	Iris	Wick	Shy, insignificant – skinny like her husband

* with Fiona's added comments

Friday, 27th April

A feeder coach will collect you from your chosen departure point and bring you to Dover where you will transfer to our luxury coach. After a lunchtime ferry crossing to Calais, we will drive to the comfortable family-run, 5-star Hotel Vermeer, just north of The Hague, for a two-night stay.

Super Sun Executive Travel

One

Fiona Mason watched the departing taxi disappear behind the port buildings and bit her lip.

Oh Bill, what have I let myself in for?

Too late for doubts now. She could already see the first of the white Super Sun coaches with its distinctive yellow stripe in the queue of traffic slowly wending its way down the steep hill road to the port gates.

It had seemed such a good idea at the time. A chance to travel and earn some pocket money at the same time. At least, that was what she'd told the family and friends urging her to get out and make a new life for herself. Of course, what they'd meant by finding herself a little job was a couple of days a week in the local Oxfam shop or hospital visiting, not gallivanting off to foreign parts for weeks at a time. Heavens knows, there'd been little chance of doing that over the last nine years. Besides, she had to get away. Without Bill, the bungalow had lost its warmth; it had become more of a prison than a home.

Time to ignore that nagging inner voice trying to tell her that it would all be too much. Of course she could cope! What could go wrong?

She tucked away the flapping ends of the yellow scarf under the lapels of her smart navy uniform, straightened her shoulders, pulled up the handle on her brand-new suitcase and trundled it towards the check-in kiosk.

Another coach pulled into one of the marked bays in the arrivals area. Perhaps the fat man would be on this one. All this waiting was making him nervous.

At last, he spotted the stout figure plodding across the concourse. Still he hung back. To have Harry clock him too soon would make his plan more difficult. Best to wait till he could get the man on his own.

Most people were now piling into the café during the long wait for the luggage to be unloaded and reassigned to the correct coach. Others joined those sitting outside in the feeble sunshine at the picnic tables alongside the main building. Harry, predictable as ever, was already making his way round the back. He would want a bit of fresh air away from the crowds; somewhere he could take a few quick nips from that flask of his without being seen. It would not look good for his fellow travellers to see him knocking back the single malt before lunch. Not that the man was an habitual drinker. Far from it. It was his heart that was the problem not his liver. But Harry was no sailor and would need a little something to steady his nerves before the crossing. Best to give him a few moments. Time to light up one of those smelly Turkish things that he smoked to disguise the alcohol on his breath.

He knew all Harry's little habits and phobias. Knew that by now the very thought of getting on the ferry was making the fat man feel ill. He'd known Harry since their days at Pinetrees Comprehensive. Not that they'd been best buddies – far from it – nor had they kept in touch. Quite by chance, they'd bumped into each other a couple of years back when his luck had hit rock bottom. By contrast, Harry was doing very well for himself with a lucrative little sideline involving frequent trips to the Continent. Harry had promised to talk to someone about putting some work his way and for once, the man had come up trumps.

'Hi there, Harry. Thought it must be you.'

'Curly, my old mate! Long time no see.'

Did he have to call him by that stupid schoolboy nickname? Still it wouldn't do to show his irritation. Not if he wanted to keep on the man's good side.

A beaming smile lit up the fat man's face. 'Didn't realize there'd be three of us on the job. That's great. Be like old times, us working together again.'

'You know the boss. Jenks is playing things close to his chest after all the recent troubles. Bit of a surprise seeing you here though. Is this the man who swore nothing would induce him set foot on a boat ever again?'

'Yeah, well. Jenks can be pretty persuasive especially with the Arabs breathing down his neck. Called me less than a week ago. Said it was an emergency. You heard about that little caper that went wrong last month? One of 'em lost his nerve at the last minute and they had to ditch the haul. Lucky not to get arrested.' He took a long drag on his cigarette. 'Coming on top of the previous fiasco, the Arabs demanded Jenks get it sorted fast or they'd find a new dealer. Which is why the boss has pulled yours truly out of retirement. Needed someone he could trust. Probably best not to enquire what happened to the previous pair, eh?'

Curly joined in the laughter. Not that there'd been anything remotely funny about what had happened, as well he knew. He'd been there! Someone had tipped off Customs and the whole coach party was being searched. There'd had no choice but to dump the lot in the nearest waste bin. Jenks had gone ballistic when he heard and had fired the two of them on the spot.

'The boss is convinced someone's out to sabotage his whole operation.' Harry dropped his dog end and ground it out with his heel. 'At one stage, there was talk of him cancelling his trip to America for his daughter's wedding this weekend. It was only when his sister agreed to stay and keep a beady eye on things that he was persuaded to go at all. You ever met the lovely Mavis?'

'No.'

'Seems like a pussy cat when you first meet her, but not a lady to be crossed, so I hear. Doesn't take prisoners so no slip ups on this one or the three of us might end up as food for the fishes.'

Curly's mind was racing. Should he abandon his plan? He'd thought that with Jenks over in California he was safe as no one else would know he'd been thrown off the job, but what if this Mavis woman had been fully briefed? Did she know that all the plans had been changed at the last minute? That Harry had been brought in as his replacement not just as an addition to the team.

No. Things had gone too far. He had to risk it. There was no way he would give up the good life, go back to working every hour there was for a pittance. Not without a fight. He'd pleaded with Jenks to let him do one more job to prove his worth, but the boss had been adamant. Claimed there was too high a risk he might be recognized after the last mess-up.

The fat man was still rabbiting on, but the sudden elbow in his ribs brought him back from raking over old grievances. 'When we get to Amsterdam, what say we slip away from the rest of the party and have a naughty night out in the Red Light District?'

He gave a weak smile. 'Afraid you'll have to count me out. Brought the wife with me. Promised her a bit of a holiday.'

'Shame.'

A sudden gust sent a paper cup rattling between them from the nearby pile of rubbish. 'Hell's bloody teeth. Now the wind's getting up. The last thing I need is a choppy crossing.'

'I'd better be getting back or the wife will come looking for me. She suffers from your problem too. Gets as sick as a dog the moment she sees the boat, but she's found these fantastic pills. Work a treat. Would you like a couple?'

'Got to be careful what I take with this dodgy ticker of mine,' Harry said doubtfully. 'Had one warning already, you know.'

'These are perfectly safe. Herbal. Natural ingredients.' He held out the small plastic drum with its gaudy green health stores label.

'Bloody hell! There're big enough,' laughed Harry as he shook them out onto his palm.

'Yeah. You'll need something to swill 'em down with. I've some juice in my hand luggage.' He rummaged in his bag and pulled out a small carton.

Harry stared dubiously at the tablets for a moment before gulping them down. He pulled a face then waddled over to the dustbins to throw the empty juice carton into one of the boxes of rubbish piled up alongside.

'Must go. The missus'll be wondering where I've got to. See you later.'

'Bye, Curly and thanks for that.'

He heard the choking cry before he reached the corner. The slow smile of satisfaction turned to horror when he heard the crash of the dustbin toppling over and turned to see Harry prostrate on the ground. Eyes already fixed and staring.

Everything was descending into chaos. Fiona watched the new arrivals pushing down the narrow aisle trying to get past those still searching for a space to put their hand luggage on the rack above. There was not a great deal of goodwill around.

There was even less when a broad, burly, red-faced man armed with an air flight holdall, camera bag, tripod and something that looked like a laptop case, bulldozed his way through, to the considerable annoyance of those sitting in the aisle seats.

'Watch it! You nearly had my eye out.' Now he'd upset the Major.

Fiona tried to ignore the choice language that could clearly be heard above the general hubbub and descended the steps back outside armed with her clipboard. Let them sort it out for themselves. They would probably turn out to be pleasant enough people when she got to know them. It was just tired-ness that was making them irritable. Some had travelled through the night to get here. She checked through the pas-senger list. Only one more person to come. With luck, they would soon be on their way and a little of the holiday spirit might seep back into the disgruntled party.

'How much longer are they are they planning on keeping us here? If we'd known we were gonna to have to sit cooped up waiting like this we could've gone and gotten ourselves a coffee.'

Fiona pretended she hadn't heard the penetrating American drawl from behind and continued to study her paperwork. The woman hadn't stopped complaining since she'd boarded the coach and discovered that the front seats had already been taken. It didn't bode well for the rest of the trip. Fiona stole a glance at her watch. Where had the man got to? The other Super Sun coaches had already picked up their new complement of passengers and had long since disappeared. Soon it wouldn't be only Mrs Oppenheimer getting restless. Fiona scanned the now empty coach transfer area but there was no sign of the tardy Mr Unsworth. Winston had checked his case from the feeder coach so the man must be around somewhere.

The disgruntled mutterings from behind were growing. She'd have to do something. Fixing a broad smile on her face, she picked up the microphone and turned to face her charges for the next seven days.

'On behalf of Super Sun Executive Travel, welcome onboard. I'm Fiona, your tour manager, and I'll be with you throughout our Bulb Fields in Bloom Tour. This is Winston, our driver, who'll be taking care of us all.'

The big black man turned in his seat and gave a cheery wave. There were a few less than hearty cries of, 'Hi, Winston,' from the back of the coach.

'We're really lucky to have him because he's Super Sun's top driver.' The only response was a sea of blank faces. 'As soon as our last passenger comes onboard we'll be off.'

Sensing her increasing nervousness, Winston put a reassuring hand on her arm. 'Plenty o' time. No worries,' he said quietly, his friendly face breaking into an infectious smile.

It didn't stop the butterflies cavorting madly in Fiona's stomach. Hardly the best of starts to her new job. After over thirty years of bringing up the boys and looking after Bill, the prospect of coming back to work was nerve-wracking enough without things going wrong before the trip had even started. Please don't let this be a disaster, she pleaded silently to some higher power. At this rate, she was going to need all the help she could get.

'Would you like me to go and check the gents?'

'You're an angel, Winston.'

With a deep throaty chuckle, Winston climbed down from coach and strolled over to the end of the long low building.

'I know many of you have been travelling for some time and must be exhausted, but I would like to run through a few things before we leave.'

By the time she'd told them about the boarding arrangements and explained how to adjust the air-conditioning and the reclining seats and pointed out the fold down leg rests, Winston was making his way across the concourse back to the coach. Without Mr Unsworth.

Five minutes later, Fiona had rung all eight Super Sun coaches to check that the man hadn't boarded the wrong one by mistake. Hardly likely as each destination was clearly indicated on the windscreen and the tour managers would have checked their lists just as she had done, but it had been worth a try.

Winston was outside delving into the luggage areas under the coach to double check that Mr Unsworth's case had been loaded and that he'd not ticked it off by mistake. Unable to sit still, Fiona clambered down to join him.

'While you're doing that I'll go and have another look around.'

The café and the shop were both empty. Even the staff had disappeared into the nether regions for a well-earned break in the lull before the frenetic spate of activity when the next wave of coaches arrived. Fiona walked up and down the aisles between the stands of newspapers, paperbacks and assorted sweets. She asked the solitary spotty youth left stacking the depleted confectionary shelves, but he had seen no one hanging around. According to him, the shop had been empty for the last quarter of an hour.

Beyond the café and shop were the tiny port offices of a couple of the larger tour companies, now closed, and one or two other unidentified offices none of which showed any sign of activity. Fiona reached the end of the building and walked round to the far side. Perhaps Mr Unsworth was a smoker and had hidden himself round the back out of sight.

At first glance, the area looked deserted. Fiona gave a sigh. Perhaps he was tucked into a doorway. She was so busy trying to work out what to do next that she didn't see it at first.

Although, given the amount of rubbish piled up by one of the rear doors, that was hardly surprising. It wasn't until she was within a few yards of the small dark object poking out from behind an overturned dustbin that she was able to make it out. A shoe! A well-polished, dark-brown brogue pointing sky-wards.

Moving closer, she could see the tan corduroy trousers mired at the knee by a growing reddish brown stain. She gasped then realised it was only the remains of the sauce in the discarded polystyrene fast-food container that had escaped from a burst bin liner beneath. Apprehensively, she edged round the second dustbin. A portly, middle-aged man lay sprawled on top of bulging carrier bags and collapsed cardboard boxes; one leg bent beneath the other, his shoulders slumped against the wall, head lolling to one side, a hand clutching at his chest. The un-blinking, startled eyes stared up at her. Even before she felt for his pulse, she knew he was dead.

Two

The port police arrived within minutes of her call, not that there was much she could tell them.

'You need a stiff drink, sweetheart.' Winston put a comforting arm around her shoulder.

Fiona shook her head. 'It was a shock of course, but I'll be fine.'

Winston looked as though he was about to argue, but she forestalled him. 'It may be a good few years ago now, but I was a nurse. I can cope.' The reassurance was as much for her as it was for the driver. Struggling to come to terms with losing Bill was bad enough without stumbling across a dead body.

'You go. Leave everyt'in' to me.'

She gladly accepted Winston's offer. The last thing she needed right now was to have wait around until the ambulance arrived.

There were several irate-looking passengers waiting for an explanation for the delay when Fiona returned to the coach.

'I'm afraid our missing passenger has been taken ill and won't be able to join us. Winston is talking to the port authorities, but as soon as he comes back, we'll drive round to the ferry.' There was no point in upsetting everyone by telling them the whole truth.

A barrage of questions was fired at her from all directions. By the time she had reassured them that this would cause no delay to the start of their holiday, Winston had returned accompanied by a man in uniform.

There was another short hold-up as Winston handed over Mr Unsworth's luggage to the port authority officer before he climbed up into the driver's seat.

16

'About time too,' came a male voice from several rows back loud enough for the whole coach to hear. Despite several tuts of disapproval at the lack of sensitivity, Edward Collins – the miserable-looking, beefy man who had caused such a disturbance with all his luggage earlier – was by no means the only one who appeared to have little sympathy for their afflicted fellow traveller. Amazing how quickly you learnt to spot the potential troublemakers.

'Right now, everyone.' Mustering a jaunty tone that she did not feel, Fiona continued, 'We're on our way. You can all settle back and relax. If you have any questions at all, I'm here for you.'

Fiona hardly had time to push down her tip-up seat in the stairwell before Mrs Oppenheimer's strident nasal whine started up again. 'Not a good start. I just knew it was a mistake to let the company fob us off with this substitute tour when they had to cancel our Rhine and Moselle cruise.'

The unexpected demise of Mr Unsworth prompted a flurry of phone calls.

Fiona had already informed the Super Sun head office before returning to the coach. The authorities would now be able to liaise with them to sort out the man's details and inform the next of kin. There was nothing more she could do for him, she told herself firmly. Best to put it all behind her and concentrate on the job in hand.

Before the coach had even driven the three hundred yards from the coach transfer area to join the long queue for the Calais ferry, Fiona could hear one of the passengers on her mobile regaling her daughter with what had happened.

'The poor man was driven off in an ambulance not five minutes ago... We don't know exactly what's happened, but he obviously won't be joining us now... Oh no. We're about to get on the ferry ... I'll call again when we get to our hotel this evening. Give my love to the children.'

Two other phone calls had to wait until the callers could ensure that there was no one around to overhear their conversation.

'I need to speak to Jenks.'

'No can do. The boss is on his way out. He's leaving for the airport right now.'

'Tell him it's urgent. Unsworth's out of the picture. He's been carted off to the hospital. What does he want me to do? Abandon the job?'

There was a short pause at the other end of the line while the news was passed on. After a few choice expletives and mutterings about sabotage clearly audible in the background, the same harsh voice was back on the line. 'Boss says to handle it.'

'What on my own? Without a backup!' It was hard to keep the panic from his voice.

Jenks launched into another tirade of swearing and cursing. Eventually a much sanitized and abbreviated message was relayed, 'It's too late to pull out now and the boss says not to worry, he's got it covered.'

With all its implied threat, Jenks's parting instruction – 'And tell him not to foul it up!' – could clearly be heard in the distance followed by the slam of the front door.

'You hear that?'

'Yeah.'

The line went dead.

A hundred yards away, beyond the ranks of vehicles, well out of earshot, a similar telephone conversation was taking place.

'It's Brooke. I need to speak to the Commander. It's urgent.'

Jenks was not the only top man who did not react too kindly on being disturbed unnecessarily, but this time the answering voice was as cultured and as devoid of emotion as the other had been coarse and full of invective. 'Is there a problem?'

'Yes, sir. It's Unsworth. The official story is that he's been taken ill and rushed off to hospital but the woman who found him came back with such a chalk white face, I wouldn't be surprised if he's dead. The ambulance has just left but there was no siren.'

'A suspicious death do you think?'

'Don't know, sir. They are letting us line up for the ferry and there's been no indication that it won't sail on time which would seem to suggest not. But there's something strange about all this. First we get an anonymous tip-off about the man and then he's suddenly taken ill before the ferry even sails!'

'I agree. It does appear a little too convenient. I think a few discreet enquiries are called for.'

'Do you want us to abandon the operation, sir?'

'Certainly not,' came the clipped retort. 'We may have lost our prime lead, but, assuming the information is correct, he would have had a partner. Moreover, it would appear that you might well now have a killer in the party. No doubt, all this will make matters more difficult, but I have every confidence in the two of you. I do not need to remind you how important this operation is. A great deal of money has been invested in it already and, if we fail, questions will be asked. At the highest level.' There was a pause. 'Jobs will be on the line.'

'Yes, sir. Thank you, sir.' As the line went dead, Brooke added to the empty air, 'So, no pressure then.'

Despite all her good intentions, Fiona found it difficult not to dwell on the unfortunate Henry Unsworth. Pulling herself back to the present, she realized she now had a more pressing problem. As they sat waiting at the back of seemingly endless ranks of cars, caravans, lorries and coaches, several of her passengers had decided to wander off. She got to her feet, anxiously looking about.

'Not to worry,' Winston's gentle West Indian drawl sounded softly in her ear. 'Let them stretch their legs for a bit. They can't go far. They soon come running back when cars start loadin', you see.'

Fiona flashed him a weak grin.

'You okay, sweetheart?'

'I'll be fine.' She looked up into the kindly, dark brown eyes. 'How could I possibly be anything else with you to look after me?'

'Das my girl. So, what make you decide to join the company?'

She knew that Winston was only trying to keep her mind from the dreadful scene she'd just discovered, but she was grateful for his concern nonetheless.

'A friend spotted the advertisement for tour managers in one of her magazines and she badgered me into applying.'

'Well tha's different,' he chuckled. 'Most folk say it's 'cause they love travellin'.'

'That too of course.'

Best not to admit that it that the real reason had more to do with getting away from all the people who wanted to run her life. It was amazing how many of them thought they knew what was best for her – urging her to join the Bereavement Group, serve on some committee or other or become a volunteer for some worthy cause. As if doing charity work or joining an evening class would fill the void that Bill had left, she thought bitterly.

'I never thought I'd be called for an interview. I was convinced the company would want young, enthusiastic dolly birds not an aging, grieving widow like me. And then when I realized I was going to have to stand up in front of two experienced reps plus seven other interviewees and give a presentation, I very nearly chickened out altogether. Believe me; no one was more surprised than I was when the company rang the next day offering me a job.'

'Now why wouldn't they? You gonna be a great tour manager.'

'I wish I had your confidence.'

'You doing fine. We gonnna make a grand team. Now let me fix your mirror. How's that now?'

'Perfect. Thanks, Winston. You're a treasure.'

Fiona had to admit she'd struck lucky with Winston. If the stories she'd heard from some of the experienced Super Sun reps were anything to go by, there were the odd grumpy drivers and one or two could be downright uncooperative on their off days. Winston had been kindness itself from the very start.

As Winston walked back down the aisle to check that the hand luggage had been safely stowed overhead, Fiona picked up the pile of passports she'd collected. At least while she was waiting she could look through them and try to put few faces to names. It was a trick she'd learnt shadowing the tour rep on her trip the previous weekend. It had only been an over-nighter to Paris but she had learnt more from Gloria on that brief outing than in the whole week's training in London. She couldn't quite see herself squealing, 'Sweetie time!' and bus-tling down the aisle handing out boiled sweets to all the pas-sengers as Gloria had done, but she had stocked up and a se-lection of mints, barley sugars and mixed fruits now lay in the bottom of the bag by her feet in readiness. Perhaps on the long drive up from Calais, they might help relieve the boredom of the journey and win her a few Brownie points.

Come loading time the inevitable happened.

'Why on earth are they letting all those rows go first? We were here long before those cars. I remember seeing that dreadful green camper van with all those noisy youngsters in the back arriving when we were waiting outside.'

'No need to worry. They won't get to France any quicker than us.' Winston's deep, resonant voice sounded a note of calm in the mounting frustration. 'The cars get loaded first 'cause they go up on the side ramps. When our turn come, we drive straight down the middle and be one of de first off at the other end.'

She had known Mrs Oppenheimer for less than an hour but at this rate, Fiona thought, I shall murder the wretched woman before we reach Holland.

Three

'As you know, there are several other Super Sun Coaches on-board so do make sure you come back to this one – Deck 5 by the red staircase – otherwise you could find yourselves being whisked off down to the Black Forest, Paris or even Rome and Sorrento.'

Curly sat in a daze, the tour manger's instructions making little impact on his consciousness. The realization of what he had done was only just beginning to sink in. Now he was a murderer. The stuff had only been meant to make the man feel ill, make him violently sick. Stop him getting onto the boat. Not cause a heart attack. How was he to know that the tablets would prove fatal? He'd been lucky to get away with it but best dump the rest of the stuff just in case.

No point in regrets. Desperate men, desperate measures. Besides, this job should have been his by rights! He had to get it back. Soon he'd have to find Unsworth's partner. Jenks had kept his plans secret and if Unsworth assumed that he was still on the team, there was a good chance that that Harry's partner wouldn't know that he'd been dropped either.

Fiona was relieved when a group of his fellow drivers came over to talk to Winston and she could make her excuses. It was thoughtful of him to offer to take her for a drink but, apart from the odd glass of wine with her meal, she rarely drank and she knew she would not feel comfortable in the smoky Drivers' Lounge. Besides, she'd revealed enough of herself already without having the man feel even more sorry for her. Best to spend the crossing getting to know some of her passengers.

Passing the duty free shop, Fiona heard a familiar voice emanating from within its recesses. Did the woman have to utter every word at full volume? Fiona hurried on. Being nice to Mrs Oppenheimer and her horsy-faced daughter was more than she could manage right now. Filled with guilt for not taking the opportunity to sweet-talk the woman who might respond better if she felt she were getting more personal attention, Fiona escaped into the cafeteria.

The place was busy and Fiona spotted several of her passengers who had teamed up together. That was something to be thankful for. Looking round for an empty table, she spotted another face she recognized.

'Mrs Pettigrew isn't it? May I join you?'

The elderly lady looked up from her magazine. The startled expression quickly changed into a wide friendly smile. 'Of course, dear. Do sit down. How clever of you to know my name already, but you must call me Margery.'

'Is this your first trip with Super Sun Tours?'

'Oh yes and I'm really looking forward to it, though I must confess I'm finding the travelling quite tiring.'

'Did you have an early start?'

'Six twenty this morning!'

'Oh dear,' Fiona commiserated.

'Those poor people who started in Exeter had to travel through the night, so I mustn't complain. I just kept thinking of all those wonderful pictures in the brochures and telling myself it will all be worth it when we get there. And these luxury class coaches really are very good aren't they? The seats are so comfy, just like on an aeroplane. I noticed the television screen; will we be having films as well?'

'I have a few DVDs lined up for later.'

'How splendid.' The round face broke into a radiant smile and she clapped her hands in girlish glee.

Once Margery had begun, it was impossible to get a word in. The poor old dear probably didn't get that many people to talk to these days. Fiona had almost finished her coffee when a man appeared at her elbow.

'May we join you? Seems half the passengers on the ship have decided to have a spot of lunch.'

'Please do, Major.' Fiona moved the remains of the tasteless vacuum-packed sandwich out of the way to let him put down the tray.

'Isn't she clever? Fiona knows everybody's name already,' Margery Pettigrew exclaimed as the new arrivals took their seats.

Fiona smiled. With his distinctive, bristly moustache, the Major was easily recognizable and the clipped tones left no doubt as to his military background.

The Major and his wife seemed a pleasant enough couple and were soon chatting away merrily. They were as enthusiastic about seeing the bulbs as Margery Pettigrew.

'One never tires of seeing Keukenhof, does one?'

'So you've been before, Major?'

It was his wife who replied. 'Cyril often pops over to Holland on business, don't you, dear?'

'Well yes,' he said quickly, 'which is why it's so nice to just sit back and leave all the organizing to someone else for a change.'

As the Major must be well in to his seventies, Fiona wondered what sort of business he might be involved in, but before she could ask, Marjory cut in, 'Are you a keen gardener, Major?'

'Well, I potter a bit, you know. Digging and mowing the lawns and whatnot, but I leave all the creative stuff to the wife. Lavinia's the one with green fingers. Wins prizes at the regional Flower Festival every year.'

'Cyril is being modest. He looks after the vegetable garden and you are very good with roses, aren't you, dear.' Lavinia Rawlings' voice was even more plumy than that of her husband although, even if she generally mixed with the county set, she appeared happy enough to rub shoulders with the other passengers.

After ten minutes or so, with a plea that she wanted to get up on deck for a breath of fresh air before they docked, Fiona managed to escape and left the three of them to their discussion about black spot and the best ways of getting rid of greenfly.

Fiona was not the only one to pore over the Super Sun "Bulb Fields in Bloom" passenger list. Unlike the brief, scribbled notes that Fiona had added to her copy as an aide memoir, this one had only question marks against five of the names. Huddled over the small table in a dark corner of the lower deck, two people sat staring at the list, lost in thought.

'Do you really think these late bookings are relevant? ' Jane gave a puzzled frown. 'Even if the Commander is right about Unsworth having a partner, it doesn't mean they both signed up at the same time.'

'Possibly, but it's as good a starting place as any, unless of course you noticed any of the passengers looking worried when Unsworth failed to make an appearance?'

She shook her head pretending to take the facetious comment at face value.

Tim lapsed back into silence. The constant clicking of the top of his ballpoint pen was beginning to get on her nerves. 'Of course, he could always have been working with one of the Super Sun staff.'

'But the tour manager and the driver have been thoroughly checked out,' she said with a frown. 'Winston Taylor has been with the company for seven years. There's never been any suggestion of anything untoward on his earlier trips.'

'But it doesn't rule him out as a new recruit. The gang must know we're closing in on them so they daren't risk using the same couriers too often. In which case, it would make sense to bring in a fresh face. And the tour manger is new.'

'Yes but Fiona Mason only took over at a few days notice. The woman she replaced was rushed to hospital with appendicitis so that can't have been prearranged.'

Tim seemed unwilling to let go of the idea and flicked open his palmtop and switched it on. 'Says here Mrs Fiona Mason is 54 and newly widowed. Housewife and mum. Two children, both grown up and left home and she's spent the last nine years nursing her terminally ill husband. Seems genuine enough,' he admitted ruefully. 'We'll have to see how things pan out but I still put my money on it being one of the women.

It's so much easier for them to alter their appearance and pass through security without being recognized.'

They both looked at the passenger list again.

'I did manage to chat to Ms Finch in the Ladies earlier. Can't work out if there's a husband lurking away in the background or not. From the caustic comments about useless men, its odds on she's divorced. She teaches German at a City Technology College so she might just have a thing about being called "Miss" all the time. Had a pretty stressful term, so she said, and made a last minute decision to get away for a short break as soon as the Easter holidays started.'

'You have been busy. Well done,' he said with grudging admiration. 'I take it she's the hippy?' All he got in reply was a puzzled frown. 'The small mousey woman, long flowing skirt and beaded jacket.'

'No. The tall fair-haired one you helped to put her things on the overhead shelf.'

'Ah hah! The good-looking blonde with the magnificent cleavage.'

'So that's why you leapt to your feet is it?' What had got into him? He didn't usually behave like some leery lager lout on a night out with the boys. Her sarcasm was wasted. He ignored her completely and sat back tapping his teeth with the top of his pen.

'With those bedroom eyes, she didn't look like a man-hater. Or particularly stressed come to that,' he mused. 'Quite a tough cookie to my way of thinking.'

'If she's a teacher, she'd have to be these days,' Jane snapped. He glanced at her, surprised at her sharpness. 'Okay. So what do we have on the late bookings?'

'First there's a Mr and Mrs Lee from,' he clicked onto another document, 'Bristol.'

'That's the couple in their fifties sitting immediately behind the driver. The guy with the grey beard and she has dyed red hair, you can hardly miss her.'

'The woman glued to her ruddy mobile all the time?'

'That's the one. And the other two late bookings are Andrew Killigan – the chap on his own obviously – and,' she glanced back at the list, 'Miss Vera Ellis. One of the older women presumably but I haven't worked out which.'

She waited but he just sat there looking thoughtful. He'd been talking to Killigan as they got off the coach. They must have been chatting for a good five minutes. Trust him not to share information! Most of the time he was a pleasant and supportive colleague; he had his off days like anyone else, but ever since he'd phoned the chief, he'd been moody and secretive. Dare she ask what next?

'Can we start by crossing off …?'

The sudden tensing of his body, never mind the look of utter distain, cut her off in mid sentence and made her feel like a raw recruit.

'Everybody is a suspect,' he snapped.

'Of course. I do appreciate that. Poor choice of words. All I was going to say was that the elderly ones, such as Mrs Pettigrew, don't exactly come under the heading of prime candidates. She must be well over eighty!'

'It would be irresponsible to rule out anyone, no matter how unlikely.'

'What I meant was,' she tried to cut short the lecture, 'let's begin with the most likely passengers.'

'The ones in dark glasses furtively glancing over their shoulders all the time.' Her sharp intake of breath must have made him realize that he'd gone too far. 'Only joking.'

The silence hung between them. If he didn't stop clicking that damned ballpoint, she'd scream. Jane picked up the passenger list and pretended to study it. Let him make the next move.

Four

There was a stiff breeze as Fiona stepped out onto the upper deck. She noticed several of her party amongst the throng milling around or leaning on the rails. Most were busy chatting, but she caught the eye of one or two who returned her wave. Making her way down the starboard side, Fiona spotted a lone figure sitting on one of the benches facing out to sea. Not the most sheltered spot for the old lady to choose. Huddled against the wind, Miss Ellis looked even more frail and tiny than she had seemed on the coach. Pale watery eyes looked up as Fiona walked over.

'A bit on the blustery side out here, isn't it?' Fiona said, holding back the hair whipping across her face.

'Yes, dear.'

Vera made no attempt to move the navy holdall beside her for Fiona to sit down. 'You'll get frozen standing around in just that thin jacket, dear. Please don't feel you should keep me company.'

'Well if you're sure.' The old lady obviously did not want to chat and she did have a point; there was a decided bite to the wind.

The ship had been sailing parallel to the coast for some time and would soon be docking. Time for her to start making tracks. She needed to be down at the coach to welcome everyone back. That piece of company policy had been drummed into her throughout her training.

Standing at the foot of the coach steps, Fiona had counted all but three of her now twenty-seven charges, when she realized there was some kind of commotion going on at the back of the coach. Moments later, a flustered Vera Ellis, emerged in the doorway.

'I'm so sorry to be a nuisance.' The poor woman looked quite distraught.

'Is something wrong?'

'So silly of me, I've forgotten my travel bag. I must have left it by the bench up on deck. I'll be as quick as I can.'

'You stay there. I'll go back for you.'

'I can manage, dear.' She went to come down the steps.

Fiona put up a hand. 'It will be a lot quicker if you let me.' Fiona hurried away before Vera could protest. Apart from the time it would take for the old lady to get up there, Vera was in such a dither that she probably wouldn't remember whereabouts she had been sitting in any case. Fiona turned to Winston. 'If you have to leave the ship without me, I'll find you on the dock.'

A steady stream of people was still disgorging from the narrow passageway onto the car deck. There was no way Fiona would be able to make her way up the stairs against the relentless flow. She caught sight of a man in overalls and hurried over to him.

'One of my passengers has left a bag behind; may I use the crew stairs to dash up and get it? I know exactly where it is.'

'No problem, darlin'. That door marked No Entry for Passengers.'

Pausing only for a quick, 'Thank you,' Fiona pulled open the heavy hatch and ran up the first flight of stairs two at a time. After struggling up several more seemingly endless sets of steps, her legs were like jelly when she staggered out onto the open deck.

So much for all those resolutions! It's definitely the gym for you my girl when we get back, she told herself sternly.

Her heart sank when she saw the empty bench. Could she have made a mistake? Racing round the corner, she almost bumped into a cleaner.

'You haven't come across a bag by any chance? A dark, canvas holdall about so big.' Fiona held up her hands to demonstrate.

He gave her a wide, toothy grin and walked over to his cart. From underneath he pulled out the bag.

'Wonderful! Thank you so much.'

In her unfamiliar court shoes, it was no easier trying to hurry on the way down. It had been so long since she'd worn high heels. Or a straight skirt and tights come to that. She'd virtually lived in comfortable flatties and casual slacks for years. Roll on the hotel when she could change into something more comfortable. There was no need dress up like some glorified airhostess until the last day and the journey home.

A great cheer went up when Fiona climbed back aboard the coach. Vera Ellis was profuse in her apologies as the bag was handed over.

'Would you like me to put it up on the overhead rack for you?'

'No, no. I'll keep it with me.' Vera seized the bag from Fiona and tucked it under the coat on the empty seat beside her. Presumably, the old dear didn't want to trouble anyone getting her things down for her when they arrived at their destination.

The massive bow doors were raised and they emerged into bright April sunshine. Within minutes they were on the motorway and heading north on the long dive up towards Belgium and the Netherlands. It wasn't the most picturesque of routes up from Calais. The only thing to break the monotony of the flat landscape was the occasional wind farm or nuclear power station. It soon became pleasantly warm in the coach and, by the time they'd reached the border, nearly everyone was dozing. The early start was taking its toll. Only Mr and Mrs Brooke had not reclined their seats and were still surveying the passing countryside. They were much the youngest passengers, probably no more than their mid-thirties, Fiona judged. The only ones, with the possible exception of Miss Oppenheimer, without undisguised, naturally grey hair.

Peace at last. Not that there was much chance of a doze herself, not with that dreadful image from earlier in the day that insisted on drifting back. Best to concentrate on something else. Perhaps this was as good a time as any to look through her notes again. It might be her last chance to run through all the bits and pieces she had put together on Delft in readiness for the tomorrow's walking tour. She pulled out the bright blue file with its garish yellow Super Sun logo.

'Why don't you just sit back and enjoy the ride?' She glanced at Winston smiling across at her. 'It's not an exam, sweetheart. You don't need to swot it all up.'

Fiona gave a rueful laugh. 'Believe me I do. Five days ago, I was just coming along to observe, see how the job was done and get to know the area before leading my own group; then I got the phone call to say the tour manager had been taken sick. Now I'm left having to lead the whole trip blind!'

'You never bin to Holland before?'

'Well, once,' she admitted. 'But that was nearly ten years ago.'

'Then you'll manage just fine.'

There was something wonderfully reassuring about Winston's easy manner. Looking up into that kindly face, she could almost believe him. Perhaps it would all come back to her when she arrived. And her neighbours, Pam and Roger, who had just returned from a very similar trip had been able to give her lots of pointers and practical tips that the guide books missed out which she would be able to pass on to her passengers.

Winston was probably right. He would think her rude if she continued and the words weren't really going in anyway. She'd already read the first page twice. After a quick run through her checklist to make sure she'd not forgotten anything, Fiona put everything back into her bag and settled into her seat. It might be as well to make a mental list of all those who would expect a postcard from her. The boys of course. Adam hadn't sounded very keen on the idea of his mother going back to work, but Martin had simply told her to go for it. A slow smile spread across her face. Thinking about the boys always made her feel better.

There were no planned stops on the way, but as the coach approached the outskirts of Rotterdam, everyone started to rouse themselves and take a look around.

A figure loomed over Fiona's shoulder. What was the name of the man with ponytail? Simon Wick that was it!

'You aren't planning on going round the ring road, are you?' Fiona looked up into the slightly bloodshot eyes peering down at her. A stray wisp of the fast-receding lank grey hair fell forward making the pasty face look even thinner. 'If you cut through the centre, we can see the famous cube houses.'

'That really is up to Winston.' The cheek of the man! A polite request was one thing but Simon Wick had made it sound more like a done deal.

Winston turned to Fiona and gave a shrug. 'Not a problem, but you're the boss.'

What could she say?

Fiona pulled out her copy of the "Eyewitness Travel Guide to Holland" and, as she studied the well-illustrated pages, berated herself for letting the pushy client dictate proceedings.

Ten minutes later, after a quiet word with Winston, she picked up the microphone. 'You might like to have your cameras ready. We'll be passing through the Blaak District in a few minutes and there are some rather unusual looking buildings. We won't be able to stop but Winston will drive slowly.'

There was a general bustle as bags were retrieved from the overhead shelves or pulled out from under the seats.

'On your left, the building looking like something out of Star Trek, is actually the metro and railway station.' Everyone was crowding to the windows, jockeying for position to take their pictures and the sound of clicking cameras mingled with the excited chatter. 'Coming up are Rotterdam's most photographed buildings; the cube houses.'

Thank goodness for the guidebook. Despite all her enthusiasm, Fiona had never heard of them before.

'Good heavens! Boxes on stalks.' Yvonne Lee, who was sitting in the front seat behind Winston, was already taking pictures with her mobile.

Like a great wave, en masse everyone turned to peer out at the next curiosity.

Before Fiona could say any more, a loud voice interrupted, 'The Dutch call them the Blaak Forest because each house is supposed to represent an abstract tree.'

Fiona glanced back at the thin face peering round Mrs Oppenheimer's seat. Simon Wick's lips parted slowly over the protruding teeth into a smug smile. Not that anyone was paying any attention to the facts the man was reeling off.

'Yes, dear... A row of bright orange giant boxes tipped onto one corner sitting on massive concrete pillars.' Not content with sending a picture of the amazing row of apartments, Yvonne was now describing them to her daughter in detail at the top of her voice. 'Can you image what it's like to live in one with all the walls at forty-five degree angles? . . . Yes, even the windows are on the slant.'

'How do they stop all the furniture sliding down to one side of the room?' came Vera Ellis's puzzled voice from further back. 'And they'd have to shorten the legs on one side of the bed or they'd fall out.'

'Silly old mare!' muttered Edward Collins as several of the others began to titter.

'I think you'll find the floors will be level and it's just the walls at strange angles,' explained Margery patiently. 'But it must still take some getting used to and I think I'd feel very uncomfortable looking out of a window at a sheer drop like that.'

'Please do stay in your seats,' Fiona urged as people started getting up and moving forward to take photographs, 'we are going to be driving underneath – through the pillars – so you will all have a good view on the other side.'

Now that everyone had perked up, Fiona felt her own tension beginning to ease. She flashed Winston a grin and, undercover of the excited hubbub from behind, said in a low voice, 'Well at least it's put a smile on all their faces.'

It was only a few kilometres from Rotterdam to The Hague. Rows of greenhouses lined the route and the picturesque traditional windmills were now outnumbered by their modern electricity-generating counterparts. Fiona pulled out her file and once more reached for the microphone. Time to give her first talk, painting a little of the geographical and historical background of the country.

'Well done,' said Winston quietly when she sat down after answering the last of their questions. She felt a warm glow inside. Despite all her earlier nervousness, the talk had gone well and her audience had seemed appreciative.

'Ladies and gentlemen, we'll soon be arriving at our hotel. When we go into the reception, if you would all find yourselves a seat, I'll check you all in and collect the room keys. Winston will see to the cases but don't forget to bring all your hand luggage.'

Fiona recognised the Vermeer Hotel from the picture in the Super Sun brochure. A modest white-fronted building set back from the road with attractive gaily-painted shutters and a short set of steps leading up to the large carved wooden double doors which stood invitingly open.

Winston was on hand to take over from Fiona helping everyone down from the coach leaving her free to go on ahead. She noticed Margery Pettigrew struggling to mount the short flight of steps. At the top, the elderly lady paused, easing her stiff limbs.

'It's so nice to be able to stretch one's legs after that long drive, isn't it?' she said to Vera Ellis coming up behind her.

'Yes, dear,' came the reply. 'It does look a lovely hotel.'

'No. I...' Vera was already disappearing through the doorway. Margery caught Fiona's rueful grin and raised her eyebrows. 'Forgotten to put her hearing aid in, I expect.'

The foyer area was not large but there were just enough padded benches and easy chairs in the same red plush velvet for everyone to sit down. Fiona heard several murmurs of approval from the less weary travellers as they surveyed the attractive oak panelling and the profusion of colourful flower arrangements. At least that was a good start.

It took some time to get everyone sorted and answer all the questions. Fiona saw the last of her party disappear to the lift and breathed a sigh of relief. She had promised to remain down in reception for the next half hour in case there were any problems, which meant that she would have to wait for the much longed for soak in the tub. What was the betting that her room only had a shower anyway? At least she could have a quiet sit down with a cup of tea. As she collapsed into the depths of one of the large armchairs, she wondered if she could get away with easing out of the unfamiliar shoes. Perhaps not. Someone would be bound to catch her.

'Hi there.'

She sat upright with a guilty start.

'Sorry. Didn't mean to make you jump.' A smiling Winston stood over her. 'Cases all unloaded so I's off to m' room. You waitin' for the complaints brigade?'

'What's the betting that the first through those lift doors will be Mrs Oppenheimer?' Fiona laughed. 'She's been given a room facing onto the road with all that noisy traffic and insists on having one overlooking the gardens at the back.'

Five

In the event, Fiona was proved wrong. The only query came from the two very apologetic Harvey sisters who had ticked the twin room box on their application form but had been given one with a double bed and wondered if there were any chance of a room change.

She was about to hand over the new room key to Phyllis Harvey, when she noticed Winston hovering at the far end of the long, wooden reception desk waiting for her to finish.

'Don't worry about moving your cases. Someone will see to those for you.'

The sisters thanked everyone profusely and disappeared towards the lift. Fiona turned to Winston.

'I've just been checkin' the travel news for tomorrow. Seems there's a political rally – some big protest march – and they've closed all the roads around the Binnenhof and the Peace Palace which means our coach tour of The Hague is off.' The alarm must have shown in Fiona's face because before she could say anything, Winston continued quickly, 'Not to worry. We'll just swap days and go up to Keukenhof tomorrow and do The Hague and Delft on Sunday.'

'But what will the company say?'

'It's no big deal.' He gave a low chuckle. 'They're used to changes, but I'll ring head office and let 'em know. You get up to your room and put your feet up for half an hour.'

Easier said than done, thought Fiona as she stepped into the lift and pressed the button for the top floor. It didn't strike her until she was in her room but it would not be quite as simple as Winston had made it sound. Keukenhof was halfway to their next hotel in Amsterdam. Did that mean they would have to cut short the tour of Delft in order to get to the hotel in time for dinner? Now she was being stupid. Holland was such

36

a tiny country, it probably added no more than half an hour onto the journey. She'd have to check with Winston later. No point in worrying about it; that wouldn't change anything. She dumped her bags on the floor, kicked off her shoes and sank down onto the bed.

'Please don't let any of the clients have a problem with this,' she prayed fervently. Changes in the itinerary were covered by the small print but this was just the sort of thing that Mrs Oppenheimer would make a fuss about. The chances of getting a column of smiley faces on the evaluation form at the end of the holiday from that particular lady were getting more remote by the minute. This job was turning out to be a great deal more stressful than she'd imagined.

'Oh, Bill! Am I doing the right thing?'

The chance to catch up on all those holidays she'd missed over the last few years, Caroline had said. She'd made it all sound so exciting. Everything had happened so quickly that Fiona had never thought about all the problems that she might have to cope with. She closed her eyes and lay back.

Dear Bill. She could picture his gentle smile and almost hear his voice telling her that she could handle it. Give it time. She'd adjusted to new situations before and in a week or two, she would look back on this and wonder why she let herself get so wound up.

Curly had been watching him for some time. Best to wait until the man went over to the bar and he could get him on his own.

'Bad news about Unsworth, wasn't it?'

'Curly?'

Curly cringed. It was bad enough Harry Unsworth calling him that without this idiot copying him. Not that he could object if he wanted to get on the man's good side.

'Didn't recognize you without the beard and glasses.'

'Really? Surely you knew I was on the trip?'

'Must have misunderstood.' He stared at Curly looking puzzled. 'I appreciate that was the original plan but then I was told I was going to be working with Unsworth.'

'He was a last minute addition to the team. Or rather not, as it turned out. You haven't heard how he is at all?'

'Only what the courier told us all at Dover.' He continued to look suspiciously at Curly but before he could ask any more questions, the barman came over to take their orders.

It was a few minutes before they were alone again.

'So do you know what the arrangements are for the hand-over?' Curly asked in a low voice.

'There's been no word from our Dutch contact yet.'

. 'Well let me know when you've got the details. In the mean time, best if we act as though we don't know each other.' Curly picked up his beer and made his way over to a group of other Super Sun passengers enjoying a drink before going into dinner.

Once she had directed the last arrivals to the five tables identified by yellow flags that had been laid out for the Super Sun party, Fiona was able take to her place. She made her way to the remaining empty chair.

'Have any of you been to Holland before?' she asked brightly once the introductions were made.

It was the first time for Phyllis and Cynthia Harvey but Joyce Collins was full of enthusiasm about a visit to Keuken-hof a few years before when they had come over for the Floriade. Edward Collins sat there looking rather bored, contributing nothing.

Vera Ellis didn't have much to say for herself either. Making small talk with Vera was no easy task. She wasn't the most communicative of people and gave the impression that her attention was elsewhere half the time. Fiona felt a vague misgiving. The woman was not just vague, she was more than a little confused at times as the earlier fiasco on the ferry had demonstrated. She fervently hoped Vera would not turn out to be a problem. Definitely one she ought to keep an eye on. Just the type to get lost.

'Do you often do this trip for Super Sun Tours?' Joyce's question caught her unawares.

'I haven't been with this company all that long,' Fiona answered, hoping the woman wouldn't press her further. It would do no good to let on that they were in the hands of a complete novice. 'I take it you've been with us before?'

'Oh yes. I'm afraid you're never going to get me up in a plane so coaching holidays are ideal, but we do like to do it in style so we always travel Super Sun Tours. The extra legroom is essential. Poor Edward finds the standard coaches much too cramped, don't you, dear?'

The Harvey sisters were also veteran Super Sun Executive Travellers and for the rest of the meal, Fiona was able to relax whilst they swapped tour stories.

'And what about you, Vera?' Fiona tried to bring Miss Ellis into the conversation.

'This is my first trip with Super Sun.'

'But not the last, we hope.'

Fiona was to remember that trivial comment for a long time after the holiday was over.

Curly knew things were going too well! That change in the itinerary would muck up all the arrangements for his little sideline. His backup plan in case Jenks refused to take him back. He could always abandon it of course, but after all the trouble he'd taken, he might as well follow it through to the end. His contact would hardly be best pleased with a call at this late hour, but he didn't have much option. Making his excuses, he made his way out of the Garden Room to find a quiet corner.

'Dag.' The voice was deep and gravelly; anything but a friendly greeting.

'There's a prob+lem. The programme's been changed and they're bringing forward the trip to Keukenhof to tomorrow. Can you still bring the stuff?'

Curly's Dutch was virtually non-existent, restricted to please and thank you and ordering a beer, but he didn't need any translation for the expletives issuing from the other end of the line.

Eventually the man said, 'I don't have the merchandise with me.'

'I'm here all week. We could arrange to meet somewhere else,' Curly persisted.

There was more muttering at the other end. 'No. Tomorrow. Same place, same time.'

The phone went dead. The man wasn't one for small talk.

'And the same to you, sunshine. With bells on!'

Saturday, 28th April

We have the whole day to explore the magnificent Keukenhof Park, the largest flower gardens in the world – 28 hectares ablaze with seven million bulbs within a beautiful landscape of established trees and flowering shrubs. Roam the seven themed gardens and linger at leisure in the peaceful water gardens. Enjoy the spectacular indoor displays of orchids, begonias, bulbs, cut flower arrangements and pot plants in the glasshouse pavilions.

Super Sun Executive Travel

Six

Fiona had just come out of the dining room after breakfast when she narrowly avoided a collision with Tim Brooke dashing through the foyer. He had obviously been out for a run. His T-shirt clung to his chest in great damp patches making his thin frame appear almost skeletal. Only the towelling band around his forehead stopped the sweat cascading into his eyes.

'Sorry! Can't stop. Quick shower, then a bite of breakfast.' He danced round her and made towards the lift.

'But we leave in half an hour...' Her voice trailed off as Tim disappeared behind the gently hissing doors.

What a start to the day! It was obvious she was going to have to be very firm about the courtesy of not keeping others waiting. What was it Gloria had said? 'If you're five minutes late, I shall make you stand at the front of the coach and sing us a song. If you're ten minutes late, you'll have to give us a dance as well and if you're a quarter of an hour late, we'll all wave you goodbye.' It may have been said in a way that had everyone laughing but nonetheless Gloria had got the point across. Did she have the confidence to try the same thing?

Whether it was the prospect of a day in the bulb fields or because they'd all had a good night's sleep, everyone appeared to be in good spirits when they clambered onto the coach. Even Mrs Oppenheimer, almost the first arrival, gave Fiona a smile when she managed to secure a front seat. The tension began to ease in Fiona and she felt more in control. She had a momentary qualm when a light-lipped Jane Brooke came down the steps on her own but it dissolved quickly when, only seconds later, Tim pushed through the hotel doors and followed his wife onto the coach.

He was by no means the last. The final stragglers came in a bunch. Once everyone had sat down, Fiona double-checked the numbers by counting the empty seats. Still one missing. She checked her list.

'Has anyone seen Miss Ellis?'

'She was right behind us when we came out of the lift. Perhaps she went back for something,' suggested Yvonne Lee looking up from her mobile.

Five minutes later Vera Ellis still hadn't appeared.

'I'll just pop back in and see where she's got to,' Fiona said quietly to Winston.

Vera was sitting in one of the large armchairs near the lifts, her head buried in her copy of the tour itinerary. She looked up as Fiona called her name.

'Hello, dear. I was beginning to wonder where everyone had got to. Isn't it time we were off?'

The misunderstanding cleared up, they set off on the road to Lisse. Fiona sank into her seat and tried to relax. For goodness sake, she told herself firmly, stop reacting to every minor hiccup as though it was a crisis and get a grip. This might well be the first proper job she had since heaven knows when but that did not make her incompetent. Everyone said what a tower of strength she'd been looking after Bill all those years and anyone who had brought up her two boys was definitely one of life's copers. Martin had been a disaster on legs from the day he was born; into everything; fearless and with no sense of danger. He'd been rushed up to hospital with broken limbs or suspected concussion so often that she should have had a permanent place in the car park. He was still a live wire. His job took him jetting all over the world and it was hard to keep track exactly where he was at any given time. Adam hadn't been quite so reckless, but he was always off on some adventure. At least now, he was settled down. A pity it was so far away but perhaps, if this new job worked out, she'd be able to earn enough to go out to Canada and see him and Kristy and the children.

Pulling herself back from her fond musings, Fiona picked up her clipboard and looked at her checklist. By now, the coach was leaving the suburbs and they would soon be on the open road. Time for that pep talk? Not really the best way to start the day. It might sound better, a little less like a telling off from teacher, if she mentioned the importance of keeping to time when she was giving them the arrangements for meeting the coach at the end of the day. That would be more natural. She pulled out her notes on Keukenhof and picked up the microphone.

'...And for a couple of euros you can buy a small souvenir booklet with an excellent map from the one of the ladies in blue mediaeval dresses standing by the entrance gates. There's a great deal to see but you have plenty of time to explore at your own pace. You'll find lots of places dotted throughout the park where you can buy a coffee and some lunch. If you're not counting calories – and we are on holiday – I can recommend the Pancake House on the terrace by the other entrance to the Park. Just follow the sound of the barrel organ. I'm still trying to decide whether to go for the pancakes ladled with hot cherries and smothered in oodles of cream or try the brandy with raisons topping. Big decision. And incidentally, the hot chocolate is to die for!'

There was general laughter and cries of, 'Sounds good to me!'

Pam and Roger had raved about them and Fiona could only keep her fingers crossed that the food would prove as awesome as her helpful neighbours had suggested.

Fiona watched the last of her charges pass through the gate and into the Park. As usual, the Smiths and the Dobsons went off together. The four friends had made little effort to get to know their fellow passengers, but that was hardly a problem. It was good to see that Margery Pettigrew had struck up a friendship with the two Harvey sisters and a couple of the other single passengers – the two younger women – appeared to have teamed up together which just left Vera Ellis on her own. She'd keep an eye out for her. Mustn't let the old dear feel abandoned.

In the mean time, there was no reason why she shouldn't have a pleasant, relaxed day herself. This was far too beautiful a spot not to take full advantage. Every now and again, she caught sight of members of the group but they were much too busy enjoying themselves to warrant her approaching them.

Later in the morning as she was contemplating stopping for a coffee, she heard someone call her name. She turned to see Margery Pettigrew, still with the Harvey sisters, waving at her from the other side of a great swathe of narcissi.

'Would you be a dear and take a photo for me? I've lots of lovely shots of these magnificent tulips but I'd like one with all three of us standing with this glorious bank of colour behind. Have you ever seen such a vast expanse of sunny yellow and bright scarlet?'

'Isn't it all wonderful? The pictures in the holiday brochures certainly don't do the place justice,' enthused Phyllis. 'We've just been in the orchid house. Absolutely breath-taking. Great cascades of delicate flowers all arranged in subtle shades of the same colour.'

They were all chattering away like excited schoolgirls and it was some time before the pictures were taken and Fiona was able to make her farewells and move on. By the time she had strolled up to the Beatrix Pavilion and spent an enjoyable half hour admiring the orchids, it was time for some lunch.

Most of the park's visitors appeared to have the same idea and all the cafés were busy. Fiona managed to find a spare seat tucked around a corner just inside the door. She was about to drink her coffee when she heard a familiar voice issuing forth at full volume from one of the tables outside. Yvonne Lee was evidently on the phone again.

'Your father and I are just about to have a bite to eat... Oh yes, we're having a great time... I haven't had a chance to speak to all the other passengers yet. There are several elderly ladies; a couple from Yorkshire and northerners are always so friendly aren't they? A Major and his wife, a bit posh but not standoffish at all if you know what I mean; and there's an

American lady and her daughter. Everyone seems very nice. Except from a rather annoying chap who keeps butting in when our tour manager – she's a real sweetie by the way – is trying to tell us something, but there's always one on every trip isn't there? I thought at first he was with his mother but, when I saw her bounding up all those flights of stairs on the ferry, I realized it must be his wife even though she does look years older. Mind you, she'd look a lot better if she did something with her hair instead of having it chopped off and clinging to her head all limp and lifeless.'

Fiona stifled a giggle. That was rich coming from a woman whose own startling bright red bouffant was certainly no advertisement for chic. No doubt Yvonne had left the dye in longer than usual in honour of the holiday but the result had turned out disastrously. Fiona wasn't sure how she felt about being called a sweetie but at least there were no complaints about her not knowing her job.

Emerging into the bright sunshine, Fiona decided to amble up to the windmill by one of the more circuitous paths through the trees away from the more crowded sections of the park. It was still pleasantly warm in the shelter of the trees and blissfully quiet. She lifted her face to the sun. There was something so supremely restful about its brightness dappled by the gently swaying branches. With such vivid splashes of colour at ground level, it was all too easy to easy to miss the subtle yellow-green haze of new growth above. Spring, the start of a new year with all its promise. For her, the start of a new life.

It was lucky that there was no one around to see the big grin on her face. It wasn't like her to be so fanciful. Time to get back to the real world.

There was hardly anyone around as she came out of the trees. Apart from the odd distant handful of people, the only person she could see was a man sitting on a bench on the far side of the river, reading a newspaper. What a wasted opportunity with so much around to see, Fiona thought. A moment or so later, another man emerged from the trees marching swiftly to the bench. His walk and upright bearing put Fiona in mind of the Major although there was no sign of Lavinia Rawlings. The man had the same distinctive clipped moustache and ring of gunmetal grey hair around the baldpate but he was far away and the sun was in her eyes. Had the Major been wearing a pale green and white striped shirt this morning? She couldn't remember.

The newcomer parked himself on the far end of the bench and appeared to strike up a conversation, though neither looked directly at the other. The first man continued reading and the other was apparently staring across the water. But not for long. Within minutes, the second man was on his feet again scurrying into the distance. How very strange.

The Brookes were in one of the pavilions when his mobile began to burble. He flicked it open.

'It's the Commander. Reception's not good in here. Back in a tick.'

Tim began pushing through the crowds heading for the door before Jane could say anything.

'Yes, sir. Sorry about the delay.'

'You were correct about Unsworth. He died of a heart attack. It would seem that there was no time to perform the autopsy on Friday afternoon so we will have to wait until Monday. As there is no evidence to suggest foul play, I could hardly insist they make it a priority. Have there been any developments at your end?'

'I'm afraid there's nothing to report as yet, sir. Although I think, I might be onto something.'

'Good. Keep me informed.'

'Certainly, sir.'

Seven

After climbing the windmill to admire the views from the top, Fiona spent much of the afternoon wandering aimlessly along the myriad paths, admiring the vibrant colours of the great swathes of chrome, scarlet and candyfloss pink tulips. Eventually she came to a small glade with an inviting bench sheltered from the occasional breeze by banks of Japanese cherry trees and azaleas. It was good to sit for a moment to appreciate the view, drinking in the clean fresh smell of the blossom. Amazing, with all those crowds streaming through the entrance, that it was possible to find spots like this that seemed almost deserted. Occasionally a hint of the heady scent of hyacinths would waft over from the seas of deep blue on the bank on the far side of the path. She closed her eyes. The sun warmed her face and she soon became quite drowsy.

Bill would have loved all this. Until the boys had grown up, all their holidays were chosen with them in mind, then funding the two of them through university had left little money for foreign travel. By the time they'd reach a stage when she and Bill could afford to live out all those dreams, the paralysis was beginning to take hold. The support group had come up with several suggestions for holidays for people in wheelchairs. They'd tried it a couple of times but she knew Bill only went for her sake so there didn't seem much point. This last year he'd never left the house.

'Hello. You look deep in thought there.' Fiona looked up to see Joyce Collins standing beside her. 'Do you mind if I join you?'

'Please do. So what have you done with Edward?'

'He's busy taking photos.' Joyce eased her amble frame down onto the bench. 'I'm a point and click person myself but Eddie takes forever lining up for long shots, close ups and panoramics and I get bored waiting. We're going to meet up for a cup of tea later. I might even treat myself to a plate of those little pancakes you mentioned. I always put on so much weight on holiday and I promised myself I'd be good for once, no naughty snacks between meals, but I don't think I'm going to be able to resist.'

Fiona laughed. 'I know the feeling. All I have for breakfast back home is a slice of toast but when the full works are laid out in front of you like that it seems rude to say no.'

'A woman after my own heart!'

Joyce was a talkative soul and Fiona let her chatter on throwing in the occasional comment. Dare she look at her watch? Something of her restlessness must have communicated itself to her companion because Joyce patted her newly permed curls and got to her feet. 'We mustn't waste this wonderful opportunity just sitting here nattering. I expect Edward is ready for that cup of tea by now. Would you like to join us?'

'Thank you but I was planning to have a look at the begonias in the Juliana Pavilion and there are several areas I haven't explored yet.'

Fiona watched the flamboyantly dressed woman wending her way to the tearoom. A friendly soul, far too nice to be married to old misery guts!

Had he got it wrong? Curly pulled out the map of the park and double-checked. This was definitely the right place; so where was the man? It was hardly his fault that all the arrangements had to be brought forward a day at such short notice. If this were the Dutchman's way of getting his own back for the inconvenience, it was more than just petty. Leaving him sitting out here all on his own, in full view, was putting them both at risk.

He'd never met this Hansen before so he had no idea of what the man looked like; no way of identifying him. It left him totally dependent on the man approaching him. He scanned the people gathered by the water's edge but they all appeared to be legitimate visitors to the park. As far as he could tell, there was no one who appeared to be on his own.

Few had bags large enough to hold the merchandize. There was a fresh faced youth barely out of his teens with a large plastic carrier emblazoned with a Keukenhof label. The way he was nonchalantly swinging it around as he laughed and joked with his girl friend, suggested that its contents did not include delicate blooms.

Curly gave a deep sigh and began folding up the map along its predefined creases. Time to go. He couldn't sit here all afternoon.

The voice at his elbow made him jump. 'Hang on a minute.'

The young man pulled out the adjacent chair and sat down placing the carrier bag on the ground between them.

'Look as though I have asked you to point out somewhere on the map. So, have you got the money?'

Curly looked into the green-grey eyes which had none of the warmth suggested by the lop-sided smile.

'Hansen?' There had been only the slightest trace of an accent in the man's voice, nothing like that of last night's phone call.

'Not quite.' Perhaps he was being oversensitive but was there was a hint of derision in the boy's chortle of laughter? 'But I have what you want.'

'So what kept you?'

Curly's attempt to seize the initiative was ignored. 'Put the money under the map.'

Best to get it over with as quickly as possible. They were too exposed out here. He slid the fat envelope from his trouser pocket but, before doing as he'd been told, he glanced down at the bag.

'There is no need for you to worry. All the goods are there. Check if you like.' Tossing back the long hair from his eyes, the young man leant over and slid the envelope across to his side of the table. The minutes stretched out indefinitely as he took his time counting the notes beneath the cover of the table.

Eventually he looked up. 'Good. All here, I see. Nice meeting you. Perhaps we can do business again next time you are over in our beautiful country. Forgive me for not stopping to, how do you say, chat? Give me a few minutes before you move away. It might look as though we were up to something if we left together.'

Curly watched the arrogant puppy saunter back to his girl friend. Best to do as the boy had said. He lifted the bag onto the table and peered inside. It wasn't easy trying to inspect the contents but it made sense not to take out the goods in a public place.

'Now what do you have there, my friend?'

His heart missed a beat then gave a resounding thump. He had been so engrossed and the man had crept up so quietly that he had not heard his approach.

'What's it to you?'

How long had he been watching? Had he noticed the exchange?

The man put both hands on the small table and leant right across trying to peer into the bag. 'More than you might think, sunshine.'

Seizing the bag away from the intruder's reach, Curly jumped to his feet and took several backward steps. The man gave a wry smile and wagged a finger then he started pulling something out of an inside pocket.

Best not to wait to find out. Curly turned and fled in the only direction possible.

By late afternoon, Fiona had met up with a good many of the Super Sun party. One way and another, she spent so much time listening to their enthusiastic chatter that the chances of her getting round the whole park were decidedly slim. If she didn't dawdle, there might just be time to look round the last of the pavilions before returning to the coach in good time to check everyone back.

In the event, she was not the first there. Jane was pacing up and down by the exit gates. When she spotted Fiona, she came rushing over.

'Have you seen Tim? He's disappeared. We were in the orchid house and when I turned round, he'd gone. Something's happened to him.'

Fiona took hold of her hands. The woman was near to panic. 'There's no need to worry. With so many people, it's easy to get separated. He knows what time we leave, believe me he'll be here any minute. He's probably been chasing around trying to find you.'

'No. You don't understand. I phoned him on his mobile and there was no answer.'

That did sound a bit more serious. 'I'm sure there'll be a good explanation. When did you see him last?

'Not long after lunch. Around two fifteen, two thirty. I've rung and rung all afternoon but nothing.' She combed back the shoulder-length brown hair with fingers.

People were already beginning to drift back. Fiona directed them to where the coach was parked but soon she would need to go herself if only to tell Winston what was happening.

Predictably, Winston was in no way fazed by the news. 'Happens all the time.'

'That's just what I told Jane, but understandably she is in a bit of a state.'

'You go back and see to the lady. I can keep an eye out for all the others.'

By twenty-five past, everyone else had returned; only Tim was still missing. Jane resisted all of Fiona's efforts to wait on the coach, pacing restlessly back and forth peering through the gates trying to spot her husband. She must have tried her mobile at least every five minutes.

Fiona was beginning to get worried about Jane never mind the errant Tim. Time to be firm. 'This isn't helping. Let's go back to the coach and ask if any of the others saw him after he left you.'

It was Barbara Shuttleworth who came up with something. 'I think I spotted him around three o'clock time.'

'Where?' Hope danced in Jane's eyes.

'We were up on that balcony bit of the windmill and I'm pretty certain it was Tim I spotted over by the corner café. He was talking with someone, but I couldn't see who because there was a tree in the way. I just assumed it was you, Jane. He seemed a bit upset, throwing his arms in the air, which is what caught my attention in the first place.' Despite the kindly woman's reticence to say so, it was clear she thought the couple were having an argument.

Jane shook her head vigorously. 'It couldn't have been me. I never got that far. You're sure of the time?'

'Definitely. I watched him hurry out of sight behind the building just as the bells on the clock began that little tune. Then it struck three and we moved round to listen to the tunes it was playing. I remember thinking how loud the music was.'

At ten to six, there was still no sign of Tim. Even Winston's habitually smiling face was looking serious. Fiona was left in something of a quandary. She would have to take the others back to the hotel soon, otherwise they would be late for dinner. Ten minutes more and they would have to go.

Jane was persuaded to sit down. Before she could change her mind, Barbara Shuttleworth slipped into the adjacent seat encircling her with a comforting arm. At least Fiona knew Jane was in capable hands.

Jane had already been to the enquiry desk so, apart from leaving a message for him, there was little else to be done. Perhaps she should ask Winston about phoning head office? No. She gave herself a shake. She knew exactly what his answer would be. Far too early to start raising alarm bells. Take it in your stride, woman. This will all be sorted soon.

At five past six, Fiona made the decision. The coach had to go. Understandably, Jane refused to go with them, but company rules clearly stated that the tour manager must not allow her party to travel without her.

'Don't worry, we'll stay with Jane.' Barbara's motherly Yorkshire openness oozed reassurance. 'When he turns up, we'll all get a taxi back. She'll be fine with us.'

Fiona wrote down the address of the hotel and her own mobile number and handed them over. 'I'll make sure they keep something hot for you when you all get back.'

What more could she do?

Curly stared out of the window. Stupid, stupid, stupid! He should never have tried to run. Certainly not behind the café to get himself cornered like a rat in a trap. But how was he to know it would turn out to be a dead end. What a disaster! The man had caught him unawares creeping up on him like that and asking awkward questions. Why hadn't he just brazened it out? Said he'd found the bag and that it was nothing to do with him.

At last, the coach was moving off. The farther away they got from this place the better. So who was this Brooke chap? Had the boss really sent someone to spy on them? Or perhaps the man was from Customs. Either way, there'd be repercussions. He took great gulps of air in an effort to steady his nerves. Now he was looking for trouble where there was none. In all probability, Brooke had been no more than a nosey parker and he had overreacted.

But if the man were from Customs, perhaps he should warn his partner. They were supposed to be a team, protecting each other's backs. But then he would have to explain everything. That would ruin all his plans. In the circumstances, it was best to say nothing. After all the trouble he'd taken getting himself back in the frame, it would be foolish to blow it now. Besides there was always the chance that if he kept his head down – kept his cool – all this might just blow over.

No point in worrying. There was nothing he could do about it now. What was done was done. Time to concentrate on his other problem. He stared, unseeing, out of the window conscious of the package trapped between his feet. Too risky to put the bag up on the parcel shelf. Once he got back to the hotel he could hide it in his room, but until then, there was always the danger of it being discovered. He could feel the sweat beginning to trickle down the side of his neck. Even with the air conditioning vent full on him, his back was clammy and he had to lean forward to ease away the damp, clinging shirt.

Eight

'Fiona!' The imperious cry rang through the foyer.

Fixing a smile, Fiona turned to face the formidable Mrs O.

'The liquid soap in the squeezy bottle contraption in our shower has run out.'

'Have you mentioned it to the maid?'

A surprised frown crossed the woman's face. 'I don't speak Dutch.'

Strangely enough, neither do I, Fiona thought. Suppressing a sigh, she replied, 'If you give me your room number, I'll mention it at the reception desk and I'm sure they'll see to it for you.'

As if she didn't have enough to worry about at the moment. If she had hoped that Mrs Oppenheimer would take the hint and do the deed herself, Fiona was to be disappointed. Did the woman ever think about anyone other than herself? Best to see to it right away.

Fiona was painfully aware of the four empty chairs over dinner. The Smiths and the Dobsons were happy enough to have a table to themselves, freed from the necessity of having to make polite conversation with a couple of strangers. There was an empty place next to Miss Ellis at a table by the window and another opposite Fiona, which acted as a constant reminder throughout the meal.

There had been no news by the time they all sat down. She had phoned not long after they'd got back to the hotel. Jane's eager voice had answered straight away and the disappointment in her tone when she realized that the call was not from Tim, only served to make Fiona feel even more inadequate. She could feel the bulge of her mobile in her pocket, another reminder, but all she could do now was wait.

The levels of happy chat and occasional bursts of laughter seemed much greater than on the previous evening. Perhaps that was no surprise. These people were on holiday and it had been a day to remember. An experience they would talk about back home for a long time. It had been far too enjoyable a day to let someone else's poor timekeeping spoil their evening.

Despite what she hoped was a look of absorbed attention on her face, Fiona found it difficult to concentrate on Yvonne Lee's raptures. 'Weren't those flower arrangements something else? I did an evening class at our local college a few years ago and believe me it's not as easy as it looks to achieve that sense of balance and harmony. It's all in the placing of the right colours alongside one another, you know.'

Fiona was not the only one to tire of Yvonne's obvious intention of giving everyone the full benefit of her expertise on the subject. Edward Collins was beginning to shuffle in his seat. Just as she looked set to start another lengthy explanation on the importance of choosing the perfect container, Gerald Lee manfully intervened, attempting to change the subject by extolling the wonderful photo opportunities they'd had. 'Those Amaryllis were fantastic.'

His wife threw him a look which did not bode well for their domestic harmony.

Before she could start lambasting him there and then, Joyce cut in, 'Did you see that chap making clogs up by the windmill? Outside his shop, there was a table with all the different types. Rounded toes for farmers, pointy ones for fishermen, but the best ones were for smugglers. Apparently the tracks they make look as though the person wearing them is walking in the other direction.'

'Load of nonsense,' muttered Edward.

'Absolutely,' beamed Joyce. 'For a start if the men were struggling back across the sand with barrels of brandy on their back, presumably the customs men would notice that the approaching footprints were deeper that the retreating ones.'

'Apart from the fact that Holland has no secret coves like Cornwall, I very much doubt that it was spirits they were smuggling.' Joyce's flight of fancy had stirred Yvonne from her short-lived, tight-lipped silence prompting her to inject what she saw as a bit of common sense into the conversation.

'You're probably right,' agreed Joyce in no way put out by the woman's rudeness. 'More likely drugs or diamonds perhaps.'

Fiona listened with only half an ear. At least her contribution was not required.

After the meal, they all moved out into the Garden Room. Gerald and Edward went to fetch the coffee whilst the three women settled themselves in a quiet corner alongside the Harvey sisters. They had just sat down when the Major came over.

'May we join your little group? It may be the done thing to have coffee with the people you shared a table with at dinner but I really don't think I can spend another couple of hours with that annoying man.'

'By all means,' said Joyce with a mischievous twinkle in her eyes. 'But only on condition you tell us which annoying man you are trying to avoid.'

The Major waited until both he and Lavinia were sitting down before answering. 'That show-off with the stupid pony tail, trying to make out he's some intellectual. There isn't a single subject on which he's not an expert.'

'Simon Wick?'

'Well he certainly gets on my wick, putting his oar in all the time. Wouldn't mind so much if half of what he said was of any interest. If you ask me, there is something distinctly odd about a middle-aged man tying his hair back like that especially when there's so little of it. If he weren't with his wife, I'd take him for a poofter the way he minces along.'

'Cyril!' admonished his wife, somewhat half-heartedly.

Fiona's pained smile had less to do with the Major's attempted parody of Simon's wriggle with raised forearms and limp wrists, than the fact that the poor man might find that he had swapped one person who enjoyed the sound of his own voice for another. With luck, Yvonne might just take the hint. And it had to be admitted that Edward was hardly the person anyone would choose for sparkling or stimulating conversation.

'Calm down, dear. He really isn't that bad.'

'The way he fusses over that mouse of a wife of his is enough to put you off your pork chops.'

'The man is an absolute pain,' admitted Joyce, 'but I think it's rather nice the way the two them always go around holding hands. You'd take them for newly-weds.'

'The Wicks haven't been married that long. It's their third wedding anniversary on Wednesday, so they were saying.' Trust Yvonne to be up with the gossip. 'I did hear someone say she's not been well, poor woman. And you have to admit, she is painfully thin.'

'She'd feel a lot better if she didn't go around looking so sorry for herself.' The Major was in a bad mood. It wasn't like him to be so unsympathetic. 'Well, how often have you seen her with a smile on her face?'

Time to change the subject. Fiona turned to Phyllis Harvey. 'Did you manage to get some good photos today?'

'If I didn't, it won't be for the want of trying.' Her round face broke into a smile and the grey-blue eyes sparkled. 'I do hope all my pictures come out especially as I used up two whole rolls of film. I'm going to have to ration myself for the rest of the holiday.'

'You should get yourself a digital camera, Phyllis. Then you wouldn't have to worry about changing film and they're so easy to use.'

Gerald Lee produced a slim, silver affair no bigger than an audio tape box from the top pocket of his jacket. 'And the real beauty of them is you can see what you've got straightaway.'

The camera was duly passed round and the pictures admired. Even Edward livened up at the mention of a subject so close to his heart. Before long there was an animated discussion about the advantages of digital cameras and, when the topic moved onto the ease of printing off jpgs – whatever they were – on home computers, Edward decided to fetch his laptop to show the bemused ladies what he was talking about.

Fiona sat back and took a look around the room. Everyone appeared to be happy enough. Even Mrs Oppenheimer had a smile on her face for once, listening to Andrew Killigan. Fiona wondered what he was talking about that both she and her daughter were so enthralled. Deirdre was looking at him with positive adulation. It had to be admitted that he was a good-looking man with that strong firm chin and striking sapphire blue eyes. The touch of grey at the temples in the thick, well-cut dark wavy hair served only to add to his distinguished air.

Some ten minutes later, Fiona put down her empty coffee cup and, with the excuse that she had to make a phone call, went out to the reception area. Before she could ask if there had been any news about Tim Brooke, she saw a taxi draw up at the door. Gordon Shuttleworth got out and went round to pay the driver whilst Barbara helped a very weary-looking Jane out of the car. As they came up the steps and caught sight of Fiona, Barbara shook her head.

'I'll ask if they'll bring your dinner through now, shall I?'

A heavy-eyed Jane waved away the attention. 'I couldn't eat anything. I'll go straight up to the room.'

'I'll take her.' Barbara's gentle reassurance was as much for Fiona as it was for Jane.

'Should we get a doctor?'

Jane turned back with a frown evidently not so distraught that she had not heard Fiona's whispered question. 'No. I'll be all right. I don't want any more fuss.'

The two women walked slowly to the lift, Barbara's arm still protectively around Jane. As the lift doors gently shushed together, Fiona turned back to Mr Shuttleworth.

'If he's still missing we really ought to inform the police.'

'We have already. That's why we've been so long, lass. We waited till they locked the gates then rang from the park when it got dark. They sent out a couple of officers but to be honest they didn't seem that interested.'

'So what are they going to do?'

'Not a lot I expect. What can they do? Jane said he didn't have much money on him. Only what he needed for the day.

The rest of their euros are in the hotel safe, but these days all you need is your credit card and you can draw money out anywhere.'

'I suppose so, but surely it's not very likely. How's he going to get home? I've still got the passports.'

'That's true. Hadn't thought of that.'

'Thank you so much for all you've done. You and Barbara must be starving. I'll go and sort out that dinner I promised, then I'll pop up and relieve Barbara.'

'No need, lass. Here's mother now.'

'She's lying down. The poor girl's exhausted. All that crying. Be asleep in no time, I don't doubt.'

Fiona left the two of them to their meal and went to phone the Super Sun head office. There should be someone on the evening desk if only to take bookings. Much to her surprise, one of the senior staff answered her call, but the only reaction she got was a bored disinterest. It seemed passengers who returned late were far from a rare occurrence. Even when she explained that Tim Brooke had now been missing for over four hours, almost seven since he'd actually been seen, all she got was a few reassuring phrases about him being bound to turn up soon and to keep them informed.

'Very useful!' she spat at the phone when the voice rang off. There was nothing more she could do.

When she got back to the Garden Room, she discovered a group of people gathered around Edward's laptop looking at his photos. Several turned and asked her if there was any news of Tim, but only one or two showed any real concern.

'All this doesn't affect our trips tomorrow, does it?' Trust Mrs Oppenheimer to put the question the others had been too tactful to ask.

'I'm sure it won't,' Fiona answered with a smile, fervently hoping she wouldn't have cause to regret her promise.

'But what about moving on to our hotel in Amsterdam?' asked Phyllis with a concerned frown. 'If Tim's not back, he'll get left behind.'

'It's a little early for us to start worrying about that just yet.' It was something that Fiona had been contemplating for much of the evening. What was going to happen? How long she could fob them off with vague clichés and well-worn platitudes was another issue.

Raucous guffaws made Fiona turn back to the computer screen. It was not the most flattering of pictures. A vast expanse of someone's bottom as she bent down to look more closely at the flowerbed filled the foreground. Although it was impossible to see the face, the henna bouffant left no doubt as to its owner.

'Sorry about that,' Edward leered at Yvonne. 'You moved at the last minute. I'll delete it when we get to the end.'

Yvonne scowled. 'I was trying to read the variety on the label.'

The programme clicked through the next few pictures and it could not be denied that Edward had taken some first-rate shots. Though most were of the flowers, both long vistas of colour and superb close-ups of individual blooms, there were some pictures of various members of the party that he had managed to catch unawares. Marjory, eyes sparkling with pleasure; an unusually serious-looking Andrew Killigan; Deirdre clapping her hands with glee at the barrel organ; Jane staring into the distance with a pensive, slightly worried expression and Edward had even managed to catch the prim and proper Mrs Oppenheimer with a genuine smile on her face. There was an unusual shot of Vera Ellis looking out into distance from behind a tree with a pensive look on her face so different from her customary decidedly vacant expression.

The pictures of the windmill were particularly good although Fiona's heart missed a beat when she saw a plump, round-faced man framed at the side of the picture who, for a spit second, she was convinced was her never-to-be passenger from Dover, Henry Unsworth. She took a few steps back and sank on the arm of one of the chairs to compose herself again.

'Come and look, Fiona. That's you there by the fountain.'

Fiona dutifully stood behind the huddle of spectators and stared at the sweeping long shot. If it were not for the turquoise blouse and navy trousers, it would have been difficult to recognize the small figure in the middle distance half turned from the camera. She hadn't known that it was being taken, but then it was a long shot of the line of fountains and water features stretching into the distance so it was doubtful that Edward had even noticed her.

The slideshow came to an end and the easy chairs were pushed back into their original positions. Edward was still extolling the features of his new and obviously expensive camera to Andrew Killigan, but when the discussion about the relative merits of the Olympus Evolt 500 versus the Canon 350D became more and more technical, the others soon lost interest. Deirdre didn't look best pleased.

Fiona spotted Winston over at the bar. 'Forgive me if I abandon you all, I need to have a word with Winston about tomorrow's arrangements.'

'I take it our missing passenger's still not back?'

Fiona shook her head. 'Mr and Mrs Shuttleworth brought his wife back about twenty minutes ago but there's been no sign of Tim. They've given all his details to the police so there really isn't much more we can do. I've just rung head office but I can't say they seemed particularly interested.'

Winston covered her hand with his enormous palm and gave it a reassuring squeeze. 'Let me get you a drink.'

'No, really. I've only just finished my coffee. So, what's the plan for tomorrow?'

Winston pulled a town map of The Hague from his pocket and opened it out. 'I've highlighted our morning route for you and marked all the stopping places.'

Fiona was happy to defer to Winston on how long to spend at the various stops. He had done the trip several times before so she could leave it all in his capable hands. At least the morning trip would give her no problems.

'Thanks for that, Winston. Now I must pop up to Jane and see if I can persuade her to have some supper. The poor girl hasn't eaten since lunch.'

There was a weak, 'Who is it?' in answer to Fiona's tentative knock.

Fiona put her head round the door. 'Only me. Sorry to disturb you. I just wondered if I could tempt you to something to eat.'

Jane sat herself up on one elbow. 'Come in. It's okay; I wasn't asleep. But I'll pass on the food if you don't mind.'

Fiona sat on the end of the bed. Jane was much calmer now, so much so that Fiona was surprised. 'If you're not hungry, can I get you a hot milky drink? Or would you prefer something stronger?'

'No, really. So what are they all saying downstairs?' There was a touch of bitterness in her voice. 'The questions the police asked at Keukenhof implied Tim's run off and I bet that's want they all think too.'

'Everyone's very concerned for you both.'

'If he's had an accident, they would have found him by now.' There was a long pause and then, in a voice so soft Fiona could barely hear, she said, 'He's not coming back.'

Fiona put a reassuring arm around the younger woman's shoulder. 'Do you think he's left you?' Jane didn't answer. 'Gone back to his...'

Jane turned sharply and stared at Fiona. 'You know, don't you?'

'That the two of you aren't married? I sort of guessed.'

'Is it that obvious?'

'No, no.' Fiona reassured her. 'It's just that most husbands know how many sugars their wives take in coffee and he had no idea about where your sister lives. But don't worry. I'm sure no one else suspects anything.

Jane managed a half-hearted smile, 'You're a very observant lady.'

'Part of the job. If you're sure there's nothing I can do for you, I'll leave you to get some sleep. Good night. Try not to worry. And your secret's safe. I won't let on to a soul. I promise. God bless.'

Sunday, 29th April

This morning, enjoy a coach tour of The Hague, the political and royal capital of The Netherlands. See the Peace Palace,
home of the International Court of Justice; The Binnenhof, used for the state opening of Parliament, and The Palace of Noordeinde, the official city residence of Queen Beatrix.

After lunch (included in your package), we drive to the historic town of Delft for a walking tour to see the Nieuwe Kerk, where the Dutch Royal Family are buried; the beautiful medieval market square and the Stadhuis (Town Hall). We end the day with a visit to a pottery factory to the see the production of the famous hand-painted, blue and white delftware.

Super Sun Executive Travel

Nine

It hadn't been a restful night. Fiona had lain awake until the small hours, her mind stubbornly refusing to lie down, only to drop off at what seemed like minutes before her alarm. Still bleary-eyed and muzzy-headed, she threw the last few things into her small suitcase and put it outside the door for collection. Time to see if there had been any news.

There was no luggage outside Jane's door and Fiona wondered if she were still sleeping. She tapped lightly.

'Come in.'

'Only me.'

Jane was already up and dressed. 'I'm going to speak to someone at the Embassy and they are sending a car round to fetch me.'

'You've managed to contact them already?'

The only answer Fiona received was a weak smile.

Fiona hovered at the end of the bed. Jane had already started packing. 'Are you going to come down for some breakfast?'

Jane shook her head. 'I'm not hungry and I'd rather not face the others if you don't mind.'

'I can understand that, but you had nothing last night. It won't help if you start starving yourself. I'll get them to send something up to your room. I'll look in before I leave.'

'Can you put the Do Not Disturb notice on the door as you go out? I'd rather not have the others knocking to see how I am.'

Fiona put her arms around Jane in a hug. For all that she was putting a brave face, the woman must be distraught on the inside. 'It will all turn out all right, I'm sure.'

Curly had spent all last night trying to decide what to do with the merchandize as they moved between hotels. In the end he'd put the DVDs in the bottom of his suitcase and spent an anxious couple of hours worrying about letting them out of his sight. Perhaps after all he should have kept them in his hand luggage.

Once Jenks had slung him out, he'd lost his source of income. He'd been left with no choice but to come up with an alternative. Of course, drugs would be considerably more lucrative, but he hadn't seriously considered that for all sorts of reasons. For a start, he didn't have any contacts, either to buy from or to sell to. True they would probably be easy enough to find. That's if he wanted to be involved with drug dealers. He trusted them even less than he trusted Jenks. But that was only part of the deterrent. He'd seen those sniffer-dogs at the Eurotunnel terminal. Absolutely hyper they were as they'd raced around sniffing in all the luggage compartments underneath the coach. Someone had told him that they trained the dogs by feeding them heroin then made them go cold turkey for a few days before working. By the time they were brought to the coaches at the terminal, they were so desperate for a fix they'd smell it out straight away. He wasn't sure if he believed the story, but you only had to watch the handler trying to hold back the dog bounding around the coach to start wondering.

Porno DVDs had seemed a much safer bet. Unless customs did a physical search, it shouldn't be a problem. There was also the possibility of hiding the package on the coach so that if they were found there was no way the authorities could identify who'd put them there. They could hardly detain a whole coach load of people.

It took some time to get the cases checked and loaded onboard, but, at last, it was time to go. On the coach, no one had appeared unduly bothered by Tim's continued absence. Fiona did catch one or two comments about the frosty relationship between him and Jane. Yvonne Lee claimed she'd seen them arguing on more than one occasion.

'I wouldn't be surprised if he decided to up and leave her the way she kept nagging at him all the time,' she said in a penetrating whisper across the aisle to Mrs Oppenheimer.

There was one small consolation in all this upset, Fiona thought guiltily as the coach drew away from the hotel. It had given her no time to get nervous about her first day actually guiding. Yesterday's talk had gone smoothly enough so there was no need to think that today would be any different. This morning, all she had to do was read the notes she'd prepared back home.

'Across the lake you can see the Binnenhof built around a central square or courtyard on the other side. It houses the parliament and several other government buildings and dates back to the thirteenth century. The Princes of Orange originally used it as a hunting lodge. We're going to have a short photo stop here before we drive on for a walk around the square.'

Armed with all his equipment, Edward Collins was one of the first off the coach, but he wasn't the only one sporting an expensive-looking camera. Eileen Finch was fixing a powerful-looking zoom lens onto hers and both the Major and Andrew Killigan appeared to be keen photographers from the additional paraphernalia they were toting. Almost everyone peeled off the coach. Surprisingly, even Vera Ellis whisked out a tiny digital camera from her handbag. Fiona wondered idly if some loving niece or nephew had bought it, desperate for an idea for a present for the relative who appeared to have everything she wanted.

Some ten minutes later, holding aloft her guide pole with its small white triangular flag emblazoned with a bright yellow smiling sun, Fiona led the little party into the inner court. With attractive buildings on all sides, the photographers were kept busy and with so many of them disappearing off to take pictures, trying to point out specific buildings and explain a little of the history proved quite a challenge. Taking up a position by the central, wrought iron fountain, Fiona brandished her pole to summon everyone to gather round her.

'Facing us, the building with the tall triangular roof and the two matching towers on either side is the Knights' Hall. To the Dutch, this is the single most famous building in the Netherlands. Back in the thirteenth century, Count Willem II of Holland – that's his statue over there – needed a palace or a castle from where he could govern the country. He chose this spot, not far from his family's country house, although he died before it was completed. The city of Den Haag or The Hague has grown up around it. Even today, the building is still used for the state opening of Parliament.'

'It looks more like a church than a castle and it's not very big.' Mrs Oppenheimer was not impressed.

'That's because what you see now is really only the main hall and the rest of his castle was never built. The building was heavily restored in the nineteenth century and that magnificent reconstruction of a medieval oak roof is unique.'

Fearful that what had been intended as a relatively short stop might stretch out into something much longer, Fiona chivvied the last few stragglers back into the fold.

'Before we leave, I'd just like to point out the Maurishuis at the end there. This beautiful seventeenth century mansion now houses a magnificent collection of Dutch Old Masters including one very famous painting.'

'The Girl with the Pearl Earring.' For once, it was not Simon Wick who jumped in but the normally timid Nesta Griffin.

'That's right. I'm sure, if only because of the film, you're all familiar with Vermeer's portrait, but in the museum, you'll also find his "View of Delft" plus paintings by Rembrandt, Rubens and Holbein. Now, if you'd all like to make your way back the coach. Our next stop will be in the main square where we are going to have coffee, but on the way, we're going to drive past the Paleis Noordeinde, Queen Beatrix's palace, although I'm afraid we won't be allowed to get out to take photos.'

On the short journey to the Groenmarkt, Fiona wondered if she should phone Jane to see if there had been any developments. Presumably not, otherwise someone would have let her know already. Best not to trouble the poor woman.

Following the last of her party, Fiona entered the café and looked around to check that none of the single travellers was sitting alone. The two younger women, Nesta Griffin and Eileen Finch, had teamed up again and the Shuttleworths seemed to have taken Miss Ellis under their wing. Margery Pettigrew was with the Harvey sisters and Andrew Killigan was sitting with the Oppenheimers. Everyone accounted for. She could relax and, after all that talking, get herself a much-needed drink.

'That seemed to go okay,' she said as she slipped into the seat alongside Winston. 'Although I'm still not sure if I'm giving them too much information or not enough. I want to keep them interested but not bore them silly.'

'You got it just right.' Dear Winston. He would say that regardless. And he'd stayed with the coach at the Binnenhof so he hadn't heard all her spiel. 'Everyone looks happy enough.'

'Well yes,' she said reluctantly, 'Although Deirdre Oppenheimer seemed a bit disappointed with the Royal Palace. After being taken to see Buckingham Palace and Windsor Castle last week, I think she was expecting something a little grander.'

'That's Americans for you.'

The waitresses were already flitting back and forth with orders. She watched with amazement trays laden not only with steaming cups but plates of pastries. Where did they put it all? It was only a few hours since they had all eaten enormous breakfasts. She had seen the piled plates as they had come back from the buffet table. Catering as it did for British guests, the Hotel Vermeer prided itself on including every thing for a full English breakfast as well as the usual continental cheeses, cold meats and breads. She contemplated saying as much to Winston but decided that making unfavourable comments about the clients was hardly professional.

Winston put his empty cup on the table and pushed back his chair. 'Time for me to go and open up the coach.'

'I'll come too. Just let me finish this.' Fiona quickly picked up her cup.

'No need. Plenty o' time, yet. You sit and finish your coffee, sweetheart. No one else is ready, so no hurry.'

Taking him at his word, Fiona sat back and relaxed. The waitresses came round offering more coffee so there was no incentive for her to get a move on. When she eventually joined the queue for the cloakroom, she caught the tail end of a conversation between the couple in front of her.

'You were positively rude to the poor man.' Nesta Griffin looked at her companion with a pained expression.

'Just because I turned him down!' Fiona could see Eileen Finch's sceptical smile reflected in the mirror.

'He was only trying to help.'

'No. He was being patronizing. Just because he has a flash camera doesn't mean he knows everything. And anyway, I didn't need his help. The clip on my shoulder holster gets stuck sometimes, that's all.'

Fiona wondered who they were talking about. She couldn't see Edward volunteering to help anyone and, as far as she could remember, Simon Wick had a perfectly ordinary-looking camera.

'I don't understand why you don't like the man. He seems very nice, to me.'

'I don't dislike him,' Eileen assured her. 'I just find all that over the top attentiveness a bit much, that's all.'

'Well, I think he's quite charming.'

Definitely not Edward or Simon.

'Smarmy more like.'

'Eileen!'

'The man's a flim-flam artist.'

'Well I like Andrew,' said Nesta defiantly.

'Umm. I can see that.' Fiona had to smile at the mischievous twinkle in the forthright woman's eyes as she turned to her newfound friend – a look which appeared to be completely lost on Nesta.

Making her way back through the café, Fiona found Yvonne Lee standing in the doorway.

'Have we got time for a quick look at the cathedral over there?'

'Grote Kerk?' Fiona looked at her watch and frowned. 'There is still a lot to see and the restaurant is expecting us for lunch at one o'clock.'

'I think you'll find quite a few of the others have already wandered over there,' her husband cut in before Fiona could refuse outright.

Damn. She should have been keeping an eye. When they'd started drifting out she'd assumed they were going straight back to the coach.

The ten-minute delay didn't seem to upset Winston at all.

'It's no big deal.' Did the man ever get irritated? Nothing seemed to faze him. 'We gonna make lunch on time, no problem.'

Apart from twelve across and nine and fifteen down, The Times crossword was complete. A personal best if he managed the last three clues in the next four minutes.

The Commander swore softly under his breath as the sudden buzzing of the telephone interrupted his concentration. For a split second, he contemplated ignoring it. Then he remembered.

'Yes,' he barked into the receiver.

'Sorry to disturb your lunch hour, sir, but it's Inspector Huygen on the line.'

'Put him through.' He'd been expecting the call all day but his heart still missed a beat. 'Dedrick. Good to hear from you. How are things in Amsterdam?'

'Have you heard from your man?' Typical Dutchman. Straight to the point. Never wasted time with pleasantries or small talk.

'Not yet.'

'I think you'd better get over here.'

He took a long breath before he said, 'Give me the details.'

Ten

Lunch was laid out on one long table. By the time Fiona came to sit down the only spare seat was near the centre.

'So what did you think of The Hague?' Fiona wasn't quite sure if the woman sitting beside her was Mrs Smith or Mrs Dobson so inseparable had the two couples become in her mind.

'Fascinating,' came the reply. 'Though I expected the Peace Palace to be a lot more modern.'

'It is nearly a hundred years old, you know,' came a voice from the far side of the table. 'Built for the first international peace conference. It became the International Court of the United Nations in 1946.'

'Oh for goodness sake!'

'You have done your homework, Simon,' Fiona cut in quickly before Yvonne Lee said any more and things got out of hand.

'I do like to read up about a place before I visit.' That smug look of satisfaction was beginning to get on Fiona's nerves and, from the reaction of all those who'd heard him, she wasn't the only one.

'Then I shall know who to ask when I get stuck, won't I?'

Oops! It would be foolish to let her irritation get the better of her, Fiona thought. She was going to have to learn to tolerate far worse than that in her new role. Take three deep breaths, smile and look interested.

A little later, Fiona was able to take a surreptitiously glance down the table to check that all was well. No glum faces. Mrs Oppenheimer had an audience; Margery Pettigrew was chatting with Vera Ellis and there was even a smile on Edward Collins' florid features. The only person not talking nineteen to the dozen was Deirdre Oppenheimer who was listening intently to Andrew Killigan and, judging from the occasional loud guffaws, she was more than happy. Fiona could relax.

It was as the plates were being cleared away that another noisy chortle attracted Fiona's attention. Eileen Finch may have taken against the man but poor Deirdre was evidently smitten. Her face was a picture of adoration. Behind the oversized black-rimmed spectacles, the watery eyes were fixed on Andrew.

It was extremely doubtful that a man with his sophistication would find the gauche, awkward Deirdre attractive in any way. Apart from being big boned and lanky, her nasal whine soon started to grate and the only observations that Fiona had heard her make were superficial to the point of being crass. The poor girl really had no redeeming features that Fiona could see. So what was Killigan up to? Was he one of these middle-aged Lotharios who go on such holidays to fleece money out of susceptible widows or, as in this case, well-to-do spinsters rapidly approaching their forties with no experience of life? Looking around there were no other suitable candidates. Eileen clearly wasn't interested and she and Nesta Griffin seemed to have formed an inseparable bond, so, if that were his game, his options were pretty limited.

You're looking for problems where none exist, Fiona told herself crossly. And anyway, there is nothing you can do about it. You're hardly the girl's chaperone. It's up to her mother to put her straight.

The walking tour of Delft was going well. On the corner of the enormous market square, Fiona stopped, holding up her guide's pole, waiting for her charges to gather round her.

Predictably, Edward Collins was still busy taking photographs of the Nieuwe Kirk and had disappeared the length of the square in order to fit in the slender tower which dominated the little town. No point in waiting for him before she began her spiel.

She had just pointed out the next stopping place at the far end of the square in front of the equally impressive Renaissance-style Stadhuis when she discovered Margery Pettigrew at her elbow.

'I don't want to worry you, but we seem to have lost Vera.'

Fiona's heart sank. 'Do you think she's still inside the church?'

'Would you like me to go back and look for her?'

Gerald Lee had overheard their conversation and stepped in. 'Don't worry. I'll nip back and collect her. You carry on.'

Fiona flashed him a grateful smile. At the pace Margery walked, it would take some time especially if she had to search around and the last thing Fiona needed was to lose her as well as Vera Ellis.

She had almost finished recounting the history of the town hall when she noticed Gerald joining the group. Alone. Damn the woman.

'Right then, everyone. We still have a little while before our visit to the little china factory. It isn't far, just off the market square. I'll meet you all here at five to three and we'll go together. That gives you ten minutes to take any photos but please don't be late because I've booked the tour. You'll have plenty of free time when we come out to look round the shops for souvenirs or get yourselves a cup of tea. As you can see, there are plenty of cafés around.'

She turned to Gerald.

'No sign of her, I'm afraid.'

'Not to worry. Thank you so much for going back. She may well turn up in time for the visit, but if not she knows where the coach is parked. The town is much too small for her to get lost completely.'

Time for Fiona to take a quick run back. There was no sign of the woman outside the church. Perhaps it was worth a look down Kerk Strat. She walked back as far as the canal but to no avail. There was no more time. She had to get back.

Fiona could see a little group already waiting as she dodged round the crowds wandering aimlessly across the open square. Gerald raised a questioning eyebrow. Fiona shook her head.

'Still no sign of her?' asked Margery as she came over. 'I do hope nothing's happened. I think the poor old dear might be getting a bit confused now and again.'

Fiona smiled. Margery Pettigrew was a good fifteen years older than Vera, if not more.

'Batty as a fruit cake, if you ask me,' said Edward Collins. 'Old girl's lost her marbles.'

'Alzheimer's,' came Simon Wick's terse verdict.

'I don't think she's as bad as that,' protested Margery. 'She may seem forgetful at times but that's probably because she's very hard of hearing and doesn't always catch where and when we're all supposed to meet up.'

Edward gave one of his dismissive laughs. 'No. I don't buy it. She can hear perfectly well when she wants to, believe you me.'

'Then she's not the only to play those games when it suits, is she, dear?' Joyce smiled radiantly and ignoring her husband's darkening countenance, turned back to Fiona and asked, 'Would you like one of us to wait here in case she comes?'

'We'll give her just a couple more minutes.'

Fiona was doing a headcount when the errant Vera Ellis wandered over as though nothing had happened.

'Where did you get to? We were all worried. Both Fiona and Mr Lee having been racing about trying to find you.' There was a touch of sharpness in Margery's normal kindly tones.

'Were you? There was no need. I fancied a sit down for a bit that's all.'

'Well you're here now,' said Fiona just managing to keep the irritation from her own voice. 'So everyone, if you'd like to follow me, I'll lead the way. Hoisting her stick aloft, Fiona set off.

As they waited for the rest of the party to gather at the end of the afternoon, Margery was keen to show Fiona her purchases. 'Weren't those artists in the workshop talented? I just couldn't resist one of those little hand-painted dishes.'

Fiona was exhausted by the time she'd mustered everyone back on the coach and, sitting in the warmth of the full sun, she had difficultly preventing herself from falling into a lazy torpor. The gradual cessation of general chatter suggested that she was not the only one. She adjusted the vent to get the full benefit of a cool blast of air.

Their journey north up to Amsterdam would take them back into The Hague. Despite all her good resolutions, Fiona soon began to feel drowsy. There was something she'd meant to do but she was finding it difficult to concentrate. With an effort of will, she leant down and pulled out the clipboard from the bag at her feet. She looked through the checklist. All done. Then it came to her, pulling her back sharply from her lethargy. Jane.

She had switched off her mobile in the pottery factory and forgotten to put it on again.

'Damn!'

'Something wrong?' asked Winston.

There was a text asking if they would all come back to the Hotel Vermeer at the end of their visit.

'It could be good news. Perhaps Tim's come back and they're ready to come on with us,' she said unconvincingly.

'So why you look so worried?'

Fiona laughed. 'I'm puzzled that's all. The message isn't from Jane but from the hotel.'

'Perhaps she asked them to call.'

'I expect so.'

It was not a long run back to The Hague and the coach was soon approaching the hotel. She picked up the microphone. 'Sorry to disturb you all but in case you're wondering what we're up to, I've just received a message asking us to call back at our hotel.'

Two police cars were parked on the forecourt.

'That doesn't look good,' she said quietly to Winston. 'Do you think it's something to do with Tim Brooke?'

'That Mercedes in front has diplomatic number plates, so it's odds on.'

Fiona stared at the big black saloon. It meant nothing to her; she'd have to take Winston's word for it.

As the coach drew up under the covered entrance, Fiona could see two policemen by the hotel doors talking with a tall, imposing-looking man dressed in an immaculate three-piece suit complete with pocket watch chain across his chest. Even before the noisy hiss of the brakes had died away, the man turned from his companions and came down the steps towards them.

'If you'd all just wait in your seats a moment, everyone, I'll go and see what's happening.'

'Mrs Mason?' Fiona nodded. 'Peter Montgomery-Jones. May I have a word?' The question was asked pleasantly but it was hardly an invitation one could refuse. 'As you have probably surmised, we still have no news of Mr Brooke's whereabouts. I apologize for the inconvenience it will necessitate, but the police will need to speak to you and all of the other passengers. Interviews will be conducted with as little disturbance as possible but, as you can appreciate, it is necessary.'

'But we're supposed to be in Amsterdam for dinner.'

'That will no longer be possible, given the circumstances. We have informed the Black Tulip Hotel and made arrangements for you all to stay here for another night. Your head office is aware of the situation.'

'I see,' Fiona replied, not sure that she did at all. What was the point of all this disruption? What possible help could she or any of the others offer? 'I'd better tell everyone.'

'It might be better coming from me.'

She stepped aside letting him mount the steep steps ahead of her. Meekly she handed over the microphone. Fine. Let him handle the flack.

Her mind was racing while he repeated the scant information he'd given her.

'The officers would like to speak to all of you which, as I am sure you will appreciate, may take some time. If any of you can remember seeing Mr Brooke after two o'clock, perhaps you would be kind enough to let them know and you will be interviewed this evening. Either before dinner, if you can spare the time, or after. The rest will be seen first thing tomorrow.'

Predictably, the voluble response he got was none too amenable. Fiona flipped down the tip up seat in the stairwell and sank onto it, leaving him to it. It was a while before the angry protests subsided.

'Thank you for your time ladies and gentlemen and, once again, please do accept my apologies for the inconvenience.'

Before leaving the coach, he turned to Fiona. 'Perhaps you would be kind enough to give me a complete list of all your passengers.'

'Certainly.' His assumption that everyone was there to do his bidding was fast getting on her nerves. She felt a sudden surge of rebellion. 'Once I've made sure that everyone has been checked in again and have their keys.'

There was a slight narrowing in the cool, grey eyes and a tension in the jaw. He gave her a cursory nod and disappeared down the steps and back into the hotel.

The barrage of questions began again. Fiona put up her hands and shook her head. 'I'm sorry everyone. I know no more than you. As soon as there is any information I assure you I will let you know. In the mean time, it would be really helpful if you would all find yourselves a seat in the reception area.'

'Will we have the same rooms as before?' Mrs Oppenheimer asked.

'I've really no idea. I very much doubt it. We could well be dotted all over the hotel wherever rooms happen to be available.'

Fiona decided to abandon Super Sun's golden rule for tour managers – last to leave the coach and first back. They could hardly get lost and she could check later for any hand luggage left behind. The sooner she could hand over their keys and let them get to their rooms the better. Keeping them sitting around in the lobby could only lead to more grumbling as they fed off each other's complaints. It would hardy look good on her very first trip if half the clients ended up demanding compensation for a spoilt holiday.

Even before she could get to the reception desk, a policeman came towards her. 'Mrs Mason? We would like to speak to you straightaway, if you do not mind.'

Yes, I bloody well do, she thought but what she actually said was, 'With pleasure. But first I need to see to my clients, I'm afraid. They are my priority. I can't keep them waiting.'

She danced round him and strode towards the waiting receptionist. And I need to speak to Winston and sort out what we are going to do tomorrow, she thought bitterly. All their plans were now in total disarray.

Fiona had just picked up the tray of room keys when Peter Montgomery-Jones appeared at her elbow.

'The passenger list, Mrs Mason?'

Had his request been a little less peremptory, Fiona might not have voiced her thoughts so tartly. 'With all your obvious organizational skills and many contacts, I'm surprised you were not able to persuade Super Sun head office to provide you with a copy.'

It was with a considerable effort of will that Fiona managed to put down the tray without banging it on the counter. The young man behind the desk hurriedly took himself to a distant corner and busied himself tidying the brochures.

'As it so happens, I did arrange for them to fax over a copy but I do need to check that the list is correct.'

She pulled out a sheet of paper from her folder. He held out a hand to take it.

'I'll ask the receptionist if it's possible to make a photocopy.'

It probably wasn't a good idea to antagonize the man but there was no way she was going to let him ride roughshod over her. She'd had her fill of pompous bureaucrats in the last few years fighting to ensure that Bill received all the treatments and entitlements that were his by right. Just because the man had snapped his fingers, she had no intention of kowtowing to him, whoever he was. She marched the length of the long counter to the young man and, with a sweet smile, gave him her request.

'Straight away, Mrs Mason. If you would like to see to your party, I will bring it over to you.' He gave her a conspiratorial grin. She obviously wasn't the only one who had had to suffer the Montgomery-Jones highhandedness.

Eleven

The keys duly delivered, Fiona had no choice but to trot off with the policeman and answer all his questions. Once it had been established that she'd not seen Tim Brooke after he went through the park gates, he seemed far more interested in the other passengers. Had she seen any of them? What had they been doing? He didn't ask about any tensions she might have been aware of between him and Jane so she didn't volunteer any information.

By the time she managed to get to her new room, there was barely time for a quick wash and change before she had to be down for dinner. So much for that cup of tea she'd promised herself earlier!

She wasn't best pleased to see Peter Montgomery-Jones standing in the lobby when she came down and groaned inwardly when he came towards her.

'I do appreciate that you have had to take the brunt of the complaints our enquiries will cause and I have been onto your head office again. As a goodwill gesture, I have booked lunch for you and your party at one of the town's best restaurants at the company's expense. I hope that will go some way to improving relations with everyone.'

He swept off before she could thank him. She had to admit that he'd done exceptionally well to persuade the company to part with the money to fund the extra meals. She didn't know whether to be pleased with the opportunity to pass on some good news or annoyed that a whole morning was now going to be wasted because there was no chance of getting away until the afternoon.

It was all very well having a posh lunch lined up but what were they expected to do all morning? Perhaps those who were no longer needed for questioning could explore The

Hague, visit some of the museums perhaps. There was the Mauritshuis and the Prison Gate Museum and it was possible to do tours of the Binnenhof and the Peace Palace. She could look up a few more suggestions and their opening times. Her heart sank. Tomorrow was Monday. What was the betting they would all be closed? She needed to talk to Winston.

'Not a problem.' As always, the man was wonderfully unmoved by all the turmoil. 'How about we drive over to Scheveningen?'

It meant nothing to Fiona.

'It's only a spit away by the sea. Folk can take a stroll along the front or on the pier and there's a few interesting old buildings to take a look at.'

'But we don't know yet how long it's going to take for everyone to be interviewed.'

'So we take those that are ready at ten o'clock and I'll drive back and pick up the rest and bring them over when they're ready. It's fifteen minutes tops, less than that if there's not much traffic; I can make as many trips as necessary.'

'Winston, you're a star. I'll tell them all tonight.' She raised herself on tiptoe and planted a kiss on his cheek before hurrying to the dining room.

They were already tucking into the main course by the time she took her seat. There was no opportunity to let everyone know the arrangements until after they'd eaten and were all together for coffee. Because the Garden Room was now occupied by another group, the only other available space large enough for the Super Sun party was at one end of the bar lounge.

By the time she had finished her meal and made her way there, half the party were already assembled. Predictably, the grousing had already begun and, as she made her way past groups of other hotel guests, she could hear Simon Wick proclaiming bitterly to anyone who would listen.

'This really isn't good enough, upsetting everyone like this, interrogating us all as though we were common criminals and all because some man's run off because he can't put up with his nagging wife any longer. My Iris is not a well woman. I won't have her upset.'

His timid little wife tried to shush him but for once Simon was not alone in his protest.

'You have to admit that this full-scale investigation is way over the top,' agreed Gerald Lee.

That seemed to be the general consensus. Cynthia Harvey's suggestion that poor Tim might have had an accident was quickly dismissed.

'In that case someone would have found him and we'd have heard. He can't have got lost so he must have left the Park intentionally.'

'Our room was next to theirs and all the rooms along that side of the corridor have twin beds.' Trust Mrs O to have spotted that. 'Twin beds! Now I ask you, what sort of happily married young couple asks for separate beds when they could have a double?'

'Are you sure? Their room could well have been different.' Lavinia Rawlings was not yet ready to assume the worst.

'Oh no. Yesterday, as I was passing, I just happened to see in as the pair of them were coming out.'

Well that clinches it, Fiona thought. Proof positive they have a bad marriage. She could hardy voice such a sarcastic comment, but she was surprised that none of the other more reasonably minded members of the party didn't come out with it.

As soon as the last arrivals had collected their coffee and sat down, Fiona clapped her hands and made her announcements about the next day's rearranged itinerary.

'I don't know how long the police intend to carry on taking statements this evening or what time they will start again tomorrow so I'm afraid we'll have to play it a little by ear. But tomorrow, if you can't make ten o'clock, Winston will keep reception informed and you can phone down and see what time the next group will be leaving.'

The general mood lightened a little but the grumbling about all the fuss rumbled on. No one seemed to have much sympathy for the missing Tim.

'So what did you think of Delft?' Fiona asked in an effort to lighten the mood.

'It's a little gem of a town isn't it? And so much history.' At least Eileen Finch was prepared to play ball.

Every time Fiona managed to steer the conversation within her little cluster onto more pleasant topics, one of the others would come back from their interview – invariably in a bad mood.

'Over twenty minutes they kept me.'

Fiona had to stop herself from doing a double take. It was the first time she'd heard Mr Karpinski say anything. For such a tiny, almost wizened, man – even his beige, polyester jacket seemed too large for him – it wasn't only the deep boom of his voice that took her by surprise. After his wife's barely-intelligible harsh Polish accent, Felix Karpinski's, broad Brummie nasal twang was totally unexpected. 'Asked all sorts of damned fool questions that had nothing to do with this missing fellow. Just nosey-parkering if you ask me.'

'At this rate it's going to take all tomorrow to get through everyone. And what is the point? Anyone'd think the man's been abducted all the fuss they're making.' Even the mild-mannered Gordon Shuttleworth was rapidly losing patience.

Fiona gave up trying to be the voice of reason and let them all get on with it.

'Perhaps he's found himself a floozie,' someone suggested.

'A weedy little bloke like him? He should be so lucky.' Gerald Lee's remark raised a few smiles from one or two of the others. 'Personally, I can't see what an attractive young woman like Jane ever saw in Tiny Tim. Moody sort of chap if you ask me.'

There were a few murmurs of agreement. Fiona wondered if she should intervene, but someone changed the subject and the conversation thankfully moved on.

At ten o'clock, Fiona was more than ready for her bed, but the others were still chatting animatedly. She couldn't be the first to leave. By half past they were all still sitting there. Don't this lot ever need sleep, she wondered?

'Another drink, anyone?' Andrew Killigan got to his feet.

Fiona shook her head.

'Not for me either, thank you. As soon as Edward comes back from his interview, I'm off to bed,' Joyce announced.

'So that's two white wines, a G and T and four beers. Anyone else?'

'I'll help you.' Deirdre leapt up knocking against the small central table as she pushed past knees in her eagerness to get out.

The two of them were still at the bar when Edward Collins returned, a smug smile replacing the habitual pugnacious expression.

'You've been absolutely ages, what happened?' enquired his wife.

'Had to go and get them all my photos, didn't I?'

'Oh?'

'Very interested they were. Had to download a copy of them all onto a CD for them to take away.' He turned to Joyce, 'Told you it would be useful bringing the laptop.'

'But what did the police want with your pictures?'

'I don't know do I, woman?' Joyce was interrupting his story. 'They were asking all sorts of pointless questions about who I'd seen during the afternoon and where. I told 'em, I don't know half the names anyway and I certainly wasn't making notes. Too busy taking photos. But I did say I took a lot of general shots for Joyce that showed members of the group.'

'I like to have pictures of the people I meet on holiday,' explained his wife.

'Anyway,' Edward seized back the conversation, 'that was when they asked if they could see them.'

'I expect they'll want copies of yours as well, Andrew,' piped up Deirdre as she pushed aside the empty glasses on the table to make room for Andrew to put down the tray. 'Andrew has some super pictures, don't you?'

All this talk of photography seemed to spark everyone back to life again. Fiona sighed. At least it made the evening end on a less fraught note.

Ten minutes later, people were starting to drift away from the other Super Sun groups. Fiona looked around her own tightly packed, little cluster. Please someone make a move, she prayed. Five more minutes and she was going up regardless.

She could have kissed Joyce when the woman wriggled her well-covered hips to the front of the deep armchair and announced, 'Well, I'm off. 'Night, everyone.'

Without protest, Edward followed in her wake, and the Shuttleworths and the Lees made their farewells. Fiona got to her feet. At last! Bidding goodnight to the Oppenheimers, Andrew Killigan, Mr and Mrs Karpinski and Vera Ellis, she made for the lift.

Twelve

Fiona had just put her key into the lock to let herself into her room when someone came up quickly behind her.

'Jane!'

'Sorry to intrude on you like this. Can we go in? I've been watching out for you and I don't want any of the others to see me.' She seemed remarkably calm. Once they were sitting on the bed, she continued. 'You've been so kind and I couldn't leave without saying thank you for all you've done.'

'You're going home?'

Jane nodded. 'First thing tomorrow morning.'

'Does that mean you've heard from Tim?'

The hazel eyes looked away quickly and she shook her head. 'We haven't spoken.'

'That's not quite what I meant. Something's happened.' There was a long silence. 'He's not coming back, is he?'

Jane gave a hollow laugh. 'Not much gets past you, does it?' She gave a long resigned sigh. 'You might as well know but please don't tell the others. As I said last night, Tim wasn't my husband, he was my boss.'

Fiona put a hand on her arm. 'Believe me, I'm not here to make judgements.'

'We weren't having an affair,' Jane said quickly. 'Nothing like that.'

'But something's going on.' There was a long silence. 'This investigation. The police would not be taking this much time and trouble interviewing the whole party for a missing holidaymaker. Assuming Tim isn't a criminal on the run, what was he up to?'

'We were on an assignment together.'

'What kind of assignment are we talking about here? Are you police officers?'

'Not exactly. Investigators for Customs and Revenue.' Jane frowned and licked her lips. She had obviously said more than she'd meant to.

'You can't stop there.'

'The point is there's strong evidence to suggest that someone is using Super Sun Tours as a cover for smuggling. We've suspected something for awhile now, but it could be any of the trips that come within easy distance of Amsterdam or Antwerp.'

Fiona stared at Jane trying to take it in. In the long pause that followed, her brain was working overtime. 'So why don't you simply stop each coach when the ferries get back to England and go through everyone's luggage?'

'If we started searching every Super Sun coach returning from Holland, the cartel would realize straight away and change the tour company. There are just too many coaches, over three hundred a day pass through Dover alone. These boys are greedy. Very greedy. And they're prepared to take risks. An undercover op seemed the best way. Besides, it may not be that simple. If the stuff is hidden onboard somewhere, even if the coach were to be taken apart and the contraband found, it would be impossible to prove exactly which passenger put it there. Sometimes the gangs stick it under the vehicle so it could well be that no one actually travelling on the coach is responsible. That's why coaches are so vulnerable. Someone on the continent plants it underneath, then when it gets back to England, another person breaks into the depot under cover of darkness and retrieves it. They need have no connection whatsoever to the tour company or anyone on it.'

'So the smuggler isn't necessarily one of the passengers on our trip?'

Reluctantly Jane answered after a long pause. 'Possibly not.'

It was obvious to Fiona that Jane knew a great deal more than she was telling but she was hardly in a position to press for details. She tried another tack. 'So are Customs putting people on all the Super Sun coaches?'

'Heavens no. We don't have the manpower. We had a tip-off, anonymous of course as these things always are, but enough to justify sinking a significant proportion of the budget in targeting this particular tour.'

'These drugs must be worth a great deal of money.'

Jane shook her head. 'Not drugs. Diamonds.'

'Really?' Fiona could not hide her disapproval. 'Don't misunderstand me, obviously I don't condone any kind smuggling. Clamping down on heroin and cocaine, I could understand. Or even child pornography, but diamonds! Does that really justify an expensive undercover operation and all this fuss?'

'Don't put these people on a par with the ones who bring in booze and cigarettes to earn a bit of extra cash. Make no mistake. These men are vicious. Criminals and terrorists use uncut diamonds to launder money because they are almost impossible to trace. We're talking conflict diamonds brought in from Sierra Leone and Angola. Huge sums of money to fund terrorist activity.'

Fiona must have looked unconvinced because Jane went on, 'We know that Al-Qaeda buy rough diamonds in Liberia, which are then brought by a series of couriers in relatively small amounts to Antwerp or Amsterdam. Our job is to track down the gangs that buy them on the black market and bring them into Britain.'

'Does that mean Tim's off chasing a lead?'

'Something like that.'

'Do you know who?' All she got was a shake of the head. 'Surely you don't still suspect someone on our coach is involved?'

'Tim was onto something. All he told me was that he wanted to follow up on a couple of hunches before he started making accusations. He may be an experienced officer, but that doesn't stop him being a bit of a maverick. I'm fairly new to the game so perhaps he just wanted to protect me. To be honest it made things difficult between us and my pestering only made him more stubborn.'

'So where is Tim now? You still haven't heard from him?'

Jane shook her head and dropped her gaze to the hands in her lap.

'Are you worried something may have happened to him?'

'As you said, he's probably off following some lead. The point is, with Tim gone my cover is blown. As Tim's wife, I can hardly continue the tour with him still officially missing. At this stage, it's far too late to put another officer into the tour. Now that you know, you can be on your guard.'

'You want me to report on anything suspicious?'

'Not at all!' Jane held up her hands in horror. 'These people are dangerous. You must do absolutely nothing to arouse suspicion. We will keep a watching brief. Our people will be close at all times. We're pretty certain we know the identity of the Dutch contact. The problem is we've never been able to prove it. Rest assured his movements are under surveillance round the clock. As soon as he makes a move, we'll be there.'

'So what do you want me to do?'

'Well, for a start we need to keep the party together until we know exactly who's involved. Whoever it is must already be very jittery and the last thing we want is for the courier to abandon the project and go home before we have the chance to make an arrest. Too much has gone into this operation so there mustn't be any excuse for anyone to start leaving the tour. Someone's got to jolly everyone along and keep them all happy.'

'I've already had a message from head office about making sure there are no causes for complaint.' Jane said nothing but her lips twitched into a rueful smile. 'I suppose that was pressure from your people,' Fiona continued.

'I expect the rest of the party are pretty miffed that they have to stay here for another night and sit around tomorrow morning until all the interviews are complete. You may have a lot of persuading to do.'

'Winston is going to drive us over to Scheveningen in relays as people are ready.'

'That's great. So you see why it's imperative that no one else finds out about Tim and me or the smuggling.'

'I'm sure they all think you are both an ordinary married couple. To be honest, at the moment all the money is on the idea that Tim's walked out on you.'

'Excellent. Encourage that idea if you can.'

Fiona sat trying to take everything in. It was some moments before she said, 'So how can you be sure that I'm not the contact?'

Jane gave a low chuckle. 'I told the Commander you are a sharp cookie. Super Sun staff are obviously prime suspects but you're new to the company.'

'You've checked up on me?' Fiona's eyes widened.

'On everyone. Remember carry on as normal. Don't tell anyone, even Winston. The department is running background checks on all the passengers so if anything comes to light I'll let you know. I will keep in contact. If there is any danger to you or anyone else we'll be there to step in straight away, I promise. Our people will be with you all the way. There is absolutely no need for you to worry.'

Easy for her to say! The doubt must have shown in Fiona's face because Jane gave her a reassuring smile. 'Here give me your mobile. I'll program in my number and if there's a problem, or if there's anything you think we ought to know, you can give me a ring. Anytime.'

This was the stuff of second-rate spy films. Any minute now, she's going to give me a code name, Fiona thought.

'I see.'

'You are obviously someone with a cool head. You have a knack of smoothing over minor hiccups. We need someone who won't panic or go into a flap.'

Fiona almost laughed out loud. If only Jane knew!

Scheveningen:
Once an old fishing port situated on the North Sea coast, Scheveningen is now Holland's premier seaside resort. Van der Valk's Pier, a modern futuristic edifice replacing an earlier structure destroyed during the Second World War, dominates its long sandy beach. Opposite the casino is the grand hotel of the Kurhaus (spa house), built at the turn of the 20th century at the time of the town's fashionable heyday. Here you can take coffee in the richly decorated central hall beneath its pendulous chandeliers and admire the frescoes sporting mermaids and semi-clad maidens.

Frobisher's Guide to Holland

Thirteen

Fiona was guiding her group through the narrow streets but the beautiful Renaissance Grote Kirk she had promised them was nowhere in sight. Only a dirty, rundown railway station with a tin roof and boarded-up windows. Angry faces loomed out of the mist, snarling and shouting. As she desperately searched for the map, all her notes were torn from her hands and ripped to shreds. She started to run. Anything to get away from the mob screaming for her blood. She turned a corner only to find her route blocked by a canal cutting right across the path and there were no bridges in sight. She turned to face her pursuers. Mr Dobson kept jabbing at her with a pitchfork and Edward Collins stood next to him slowly passing a scythe with a lethal-looking, shining blade from one hand to the other, as he demanded she hand over the diamonds.

The next moment, she was the one wielding the scythe lashing out at a man in front of her. Blood was spurting from cuts across his chest as Tim Brooke stretched out his hands in supplication. But still she did not stop, hacking away until he sank to the ground. When she looked down at the remains at her feet, it was not Tim but Henry Unsworth whose dead eyes stared back up at her in accusation.

She woke with a start at the sound of her own scream, drenched in sweat.

She staggered to the en suite, clattering the glass against the sink as she filled it with water. Still shivering, she downed two full tumblers and looked at the drawn, ashen face staring back at her in the mirror.

So what would Freud have made of that? The first part was explicable enough. Despite Winston's frequent reassurances, it took very little to knock her confidence in her abilities for this new job and this smuggling business wasn't making it any easier. But what about Tim? Deep down, did she fear that the poor man was dead? But what did all that have to do with Henry Unsworth?

And why, in the name of all that was holy, was she standing shivering in a freezing bathroom in the middle of the night trying to analyse her nightmare?

'For pity's sake, woman! Pull yourself together.'

As she crawled back to bed, she glanced at the digital clock. 02.18.

If she'd been at home, she could have made herself a soothing cup of hot milky chocolate. She snapped off the light and snuggled down pulling the covers up under her chin. Thoughts kept racing through her brain. Which of her motley assortment of passengers could possibly be a smuggler? How could anyone become involved with activities that furthered the cause of any kind of terrorist group? Were they so desperate to make money that they would willingly help in a scheme to finance the deaths of innocent people? Or perhaps, if they were simply middlemen, they did not realize exactly who they were working for. Surely, that must be it.

There was so much she didn't know. If only Jane had told her more. Just who was supposed to be keeping an eye on them all and how? There were so many questions she wished she'd asked last night, but it had all been so hard to take in.

The more she tried to push away all thoughts of Jane's revelations from her mind the more they kept coming back. Pink elephant syndrome! Try as she might, it was the only thing she could think about. Perhaps she could read for a while, but the room was too chilly to sit up in bed. And she'd only just warmed up again curled up in a tight ball under the thin blankets on the hard, unfamiliar single bed. Oh to spread out under her lovely down duvet on the king size back home!

The cases did not need to be outside the door until nine o'clock; an hour later than the previous day. There was no need to put them on the coach until lunchtime, but as the rooms had to be vacated by ten, there was no point in leaving them any later. At a little after eight thirty, she looked out and there were already several cases in the corridor.

When she got to the lift, she found Vera Ellis waiting. 'They take forever, don't they?'

'Yes thank you, dear. And you?'

Fiona smiled and nodded though quite what she was admitting to was something of a mystery. 'I think we're in for another lovely day.'

'Sorry, dear, I didn't catch that.' Vera's face broke into a smile. 'Getting old and my hearing isn't what it was, I'm afraid.'

You're not that old, Fiona wanted to say. She could only be in her mid sixties and she still had a beautiful skin. True there were a few wrinkles around her eyes but, as Vera stood clutching her bag to her chest, Fiona felt quite envious of the smooth, unblemished backs of the pale hands all too aware of her own prominent veins.

'Are you coming with us to Scheveningen this morning?' Fiona asked raising her voice a little.

A puzzled frown came over Vera's face. 'I thought we were going to Amsterdam today?'

'We are, but not till after lunch. We have to wait until all the interviews are over.'

Vera still looked confused. 'It said in the itinerary we had some time to look round Amsterdam on our own. I was planning to visit the flower market.'

'You can this afternoon, but the police need to speak to everyone first.'

'Oh yes. How silly of me. I'd forgotten all about that. Though I didn't quite catch what about.'

'Mr Brooke went missing. Do you remember? They want to know if any of us saw something that might help find him.'

'Oh I see. I couldn't really follow what all the fuss was about last night. I didn't realize it was to do with that poor man who got lost. His wife must be terribly upset, poor lady. Let's hope the police find him soon.'

'Yes, indeed.'

She really would have to make sure Vera heard all the important information in future. As they stood facing each other in the confined space of the lift she asked, 'Have you put your case outside your room?' Not very tactful but it was best to check.

'Oh yes.' Fiona was given a cherubic smile.

Forgetful she may be, but yesterday's verdict that Vera was in the early stages of some kind of dementia was surely far too harsh. Margery Pettigrew was obviously right. The woman is deaf not daft, Fiona thought as she watched Vera amble towards the dining room. Still, there were enough problems to worry about without having to keep a constant lookout for Miss Ellis.

The Super Sun section of the dining room was already quite busy by the time Fiona walked in. She walked round checking that all was well and wishing everyone good morning.

Margery was at the buffet looking longingly at the hot trays of sausages, bacon, fried tomatoes, mushrooms and scrambled eggs.

'Smells wonderful, doesn't it?' she said to Fiona, 'So tempting. But I suppose I really ought to stick to cereal and toast especially as we're going to have a nice lunch as well.' The hand continued to hover over the serving spoon.

'Well, you are on holiday.'

'Perhaps just a little.'

Were all Super Sun clients obsessed with food? Fiona pulled herself up short. For goodness sake woman, get a grip. The poor old dear was probably just making conversation. The strain of keeping up the farce that everything was hunky dory was going to be no mean accomplishment. I don't know about making sure none of them escape back home, she thought crossly, How about me? If I had any sense, I'd chuck the job and catch the next ferry home myself.

Taking her fruit and yogurt, Fiona made her way to a table at the back of the room where she could pull herself back together in peace. From where she was sitting, she had a good view of all the party. Surely, it wasn't possible that one of

these ordinary people could possibly be an international diamond smuggler?

Certainly not nice Gordon Shuttleworth and Gerald Lee
seemed harmless; the poor man had enough to worry about
with Yvonne for a wife. Now she was being downright bitchy.
Simon Wick was a real pain and his little outburst last night
had incited quite a bit of resentment amongst the others at
having to be interviewed, but it was difficult to picture him as
a smuggler. Then there was Felix Karpinski. Although he
claimed most of his work consisted of mending watches, he
did work in, possible even own – he hadn't been too specific –
a jewellers of sorts. Birmingham had a famous jewellery
quarter. It would not be difficult to for him to dispose of the
diamonds once he got them back to Britain. He would presumably have all the necessary contacts. Fiona gave a deep
sigh.

There had been that strange business in Keukenhof with
Major Rawlins. Had that meeting with the man on the bench
been pre-arranged with some Dutch contact? It was a pretty
elaborate plan finding just the right bench and besides, the
itinerary had been changed only the night before. Plus of
course, by his own admission, he was a frequent visitor to
Holland and she never had discovered what sort of business
brought him over here.

And what about Edward Collins? If it had to be anyone, she
would quite like it to be him. She rarely took against people
but the man could be downright disagreeable at times. He was
always off supposedly taking photos. However, that really
wasn't enough to put him in the frame. Mind you, if Barbara
Shuttleworth was right about seeing Tim arguing with someone, it could have been the smuggler. It was around three
o'clock that she'd been talking to Joyce so Edward certainly
wasn't with his wife at the critical time. Now you're being
ridiculous, woman. You've been reading too many second-
rate crime novels.

As the only unaccompanied man in the party, the most
likely suspect surely had to be Andrew Killigan. But was that
relevant? If the organization were as slick as Jane had sug-

gested, there was no reason to suspect the courier was working alone. It could just as easily be a group. The Dobsons and the Smiths kept themselves pretty much apart from everyone else.

Time to stop playing amateur detective. Was a smuggler really worth all this bother? Surely she had better things to think about? Fiona poured herself another cup of tea and tried to think of the day ahead. She glanced around the room. Had the waiter in the far corner been staring at her? He'd looked away as soon as their eyes met, but he seemed in no hurry to be off anywhere else. All the other staff were busy clearing tables or bringing fresh pots of tea and coffee, but the man continued to stand by one of the side tables leisurely folding a pile of napkins in marked contrast to the bustle going on around him. Without trying to make it too obvious, Fiona tried to keep a watch on what the man was doing. Though his hands moved slowly, his eyes were darting round the tables as though was he was checking out all the people sat in the dining room. But why only the Super Sun party? Was he the Dutch contact? Was he looking out for the smuggler? Hardly likely! Breakfast time in such a public place was hardly the best spot for a rendezvous of any kind let alone passing over diamonds. She must have subterfuge and intrigue on the brain.

With a sigh, she put her empty plates together and glanced at her watch. If she didn't make a move, she'd be late. Time to clean her teeth and throw the last few things into her hand luggage before checking to see how many people were ready for the ten o'clock departure.

Perhaps it was because her mind was still in overdrive, but Fiona found herself almost colliding with someone as she turned sharp left coming out of the dining room. 'I'm so sorry.'

'Good morning, Fiona.'

Why did it have to be Mrs O?

'And to you. Did you sleep well?' Fiona gave the woman her brightest smile but it did nothing to lighten the grim expression still darkening Mrs Oppenheimer's face. Fiona's heart sank.

'One doesn't really expect to get a restful night away from one's own bed, especially with the church clock chiming every quarter hour. And why they have to make deliveries at such an unearthly time in the morning is beyond comprehension.'

'Oh dear.' Quite what Fiona was expected to do to improve the situation she couldn't even hazard a guess. 'At least we seem to be lucky with the weather this morning. A lovely sunny day and it's quite warm out.'

With a little snort, Mrs Oppenheimer replied, 'The forecast on CNN was for rain.'

Deirdre looked a little embarrassed at her mother's determined pessimism and tugged at her arm. 'We'd better get going, Mom or we'll be late.'

Fourteen

'You have done what?' He spoke very slowly, a marked pause between each word.

It was the total absence of emotion that sent a shiver down Jane's spine. That and the steely grey eyes boring deep into her innermost being. She had anticipated that he would be angry; knew she was in for the biggest dressing down she'd ever had, but this white-hot, controlled fury was terrifying. If it should bubble over – if that iron self-discipline should suddenly give way – the consequences were too horrific to contemplate.

It took a great deal to unsettle the Commander. No matter what the emergency, he was never one to lose his cool. Mr Unruffled. But then he'd never lost one of his men like this before.

'As I said, I didn't really have any choice, sir. Fiona Mason is a very observant woman. Not much gets past her. She'd worked out most of it for herself anyway. Straight away she recognized that Tim and I weren't a kosher couple,' she was gabbling and she knew it. 'That we weren't married, I mean. And it was very clear that she wasn't going to fall for any story about a boss and his secretary having an illicit week away. I had to tell her something and she knows nothing about Tim being shot.'

'And exactly how long do you think it will take her to work out that Brooke is dead?' It was a purely rhetorical question and one that Jane had been asking herself half the night. She could have bitten off her tongue the moment she had blurted out about the two of them being Customs Officers. How could she have been so inept, so unprofessional?

But this was no time to back down. 'There was always the possibility of her voicing her doubts about Tim and me to the wrong person and blowing our investigation sky high. There really was no alternative.'

'And what if she should be the contact?'

'All the background checks point to her being exactly what she claims to be. This is her first assignment for the company and she hasn't left Guildford for more than a few days at a time in the last nine years. Not since her husband was diagnosed with motor neurone disease. Taking this job would seem to be more of a way of trying to make a new life for herself than because of any financial necessity. In all the reviews we've had, her name has never been raised as a serious contender.' There was a long pause. She could hear the thumping of her heart. His jaw tightened but before he could protest again, she tried a new argument. 'She's resourceful and thinks on her feet. I really believe it would be an asset having someone like her on the inside. If any of the other passengers stumble across something and start asking awkward questions, she can let us know immediately.'

'The woman has had no training whatsoever. One false move on her part could put her and everyone else in real danger. You had better pray that she is all you claim and that she is not the type to fall apart in a crisis. The knowledge that she has a smuggler onboard could unsettle the woman and push her into doing something stupid. Have you given any thought as to how vulnerable she must be feeling right now? What is the likelihood of any ordinary person being able to act naturally in such circumstances?'

She hung her head waiting for him to tell her she was dismissed from the service or at the very least sent back home in disgrace. The Commander was silent for what seemed like an age.

'As there is no possibility of undoing what you have done,' he said eventually, 'we are going to have to work out some serious damage limitation. I suppose you had better stay on hand to give the poor woman some kind of reassurance.'

'Yes, sir.'

'If this all goes wrong, you do realize that it is your career on the line.'

'Yes, sir.' Time for a quick exit.

Jane closed the door and collapsed against it, utterly exhausted. She was reprieved, at least temporarily.

Only a handful of people had gathered in the lobby when Fiona went down but there was still plenty of time before the first departure. There were no messages for her at reception so presumably head office was leaving her to cope with things. At least it was good not to have them constantly checking up on her and, on the bright side, it did seem to imply that they had sufficient confidence in her ability to cope with the situation. Just how much they were aware of, was anybody's guess. No messages from the police either so she had no idea how the interviews were progressing or how much longer they would take.

Fiona glanced at her watch. Perhaps it was still a little early for Winston to drive the coach round from the car park to the front of the hotel, but he wouldn't be long. Winston. Why hadn't it struck her before? In all her deliberations over breakfast, she hadn't considered him as a suspect even though last night she had been the one to point out the logic of Super Sun staff being the most obvious candidates. It was difficult to think of the ever-smiling, easygoing Winston as a possible smuggler. But who had a better opportunity? As a coach driver, he was back and forth to Holland on a regular basis and, out of all them in the party, he was the only one whose presence couldn't be accounted for. For most of the day, he was off on his own leaving them to their sightseeing. The person best placed to make contact with his Dutch source with no danger of being seen by any of the others in the party. So what did he do with himself for hours at a time? He'd said something about sweeping out the coach and washing down the windows, but that couldn't take too long each day. If she started asking questions, there was no guarantee she would get truthful answers. He might begin to wonder why she was prying into his affairs. At best, she could put their congenial relationship in jeopardy and, if he were guilty, all she would achieve would be to put him on his guard.

Stop trying to play detective. Leave it to the professionals. The worst thing she could do was to alert suspicion by behaving differently towards people and the only way to stop herself doing that was by resisting the temptation to start imagining all sorts of things.

He was feeling more relaxed this morning. Every day that passed had to be a bonus. Seeing the police waiting when the coach got back to the hotel last night had given him a nasty jolt. For one heart-stopping moment, he'd expected them to march straight onto the coach and clap him in handcuffs, but it turned out all right; there had been no revelations. It looked as if they hadn't even found the body. Most likely the police were only there at all because they had the British Embassy breathing down their necks and had to be seen doing something. On the other hand, all these blessed interviews indicated that the authorities were not happy with the explanation about Brooke having run out on his wife. And why were the police asking so many questions about where everyone was?

If they had any real suspicions, he tried to reassure himself, the police would have conducted searches of all their rooms. Then he would've been well and truly scuppered. Apart from the DVDs, there was the matter of the gun. He should have got rid of it there and then but he'd been so terrified at the time that all he could think about was getting away. There was no possibility of it being traced back to him. It wasn't as though he'd bought it in a shop on his credit card.

It had been a last minute decision to bring his father's old wartime pistol. A Lugar picked off some dead German and brought back as a souvenir and hidden away in a shoebox at the back of the wardrobe. He'd only brought it to bolster his confidence. That last phone call to Hansen had unnerved him. He didn't trust the man and it had seemed sensible at the time to take along the gun as security in case he needed protection. He'd only meant to frighten him. How was he to know that the bloody thing still had a couple of cartridges left in the chamber?

Amazing how bulky these things were. Eight and a half inches of pistol didn't fit easily into a pocket, never mind the weight.

He needed to dump it as soon as possible. The plan had been to drop it in a canal somewhere yesterday, but there had been no chance. They didn't go near any water in the morning and then in Delft, when they weren't being walked round the centre, it had proved impossible to find a quiet moment with no one around to spot what he was doing. Perhaps today would be better. He could chuck it in the sea. If not he'd have to dump it in a litterbin. As long as it was well wrapped up inside an old plastic carrier bag, it was unlikely to be discovered. With the police breathing down all their necks it would be a mistake to hold onto it.

At ten o'clock, there were still only a dozen passengers sitting in the coach. At this rate, the interviews would last into the afternoon and they would be held back even longer. Fiona was just about to return to the lobby to check there was no one else when Cynthia, the younger of the Harvey sisters, came scurrying out of the lobby.

'Phyllis is on her way,' she said breathlessly. 'Sorry we're late. She's only just finished talking to that policeman and had to dash back to our room for her things.'

'Don't worry. Take your time. I need to let reception know when Winston is going to make a second run.'

Simon Wick was helping his wife up the steep coach steps by the time Fiona returned. She had to wait until he had finished fussing around seeing that Iris was comfortable before she could do a quick count. Seventeen! Not bad at all in the end. It really was about time she learnt to stop anticipating problems. There were enough real ones to worry about without inventing more for herself.

As the coach pulled out onto the main road, Phyllis called out, 'Fiona. I didn't quite catch the name of this place we're going to?'

'Scheveningen.'

'During the war, the local resistance used the name to test out anyone they suspected of being a German spy because apparently only the Dutch could pronounce it properly.' A chorus of groans greeted Simon's contribution. Would the man never learn?

'In that case, you'll forgive me if I don't get it right either,' Fiona said with a smile. 'Though I do know that the v is pronounced as an f and you're not supposed to sound the n on the end.'

There were no more than a brief couple of paragraphs on Scheveningen in either of Fiona's guidebooks; and no photographs. She would have to trust to luck that places such as the Kurhaus and the Casino were easily identifiable. A hotel grand enough to have been used by several of the crowned heads of Europe, not to mention Marlene Dietrich, Edith Piaf, and Maurice Chevalier would presumably stand out.

There was an arcade area inside the first of the great glass spaceship domes that constituted the pier. Curly hovered on the edge of the group and, when one or two of them began feeding the slot machines, others crowded round to watch. He slipped away leaving them all to it. He made no attempt to linger at any of the shops, hurrying past not even bothering to glance at their wares.

There were fewer people in the second dome and, much to his relief, hardy any in the last one. At the far end of the building, Curly climbed the stairs to the upper story, glanced over his shoulder, then pushed open one of the heavy doors and went outside.

His clothes flapped in the blustering wind and he had to stand a moment or two leaning forward to prevent himself from being blown over. He battled his way to the rail and peered down into the sea below. Keeping one arm hooked under the rail for support, he unzipped the bag slung over his shoulder and, with difficulty, pulled out the package. Then, in a great over-arm swing, he flung it into the water.

He was still leaning over the rail looking into the turbulent waves when a hand clapped him on the shoulder.

'Hi there, Curly. How's tricks?'

'Do you have to call me that?' came the irritable response. 'You know how much I hate it.'

'Sorry, old boy. Force of habit. It's how Jenks always refers to you.' It was obvious that he wasn't in the least bit sorry. It was stupid to let the man get under his skin and put him at a disadvantage. 'So what have you been up to then?'

'Are you snooping on me?'

'Guilty conscience? Just wanted to get you on your own to let you know I've spoken to Almas and arranged a handover. We'll have the diamonds by tomorrow. You are still up for it, I take it?'

'Of course I am.'

It wasn't easy trying to talk quietly with the wind howling around and so they made there way back inside where they no longer had to shout at each other.

'So what was it you were so keen to get rid of back there?'

Curly rounded on him angrily. 'What the hell's it got to do with you?'

'All right, sunshine! No need to ring for the fire brigade! Just curious that's all.'

'I don't like being spied on.'

'With the police snooping around, we need to watch our step. Heaven knows why they're so interested in this chap that's disappeared. If you ask me there's more to this than meets the eye.'

'Because he's run out on his wife?'

'I don't buy that and it's obvious the police don't either, otherwise why hold back the tour to interview everyone.'

'They have to be seen to be doing something.'

'My guess is that they've found the man's body.'

'What!' Curly literally jumped into the air.

'Calm down, old man. You'll give yourself a heart attack like poor old Unsworth.' Curly felt his eyes widen and tried desperately to conceal his panic. 'What's up? You don't know anything about it do you?'

'Why should I?' With that, Curly turned and scurried away at a fast trot, almost breaking into a run in his eagerness to put distance between the two of them.

It was quite a bracing walk along the front so it was no surprise to see several Super Sun folk had already found a haven when Fiona went into one of the little beach cafés facing the grey-brown sea. She was still chatting with Margery Pettigrew and the Harvey sisters when Mrs Oppenheimer came in.

'Deirdre not with you?'

'She and Andrew have gone for a walk on the beach.' The thin-faced American looked none too pleased at being abandoned. Probably not a good idea to probe any further.

'I did think about going down for a paddle, but for all the sun is doing its best, that water still looks far too cold for my old bones,' said Margery.

'It's getting your feet dry again that I always find the problem. And no matter how hard you brush it off from between your toes, you always end up with sand in your shoes.'

Even Mrs Oppenheimer managed a polite smile at Phyllis's lament even if it did lack any warmth.

Some five minutes later, Cynthia Harvey began to wave vigorously and everyone stared out of the window to see what had caught her attention. Deirdre and Andrew were strolling at the water's edge. He had rolled his trousers half way up his calves and was splashing in the sea. Deirdre was keeping pace with him, zigzagging up and down the firm wet sand to avoid each approaching wave.

When Deirdre turned to face in their direction, everyone waved, but she turned back and carried on dancing back and forth.

'I thought she'd seen us then,' said a disappointed Cynthia. 'But obviously not.'

There was little doubt that she had, but the girl clearly had no intention of spoiling her fun, thought Fiona. Deirdre ran over to Andrew and pointed to something out at sea. The last thing she wanted was to have Andrew glance towards the café in case he should suggest the two of them join the others for coffee. She didn't want to have to share her man with anyone. From the grim expression on her mother's face, Fiona judged Mrs Oppenheimer had come to the same conclusion.

'He's such a pleasant man.' He'd obviously added Phyllis Harvey to his list of admirers. 'Don't you think?'

'Real nice,' came the reply with just a hint of sarcasm.

Fifteen

Mrs Oppenheimer had even less to smile about on the journey back. Much to her mother's consternation, Deirdre abandoned her and made straight for the rear of the coach to sit next to Andrew when they all clambered onboard. In response to every burst of hee-haw laughter from the back, Fiona could feel powerful angry vibes emanating from the woman in the front seat behind her as they drove through the town.

'I've got all the information about the Kurhaus from the guide book, but I'm a bit worried that I might not recognize it. Is it a big hotel?' Fiona admitted quietly to Winston. The man was such a treasure; she knew he would point it out.

'No problem.' He gave her one of his beaming smiles. 'You can't miss it, sweetheart. Looks just like a mini Brighton Pavilion.'

When the coach trundled into the main square, Fiona could see exactly what he meant. With its domes, patterned brick-work and all those ornate arched windows, it had all the over-the-top opulence of a bygone age. Fiona was in the process of reeling off the names of some of its rich and famous former guests when the familiar voice cut in.

'And the Rolling Stones!'

Fiona stopped short of an audible groan but her eyes rolled heavenwards. 'Thank you for that, Simon. Now if you all look over to the right on the far side of the square you can see the Casino. The building was designed to resemble the rounded hull of a ship.'

Once the clicking cameras had stopped and she had their attention again, she announced, 'Now for some lunch. I hope you are all feeling suitably peckish after your morning in the fresh air.'

Despite the interruption, her hastily prepared snippets of information appeared to have gone down well enough. Fiona sat back feeling quite pleased with herself. With every talk, she was gaining in confidence.

It would have been difficult not to be impressed by the restaurant that the man from the embassy had chosen for them. Phyllis Harvey stopped inside the doorway to gaze around the elegant room admiring the surroundings. 'Just look at those huge gilt mirrors all round the walls and those curtains! Aren't they magnificent? All those beautiful draped pelmets. It's like a palace.'

'If I'd realized we were coming to somewhere as grand as this, I would have worn something different. I feel horribly underdressed,' cried Margery.

The maitre d' led them over to the reserved tables by the enormous picture windows overlooking the attractive gardens. As soon as they sat down, the waiting staff – all in smart blue waistcoats – were on hand to give out the menus and take their orders for drinks.

When Fiona cast a quick eye over her charges, she was relieved to see that Mrs Oppenheimer was sitting at the same table as her daughter. Andrew was being particularly attentive to the older woman who quickly succumbed to his charm. By the end of the first course – a rather good duck pate – like everyone else around her, she was smiling and laughing.

'Does anyone know what sort of dish they mean by hodge-podge?' asked Cynthia Harvey, peering over the top of her menu.

'The English translation is in brackets after, dear,' volunteered her sister.

'That is the English! I can't even begin to pronounce the Dutch.'

'I presume it's a mixture of some kind.' Fiona looked down at her menu. 'Do you think "hutspot" is hot pot? "Met" is obviously "with" and "klapstuk" could well be steak or some cut of beef. We'll have to ask the waiter.'

Fiona's suggestion turned out to be correct and those who opted for the hodgepodge were not disappointed.

'This is absolutely delicious. The meat is so tender and the sauce is very good.' Margery certainly loved her food. Fiona couldn't help smiling at the look of rapture on the elderly lady's face. 'How is your fish, Fiona?'

'Perfect, thank you. It's ages since I've had sole. This gebakken tong was an excellent choice.'

'The waiter did say that all the fish used in the restaurant was brought straight from the dockside every morning.'

Everyone was tucking in with gusto, so much so that the general chatter all but ceased. When the knives and forks were finally laid down, there were satisfied smiles all round. Good food certainly brought out the best in her passengers.

Fiona gave a contented sigh. Things were back on track and going well. Last minute changes to the itinerary and awkward passengers she could now take in her stride. Even the dreaded talks appeared to be hitting the right note. And it wasn't only Margery who made complimentary remarks about them. 'Just enough information to be interesting and not so much that it starts going over the top of our heads,' Barbara Shuttleworth had said. Even Lavinia Rawlings had stopped her on their way into the restaurant to say much the same thing.

For once, she had nothing to worry about. She felt a sudden knot in her stomach. How could she have let herself forget all about the smuggler in her party never mind poor Tim? Had he made contact yet? Would she ever find out? What was the point in letting such things prey on her mind? It would be foolish to allow such thoughts to ruin this magnificent meal. After all, as Bill used to say back in those dark days, 'Worrying about matters you can do nothing about won't make them any better, so concentrate on the good things.' The smuggler could stay someone else's problem.

She raised her glass in a silent toast to Bill.

The Major was looking at her quizzically. He must be wondering what on earth she was up to. She gave him a broad smile and said, 'Not bad for a house wine, is it?'

He grinned back. 'Must confess, more of a beer man myself, especially since m' son-in-law talked me into joining the board of his family brewery. Still, mustn't complain. Keeps me occupied and means I get frequent trips out here to visit our Dutch partners all on expenses.'

Fiona felt a surge of relief. Another mystery solved. He could be lying of course, but how could he know that she'd been worried about his possible involvement in diamond smuggling?

Best to move on. She picked up the dessert menu. 'Now, what's everyone going to have for pudding? Looking at this wonderful selection, I think we have may some difficult decisions to make, folks.'

After much discussion and a long conversation with their helpful waiter, nearly everyone settled on the broodschoteltje met amandelen, which, although it translated on the menu as, a bread dish with almonds, turned out to be a very rich, scrumptious egg custard.

'I am absolutely stuffed,' said the Major as he got to his feet at the end of the meal. From the murmurs around him, it was evident that he was not the only one.

'That really was the best meal I've had in a long time,' agreed Lavinia. 'I doubt I can manage another mouthful for at least twenty four hours.'

It was a very contented group of people who left the restaurant. But then the food had been superb, the service exemplary and the décor positively sumptuous. How Super Sun had ever been persuaded to fork out for such luxury was a mystery.

As they were leaving the restaurant to get back onto the coach, Fiona received a message from Peter Montgomery-Jones. Against all her expectations, his promise to see if he could find another sweetener in an attempt to placate the passengers for their disturbed morning had not been an empty one.

'We have a little surprise lined up for you in the hotel this evening.' Fiona announced. 'After dinner tonight there will be a show of traditional Dutch songs and dances.'

'If that means we're supposed to join in with "Tulips from Amsterdam" and sing rousing choruses to "Little Mice with Clogs on!" you can count me out.'

'Old though those particular numbers might be, Edward, I don't think they quite rate as Dutch Traditional. Though if they do ask for volunteers to join in the dances, we'll all know who to push forward, won't we folks?'

Fiona's quick retort provoked laughter and clapping from the rest of the coach. Edward Collin's face went an even more unpleasant shade of red. So she hadn't made a friend there, but it was his own fault for trying to put a damper on things, especially when they'd all been in such a good mood.

If anyone else were unimpressed with the proposal, they didn't show it.

'If there are no more questions, we'll head up to Amsterdam and our new hotel.'

Soon they were passing picturesque windmills and fields with strips of vibrant coloured bulbs and there were frequent demands for photo stops. One of the lay-bys had small stalls laden with packets of bulbs, cheap painted clogs, key rings and row upon row of porcelain windmills and other ersatz delft pottery souvenirs, no doubt imported from China. It took some time for Fiona to usher both photographers and shoppers back onboard again.

'Couldn't resist them. Slippers made to look like clogs. I just had to get a pair for each of the grandchildren. Look, aren't they adorable?' enthused Yvonne to her husband as she dropped into the seat behind Winston.

'But you bought them both t-shirts this morning when I left you at those shops on the pier,' protested Gerald. 'Ones that change colour in the sun, you said.'

'Well yes, but these are so cute. The girls won't have anything like this.'

Fiona had to hide her smile. Gerald was muttering something about not letting her out of his sight in future, but it was odds on that these would not be the only presents that Yvonne would be unable to resist buying for their granddaughters.

As the last of her passengers clambered onboard, it became apparent that it was not only Yvonne Lee who had come back laden. As Fiona had discovered on their first day, there were several inveterate shoppers in the party who returned with bulging packages at every opportunity. At this rate, the luggage compartments under the coach would be sadly inadequate. Perhaps she ought to say something. Best to leave it until they reached the hotel, but she must not forget to mention it before they all disappeared into Amsterdam for the rest of the afternoon.

Perhaps this was as good a time as any to put on some entertainment. Fiona stretched up and lifted down the box of DVDs from the overhead rack.

'That's strange,' she muttered to herself as she sat down again.

'Somet'ing wrong?' Winston glanced across.

'It's just that there's a loose one here. And,' she said turning it over, 'it has no label. I wonder what it is.'

'Best not to play it,' Winston said quickly. She turned to look at him but it was difficult to read his expression as he stared fixedly at the road ahead. 'It could be anyt'ing and company policy is very strict. No films with swearing, violence or explicit sex.'

'That doesn't leave too many options,' she laughed as she flicked through the pile. 'Look at these! Calamity Jane, An American In Paris, The Sound Of Music. They're all yonks old! Pride and Prejudice! That'll do.'

Everyone either donned their earphones or settled down for a quiet doze as the coach trundled its way north.

The news from Keukenhof was not good. Police and customs officers had spent the whole of the previous day searching the park, even raking through the litter collected from every bin, but to no avail. The gun had not been found.

'Does that mean you are going to order a search of all their luggage, sir?'

The Commander turned his gaze on Jane and slowly shook his head. 'No point. Our murderer has had ample time to get rid of it by now.'

'Isn't it worth a try?'

'In the normal course of events, most probably, but it would be counterproductive to put our smuggler on the alert.'

'But surely if you made up some story about a valuable piece of jewellery being stolen...' The look he gave her made her stammer to a halt. He must think her a complete idiot! 'Sorry, sir,' she muttered, 'Let my tongue ramble on before I engaged my brain.'

Sixteen

The Black Tulip was much larger than their previous hotel, part of an international chain. From the outside it looked a characterless glass-and-brick affair typical of many such hotels to be found near the centre of a large city anywhere in the world, but inside, what it lacked in the more cosy atmosphere of the family-run concern they had just left, it made up for in gleaming, spacious modernity. Welcome drinks were handed round in the comfortable, well-lit reception seating area while all the preliminaries were dealt with. Not that people lingered. As soon as they collected their room keys, they disappeared in the direction of the many lifts with the alacrity of a bomb scare evacuation.

Breathing a sigh of relief, Fiona made her way back to the reception desk.

'Fiona, do you have a minute?' She turned to see a sheepish-looking Andrew Killigan.

'Of course. What can I do for you?'

He looked around. 'Could we go somewhere a little more private?'

Fiona was wary. What game was he playing that he wanted to involve her? 'There's a quiet corner over there. Will that do?'

They walked over to the easy chairs in the quieter recess beyond the lifts on the far side of the spacious lobby. Fiona sat down on the settee in clear sight of the reception desk.

He licked his lips. 'It's about Deirdre Oppenheimer.'

'Oh?'

'I don't know if you've noticed but... How can I put this?'

'You seem to spending a lot of time together. Her mother doesn't seem to be too happy about it.'

'That's the least of my worries. Deirdre is a nice girl, but she's not exactly what you'd call worldly-wise.' Another pause.

'I'd agree with that,' she said, still somewhat apprehensive.

'She obviously hasn't had a great deal of experience of men in her life and, to be honest, I felt a bit sorry for the girl when no one seemed to be talking to her. But she's totally misinterpreted my friendly gestures.' He looked pleadingly at Fiona. 'She seems to think they mean a great deal more than I ever intended.'

'Oh dear.' Served him right, the silly man.

'I can't get rid of the girl.' It came out as a desperate wail. 'Everywhere I go she's there. She appeared out of nowhere this morning and asked if I'd take her down to the sea because her mother hates walking on the sand. I didn't know how to refuse. Then after our paddle, she stuck with me for the rest of the morning. I couldn't get away. To cap it all, when we got back onto the coach, she came and plonked herself next to me,' he finished with a little crescendo of anguish.

'I did notice.' Fiona tried hard not to laugh. Andrew certainly couldn't see the funny side.

'So did everyone else!' he said bitterly. 'It wasn't my idea I can assure you. I tried telling her that she should be with her mother, but she just said that her mother wouldn't mind. What could I say? I genuinely don't want to hurt the poor girl but what can I do?'

'I do see the problem, but I'm not sure what I can do to help.'

'Could I possibly sit with you at dinner tonight? Not at the same table as the Oppenheimers.'

It sounded a genuine enough request though whether it would be enough to deter Deirdre was another matter. 'Make sure you're down at the restaurant early and we'll see what we can do.'

'Fiona, you're a star.' Before she could change her mind, he leapt up and hurried over to the lifts.

Perhaps she'd been reading him all wrong. Just because the man oozed debonair charm was no justification for branding

116

him an out-and-out philanderer. Of course, there was always the chance that he was a damned good actor and this was all to draw Deirdre even tighter into his net by making the poor girl jealous, but she didn't think so. His dismay at the girl's infatuation appeared genuine. And in any case, from the way Deirdre was now behaving – eyes lighting up whenever she saw him, hanging on his every word – the girl was not just hooked, she was well and truly landed.

Fiona's smile quickly disappeared as another thought came into her head. Should she be doing this? After all, he was high on her list of suspect smugglers, which gave him a powerful incentive for shaking the girl off. Having Deirdre tagging along all the time would make things much more difficult for him. The idea that she could possibly be aiding a man to pursue his criminal activities was just too ridiculous to contemplate, she told herself crossly. If only Jane had never mentioned the smuggling ring in the first place. As if she didn't have enough to contend with.

Andrew usually went into the bar for a drink before dinner, but he wasn't there when Fiona went down. Not surprising really, she thought, he wouldn't want to hang around where he could be waylaid; though, as yet, there was no sign of Deirdre or her mother amongst the little groups of drinkers either.

'What are you having, Fiona?' Gordon Shuttleworth was standing at the bar.

Fiona hesitated. She didn't want to get caught up, but not only would it seem odd to walk in and straight out again, it would be churlish to refuse.

'Thank you. I'll have an orange juice please, but I mustn't stop long.'

As the two of them joined Barbara, Fiona took a seat facing the door where she had a good view of who was coming into the bar and across the lobby to the restaurant. She had only taken a few sips when the Oppenheimers arrived. Deirdre had made no small effort. Fiona had never seen her looking so attractive. She was wearing a simple dress in an attractive, jewel

117

green, which suited her dark colouring. The long black hair, which during the day she wore scraped back into a severe ponytail, now cascaded down her shoulders and had been newly washed and brushed until it shone. The large, square, heavy-framed glasses had been abandoned. Perhaps she was wearing contact lenses, but from the way she was screwing up her eyes as she peered intently at each of the bar's male occupants, Fiona doubted it. The girl was also wearing makeup. The full works, green eye shadow to match the dress, eyeliner and vibrant red lip-gloss. Was that a first on this trip? Fiona couldn't remember, but she was fairly certain Deirdre had not gone to this much trouble on the two previous evenings or she would have noticed. Tonight, what made the girl really stand out was a kind of internal radiance, a sense of self-assurance. Poor girl, Fiona thought with a pang of conscience, I am going to be a party to bursting your bubble.

Fiona finished her drink, gave her apologies to the Shuttleworths and made her way to the door. Seeing her on the move prompted several of the others to follow. There were a few people already sitting in the restaurant and, by the time Andrew appeared, the section assigned to the Super Sun party was beginning to fill rapidly.

There's a couple of seats over in the corner,' she suggested.

Andrew glanced over and frowned. 'I'm not sitting with Wick! Can't stand the man. How about over there?'

He led the way to a table in an alcove by the window to join the Smiths and the Dobsons. Fiona was so busy watching for the Oppenheimers that she missed the introductions. There was a Sue and a Tricia though which was which she had no idea. The shorter, sandy-haired man was Kevin and the other's name she hadn't heard at all. She'd have to check her list when she got back upstairs.

Nearly everyone else had arrived by the time the Oppenheimers appeared in the doorway. Deirdre was holding back still looking over her shoulder. Her mother said something to her and took several steps into the room. Deirdre had no choice but to follow. She stood myopically scanning the occupied tables. She hadn't noticed Andrew who was leaning back so as to be almost hidden behind the trellising that separated the outer tables into little bays. They were too far away for Fiona to hear the exchange, but even at this distance, Mrs Oppenheimer's insistence that they sit down was readily apparent. Though Deirdre reluctantly conceded, she took a place at a table with three spare seats and sat herself facing the door all set to attract Andrew's attention when he came in.

Fiona forced her attention back to her own table. After the first few pleasantries had been exchanged, the four friends reverted to their usual pattern and chattered amongst themselves allowing Andrew to ask Fiona what was happening.

'Hurdle one over. You're safe for now,' Fiona said quietly.

Andrew let out a great sigh of relief, but Fiona felt guilty. It was little consolation to tell herself that it was better for Deirdre to be let down now rather than a few days later when her expectations would no doubt have risen even higher.

As the meal progressed, with only the occasional polite exchange from the Smiths and the Dobsons, Fiona and Andrew were left to entertain each other. It was all too easy to see how Deirdre had become so infatuated. Those attractive vivid-blue eyes seemed to be totally focused on Fiona as she talked. He had the knack of making her feel she was somehow the only person in the room. Fiona found herself flattered by his attention, responding to his magnetic charisma.

It was only when the waitress came to clear the plates that Fiona realized hers was empty. She must have been so preoccupied with Andrew that she had polished off every scrap of the pork casserole placed in front of her. So much for all her earlier protestations that, after their magnificent lunch, she would not be able to manage more than a few mouthfuls.

Had she really told Andrew all about Bill, the boys and her two adorable grandchildren? She had not meant to share such things with any of these people, but Andrew had the knack of getting her to do most of the talking. He was such a wonderful listener. If she and even a tough, old cookie like Mrs Oppenheimer had melted under his gaze, then the inexperienced Deirdre hadn't really stood a chance. Time to remind herself very firmly that, as the sole unaccompanied man, Andrew was number one on her smuggler suspect list.

'You must get to go to some interesting places in your work,' he prompted.

'You could say that.' Dangerous ground. No point in letting on about her total lack of experience even to someone as apparently understanding as Andrew. Perhaps she should do a bit of probing herself. 'So what about you? Are you married?'

'Divorced.'

'What about children?'

He shook his head.

'So what line of work are you in.'

'I'm in insurance. Terribly boring really.'

He seemed as reticent to talk about himself as Fiona was about her job. Was he trying to hide something? It was perhaps fortuitous that the waitress appeared with dishes of a decidedly lurid, pink concoction masquerading as mousse. Their table was one of the first to be served, so they were also one of the first to finish their meals.

'Now comes the difficult bit,' Andrew gave Fiona a rueful grimace, 'getting out of here.'

Deirdre must have worked out where they were sitting by now. The trick would be to leave without her rushing over to insist he sit next to her at the concert. Luckily for Andrew, there were several tables leaving at the same time and he managed to skirt round the outside if not undetected, at least sufficiently distant for Deirdre to be unable to speak to him.

'You will sit next to me won't you?' Andrew asked Fiona quietly once they'd escaped the restaurant.

Fiona hesitated, 'I really ought to...'

'All this will be a waste of time if she manages to ensnare me for the rest of the evening,' he pleaded.

Coffee was laid out in the room set aside for the entertainment and tables and chairs were tightly packed around the small square of wooden floor in the centre. Andrew and Fiona found a couple of empty seats in the midst of a small group. Deirdre and her mother, having been some of the last to sit down for dinner, were inevitably among the tail-enders coming in for the concert.

Neither Fiona nor Andrew dared look to see where the couple were sitting and kept hunched down as much out of sight as possible, fervently trusting that Deirdre would not come over to invite him sit with them. They both breathed a sigh of relief when a blond girl wearing a bright yellow dress, enormous white apron, distinctive winged cap and the inevitable clogs clattered onto the stage area. The show had begun.

The first item was introduced – a group of dancers from the west of the country near the German border. As the accordion started to play, the six couples made their entrance. In marked contrast to the young girl, the women were soberly dressed in dark blue and white print blouses over navy skirts and large grey-blue aprons. Their pleated white bonnets tied under the chin were also very different. The men, in navy trousers and waistcoats over blue-grey shirts, sported navy, peaked caps. The gleaming, white, wooden clogs made surprisingly little noise as the dancers skipped around the floor.

After three or four dances, came the inevitable call for members of the audience to join in. Fiona was grateful that she was hidden away at the back. One of the men held out a hand to Deirdre, but she shook her head. Everyone shrank back. Fiona sighed. There was nothing for it; she would have to get up and be the first to make a fool of herself.

'Come along now,' encouraged the pretty, young announcer.

'Let's show these youngsters how it's done.' Margery was on her feet. Everyone clapped enthusiastically as she put on the pair of clogs held out to her. For such a large lady, Margery was surprisingly light on her feet and for someone in her eighties showed remarkable energy.

Everyone was cheering and it wasn't long before she was joined by others. Even Mr and Mrs Collins were pulled onto the floor.

'Our Edward seems happy for once,' laughed Fiona. 'That's the first time I've seen him with a smile on his face since we got here.'

'Our turn now,' said Andrew pulling Fiona to her feet.

Soon nearly everyone was clattering around in the unaccustomed heavy clogs some swinging their legs quite expertly as they sashayed around the circle. Andrew inevitably proved to be a dab hand at the newly acquired skill, and, once she had seen him on the dance floor, Deirdre changed her mind. Not that she was able to get anywhere near Andrew as all those who took to the floor were taken under the wing of one of the Dutch dancers.

There were general sighs when the dancing came to an end and the clapping and cheering as the accordion played the little group out of the room was more than polite applause. The entertainment was going to be a success, Fiona thought to herself, which, given the initial lukewarm response to the idea, was a considerable relief.

'I enjoyed that.' Andrew sounded mildly surprised.

Before Fiona could reply, their mistress of ceremonies announced the next act and a dozen or so singers lined up to continue the evening's performance.

Some half an hour later, when everyone began to wander through to the bar, the only person who looked less than happy was Deirdre who had positioned herself by the doorway, glaring at Fiona with a look of pure venom.

'Oh dear, I think I've made an enemy tonight,' Fiona whispered to Andrew. 'If I'm found floating in a canal with a knife in my back in the next day or two, it will all be down to you.'

In the jostle of people funnelling to go out, Fiona and Andrew became separated. Fiona exchanged a few words with Mr and Mrs Karpinski and tried not to glance in Deirdre's direction in the vague hope that she would be able to get through the door without being accosted. She was only a few feet from the girl now. It was stupid to do so, but Fiona couldn't help glancing back over her shoulder to see where Andrew had got to.

'You're much too old for him,' a voice hissed in her ear as she passed.

Best to pretend she hadn't heard.

Seventeen

By the time Andrew caught up with Fiona and their little group had reached the bar, Deirdre had wormed her way in and was at his elbow. Fiona glanced back and caught the look on Mrs Oppenheimer's face. Their eyes met. Oh well, Fiona thought, she had never been in that particular lady's good books anyway.

Andrew could hardly ignore Deirdre and her mother. 'I'm in the chair. What's everyone having?'

Once the orders were taken, Andrew suggested that everyone go and find somewhere to sit and he would bring over the drinks.

'I'll stay and help,' Deirdre offered before anyone else had a chance.

'There's no need. They'll give me a tray.'

'It's no trouble.' Deirdre had no intention of letting him get loose again.

The lounge bar was filling up fast and the only free area large enough for their party was by the door. More chairs were found and pulled round the small table and Fiona deliberately made sure that she had someone on either side of her, which left two empty chairs on the other side of the circle. If she were not careful, it wouldn't be only the Oppenheimers who would think that she had designs on the group's only available man.

Fiona could see Andrew's fleeting look of dismay when he came over. Deirdre sat down with a look of smug satisfaction on her face. There was no way he could get out of sitting next to her. He looked around for inspiration.

'Miss Ellis. Vera. Why don't you join us? What will you have? There's a seat just here.' He all but grabbed her by the arm as she passed by.

Solicitously, he fussed around her then made for the bar.

Mr Karpinski was on his feet. 'I'll rustle up another chair.'

The nearest spare one was alongside the wall and everyone shuffled round so that he could pull the heavy seat into the circle between his own and Fiona's. She would be sitting next to Andrew again! At this rate, as soon she was back in her room, Deirdre would be sticking pins into that Dutch doll she'd bought earlier as part of some black voodoo rite.

'So what did you all think of the show?' Fiona asked. Best to keep the conversation open so that people didn't just chat to those on either side.

Her ploy worked well enough and, much to Fiona's relief, Andrew must have had the same idea. Between him and Margery there was soon a lively discussion across the circle and everyone was joining in. Andrew even managed to draw Deirdre into the general chat. The sulky look disappeared. Even the normally quiet Vera Ellis was laughing and joking with them all. Fiona could relax.

When the glasses were nearly empty, Fiona got to her feet. 'My round I think. Same again, everyone?'

'Not for me.' Margery Pettigrew shook her head. 'I'm off to bed when I've finished this one.'

'Me too.' Vera looked around for her handbag.

Fiona would dearly have loved to beat a retreat as well, but, having offered to buy drinks, she could hardly disappear now.

Andrew yawned ostentatiously. 'If you don't mind, Fiona, I think I'll change my mind about that beer. I'm ready for some shut eye too.'

When Fiona returned with the tray of drinks, she realized that Deirdre was also missing. Mrs Oppenheimer was still sitting there, staring out from under close-knit eyebrows into the lobby, lips pursed. Fiona followed her gaze. Andrew and a wildly gesticulating Deirdre were standing by the lifts.

'Oh dear.' Fiona hadn't meant to say the words out loud.

Though the couple were too far away to hear what was being said, it was all too obvious that she was pleading with him. The lift doors hissed open giving Andrew the chance to escape. Deirdre stood there motionless with her back towards them facing the closed doors as Andrew was whisked skywards. What thoughts were going through the poor girl's mind? The heavy shoulders began to shake. She dropped her head in her hands and, even at that distance across the whole length of the lobby, the sound of harsh, wracking sobs could be heard.

Fiona took a couple of paces before pulling herself up short. Her every instinct was to go to the girl and put comforting arms around her, but she was the last person – the very last – from whom Deirdre would accept any consolation. Besides, her mother was already hurrying to the rescue. As the girl's sobs turn to a high-pitched wail, Mrs Oppenheimer punched the lift button and hustled the girl inside, the moment the lift doors opened.

The noise had attracted the attention of others. Fiona, still on her feet, smiled at everyone. 'Not to worry; everything's in hand.'

The buzz of chatter continued as Fiona placed the tray of drinks onto the table and sank down onto her chair. Smiling at the Karpinskis, she asked 'So, did you get to see much of Amsterdam this afternoon?'

Fiona kicked off her shoes and collapsed onto the bed. This job certainly didn't get any easier. She may have helped solve Andrew's problem only to create one for herself. Mrs Oppenheimer and her daughter were probably busily penning a letter of complaint to head office about the appalling behaviour of their tour manager at this very moment. Either that, or the two of them would be leaving tomorrow which would not endear her to Jane and the Customs and Revenue Service.

Despite all her promises, Jane had not been in touch. No point thinking about that. She felt depressed enough as it was. Time to get ready for bed while she still had enough energy to get undressed.

She had only just padded through to the bathroom when her mobile began to burble. 'Talk of the devil,' she said out loud as she bent down to pick up her bag from the floor where she'd dropped it. Only one person would be phoning her at this hour.

'Hi, Fiona. It's Jane. Is this a good time to talk?'

'I've just come up to my room.'

'Good. I wanted to get you on your own. How were the lunch and the show tonight?'

'Excellent. Everyone thoroughly enjoyed both.'

'That's good.'

'Tell me, did they really come out of Super Sun's coffers or from your budget?'

There was a pleasant chuckle at the other end. 'No fooling this lady is there?'

'Have you heard from Tim yet?'

'Not personally but we do know where he is now. So how is everyone? Have you managed to gag that boring idiot who keeps interrupting? And what about old Ma Oppenheimer? Is she still whinging on at every little thing? You certainly have your hands full with that lot!'

'Actually she's been no problem today though I can't say the same thing for her daughter.'

'Oh? Do tell.'

Fiona kept up the light-hearted pretence, making the whole saga sound more like a farce than a cause for concern. After a few more minutes of chitchat, Jane brought their conversation to a close.

'We are making progress so there really is nothing for you to worry about. I will keep in touch, but if you have any worries give me a ring. Any time. And remember, just act normally. Don't do anything that might put our smuggler on his guard. Bye.'

Their exchange had been deeply unsatisfying. Jane had been so quick to answer Fiona's question about Tim that it was obvious she had prepared her words carefully, skirting over any detail and hurrying on with all that trivial banter before Fiona could ask any more questions. The jocular charade that had followed had been purely superficial and it was all too evident that Jane's joviality had been as false as her own. So where was Tim? All this mystery was deeply unnerving.

Tuesday, 1st May

Surely one of the best ways to see the glorious architecture of Amsterdam's city centre must be by boat, which is exactly what we have lined up for you this morning. Glide past elegant merchant houses, carillon-crowned churches and warehouses dating back to the Golden Age on an unforgettable canal cruise. Later, at the Diamond Centre, you will be able to see how these precious stones are cut and polished and marvel at the exquisite jewellery fashioned by expert craftsmen. In the afternoon, we take a sightseeing walking tour along cobbled streets beside the network of canals crisscrossed by charming humpbacked bridges. We end our day with a short drive to the pretty old fishing village of Volendam on the shores of the scenic Zuider Zee with its picturesque harbour and quaint streets lined with gaily-painted, wooden houses, which attracted artists such as Picasso and Renoir to the area.

Super Sun Executive Travel

Eighteen

Fiona awoke to the alarm. She stretched out in the unfamiliar bed and tried to pull herself from slumber. Amazingly, she had slept right through. After all the upset last evening, she had been exhausted both physically and mentally when she'd eventually crept into bed, and, for the first time all week – several weeks in fact, if not months – she must have dropped off to sleep as soon as her head hit the pillow.

What a trip! Finding a dead body before she'd even started; day two she lost a passenger; day three the whole party had been questioned by the police and she'd learnt she had a smuggler in her party and day four there'd been the Andrew-Deirdre fiasco. Not to mention all the hassle of rearranged schedules and major changes of itinerary. Talk about a baptism of fire.

It was unbelievable that so much had happened in so short a time. Was it only yesterday that she had sat at breakfast trying to work out who the smuggler might be? Less than twenty-four hours, but it all seemed such an age ago. Andrew had been high on her list of suspects back then, but after dinner, there she was, almost as captivated by the man as Deirdre had been. Jane had told her that her only task was to keep everyone happy and not to play detective. As things had worked out, she had been kept far too busy to even think about Tim, let alone carry out any investigations for herself.

What was in store for today? Surely she was entitled to one day that went according to plan with no major disaster? Oh well, no point in lying here. Onward and upward, as Bill would have said. What with last night's show and all the upset that followed, she had not made the time to chat with Winston about the day's programme. That would have to be a priority even if it were no more than a quick chat to check there where no last minute changes. And at this rate, there would be no time either to look through all her notes for the walking tour. At the very least, she needed to study the map again or today's disaster would be getting the whole party lost, no doubt in the Red Light District!

Breakfast was served in the Black Tulip Hotel from seven thirty until nine so Fiona had no way of knowing if either Andrew or the Oppenheimers had already been and gone or were yet to come down when she arrived in the restaurant a little after eight o'clock.

'I think he's already eaten. You've missed him, I'm afraid.'

Fiona swung round to the woman a few feet from her at the breakfast buffet counter. 'Sorry?'

'Andrew Killigan. Wasn't that who you were looking for?' Yvonne Lee ran a hand though her vibrant flame-coloured curls in an attempt to look coy.

Fiona did her best to smile. Good grief! Surely having dinner with the man and sitting next to him during the entertainment was hardly just cause for the tongues to start wagging? Did everyone think she was now as besotted as Deirdre? 'Actually I was just looking to see how many of our party were here and if they needed anything,' she lied.

'Oh, I see.' Yvonne looked far from convinced.

Someone really ought to tell the woman that the gash of fuchsia pink lipstick she'd applied so inexpertly clashed horribly with her ridiculous hairdo. Something of Fiona's mood must have reflected in her face because Yvonne eyes suddenly widened.

Forcing a smile, Fiona said, 'May I join you and Gerald?'

It was the last thing Fiona wanted, but apart from making amends for scowling at the woman, it might be a good opportunity to ensure that she had no chance to spread that little piece of juicy gossip to any other of the Super Sun group. No doubt, she had already been on her mobile regaling her daughter with lurid tales.

'Sir, it's O'Hanlon on the line. Would you like to take it yourself?'

Without a word, the Commander turned from the small group of his Dutch colleagues and walked across the room to take the receiver.

Jane returned to her own desk and bent her head over her papers in an effort to disguise the fact that she was listening in. As always, his face was expressionless, but she could see the sudden slight tightening of the jaw. Clearly, the news was not good. He made no comment, only the occasional murmur of acknowledgement. It was not a long call and when he put down the receiver, he stood motionless looking at the phone, a slight frown on his forehead.

Dare she ask?

He glanced up and caught her looking at him.

'Did London have any useful information, sir?'

'The results of the autopsy on our Mr Unsworth.' For a moment or two, she thought that was all she was going to get. 'It seems Brooke was right. He said at the time that he thought the man had been murdered.'

Pity he never told me that, she thought resentfully, before a wave of remorse hit her. What was she doing letting herself get irritated by a man who could no longer defend himself?

'An overdose of potassium chloride. The man had a weak heart and was on beta-blockers so death would have occurred within minutes.'

'Which means it's almost certainly one of the other passengers. So we have a double murderer on our hands.'

'That would appear to be the case.' There was another long silence.

'Are you going to pull the whole operation, sir?'

'Unfortunately we have not been given that option. Too much time as well as money has been invested in this operation. We have to trust that Mrs Mason does not starting asking awkward questions or doing anything else to arouse suspicion. It might be a good idea for you to telephone her to stress how important it is that she acts normally. Reassure her that we have the situation in hand. In the meantime I must go and see if I can persuade Inspector Huygen to assign a few more men to keep a watch on things.'

It was only a short hop from the hotel to the top of the Damrak and the embarkation point of their canal cruise, but at this stage of the tour everyone tended to sit in the same place on the coach and that morning was proving to be no different. Except that is for Andrew.

He arrived early and came out of the hotel with Margery Pettigrew. The two were chatting away and, as she usually sat in the seat opposite him on the driver's side of the coach, what more natural than that he should forgo his usual place and sit next to her to carry on their conversation?

Fiona couldn't resist a smile. How had he contrived that, she wondered? All the single rooms were along the same corridor and she could imagine him waiting for Margery to emerge so that he would not have to come down to the coach alone.

He only just made it. The Oppenheimers emerged in the hotel doorway seconds after Andrew had sat down. Deirdre was still looking around the lobby. Her mother said something to her then swept down without a backward glance at her daughter and climbed onboard with a distinct sucking-lemons expression on the narrow face. Deirdre still hovered by the hotel entrance. Fiona realized with a sinking feeling that, despite all last's night's little pantomime, the situation was far from being resolved.

Whatever Andrew had said to Deirdre last evening before the lift had whisked him up to his room, had not been enough to deter the girl who clearly had only one thing on her mind. Though she'd put on the heavy-framed spectacles, even from the coach, Fiona could see that she had made a special effort. The normal daytime baggy T-shirt had been replaced with a smart blouse and, instead of the customary ponytail, her hair had been pinned up with great waves around her face to soften its angular shape. And she was wearing make-up.

Deirdre walked along the pavement peering into the coach checking that Andrew had not arrived. The poor girl probably hadn't considered that he might not be sitting in his customary place. She disappeared back into the hotel.

Ten minutes later, everyone else had arrived. Should she go and find her? Fiona looked across at Mrs Oppenheimer who was talking to the Karpinskis in the seat behind. It would be so much easier if her mother went to fetch her, but Fiona had the distinct impression that Mrs O had all but given up on her wayward daughter. In the event, Fiona didn't have to do anything. Deirdre threw open the great, glass doors and ran to the coach. Whether she looked to see if Andrew was onboard before she flung herself into the seat next to her mother, Fiona couldn't tell.

Fiona pushed away all thoughts of Deirdre and what the girl must be feeling and pulled her attention back to more important matters. With a nod to Winston, she picked up the microphone.

Being right at the front, Deirdre and her mother were among the first to follow Fiona off the coach, but, when Fiona turned round holding aloft her guide's pole, she saw that Deirdre had remained standing by the door ready to catch Andrew as he came down the steps. There was no way of knowing if he had spotted her, but, from the way Andrew had his back towards the girl, half turning to help Margery down the steep steps, Fiona decided it was more than likely. Solicitously, Andrew put out a hand. Perhaps he had confided in Margery and had persuaded her to help him, although from the slight tinge of colour in her cheeks and the contented smile it was odds on that he had simply used his magic charm. The man certainly had a way with women no matter what their age; one look into those magnetic blue eyes and they were putty in his hands. Was that a tinge of green-eyed jealousy surfacing from the pit of her own heart? Surely not!

It was best not to linger so she led the way to the landing stage. If there were going to be a confrontation, it would be better if the others didn't hear it, if at all possible. Fiona had confirmed the booking the previous afternoon and the glass-covered, sightseeing boat was already waiting, which meant that she was able to usher everyone onboard with the minimum of delay. By dint of sheer determination and not a little elbow power, Deirdre managed to squeeze in alongside Andrew on the bench seat and began to monopolize him. If she bore any resentment at his desertion of the previous evening, it was well disguised beneath all the adoring glances.

Short of getting up and moving to another seat, there was little Andrew could do. It's not your problem, Fiona told herself firmly. As long as there is no scene to upset everyone else, just let them get on with it. There were plenty of spare seats and Fiona made her way to one at the back, as far away from the pair as possible. Time to sit back and enjoy someone else's commentary for a change.

The tour began in the Eastern Dock, which was obviously a disappointment to those who were eager to glide down the historic canals straight away. Interest perked up when a magnificent three-masted clipper came into view.

'Moored at the wharf in front of the Ship Museum, you can see a full-size replica of the Dutch East Indiaman ship, The Amsterdam which foundered off Hastings in 1749 on her maiden voyage to the fabled Spice Islands of Indonesia,' came the piped commentary over the loud speakers.

The sliding side windows were drawn back and the sound of madly clicking cameras continued throughout their journey along the network of canals but it was not the picturesque narrow houses and attractive bridges that claimed all her attention. Despite her best efforts, she found herself thinking about Tim Brooke. So what had happened to him? Where was he now? The puzzle was like some persistent mosquito buzzing away in the background, not so much demanding her concentration as distracting her from getting on with the job in hand. The more she tried to bat it away, the more frenzied it became.

She forced herself to listen.

'We are now approaching the most photographed bridge in Amsterdam the Magere Grug or skinny bridge. The story goes that it was built by two sisters who lived on either side of the river ...'

The sight of Edward leaning precariously out of the window a couple of seats in front of her in order to get a better shot suddenly distracted Fiona's attention.

'Do be careful, Eddie,' urged his wife, 'You'll drop the camera.'

Joyce's plea went unheeded and she was not the only one to breathe a sigh of relief when he had taken sufficient pictures to satisfy his obsession and sat back down. The prospect of trying to pull the sodden, heavily built man out of the canal was not one Fiona wished to contemplate.

The area alongside the Victoria Hotel facing the imposing Central Station was a popular pickup place for many coaches and, as Fiona brandished her guide's pole high in the air, she looked anxiously around. She could not afford to lose anyone here. A quick glance at her watch told her that Winston would be another few minutes. Coaches were not allowed to wait. It was far too busy and noisy to attempt any kind of talk to keep her charges amused. She would have to trust that no one would decide to start wandering off.

'Where are we going now?' Cynthia Harvey was almost as vague as Vera Ellis.

'It's the diamond factory next, dear,' said her sister.

Edward, who was standing next to them, nudged Cynthia and said, 'Do you think they'll be giving away any free samples?'

'Bet they haven't heard that one before,' said the Major in a deadpan voice.

In the same dry tone, Eileen Finch added, 'At least not in the last five minutes anyway.'

As Edward's eyebrows met above his shiny, bulbous nose and he puffed out his cheeks with a sharp intake of breath, Fiona decided that perhaps a short spiel would not come amiss after all.

'Amsterdam's diamond industry began at the end of the sixteenth century when Jewish refuges came to the city to escape persecution in the Spanish Netherlands or what is today's Belgium. Diamond cutting and polishing remained a Jewish trade for some time, right up to the Golden Age.'

'Did you know,' cut in a loud voice from the back of the huddle around her, 'that during the war more than 2000 Jewish diamond polishers were taken from Amsterdam to concentration camps in Germany and Poland.'

There were raised eyebrows followed by titters from nearly everyone when the Major muttered, 'And if Mr Know-it-all doesn't learn to button it, there'll be one more body bundled onto a cattle truck and sent to meet a nasty end.'

'Yes, well.' Fiona frowned. Best not to encourage the Major. 'When the Germans occupied the country, the thriving Jewish Quarter of the city was denuded.' She shouldn't let Simon get under her skin. There was no need for her to keep proving herself. If they wanted more facts and figures, they would have to wait until she was back on the coach and had her crib sheets to hand. Figures had never been her strong point at the best of times and if she started reeling them off now, she'd be bound to get them wrong.

'There's our coach,' went up a cry from some eagle-eyed person.

Fiona breathed a sigh of relief and everyone shuffled to the edge of the pavement.

'Careful now! We don't want any accidents.'

Fiona counted them all onto the coach and double-checked when she climbed onboard herself.

'All present and correct,' she said with a smile to Winston.

Curly was feeling much more like his old self again this morning. There'd been no news of their missing passenger. Surely they would have been told by now if there was. If the police were concerned about any suspicious circumstances, at the very least, the whole party would have been held back in The Hague. Perhaps the bin had been upended into the refuse cart without anyone looking inside first and, when it was dumped on the tip, the body had been covered with rubbish straight away. That must be it. As more and more refuse was tipped on top, the likelihood of it ever being discovered was getting more and more remote as each day passed. Perhaps he could begin to relax at last. After all, he was still here and still free.

Now that the DVDs were locked away in his room safe, he had nothing to worry about on that score either. He felt much happier about that little enterprise too. With all the publicity about how easy it was to trace web sites, people were much more wary of surfing for any kind of pornography never mind downloading it, so there should be a good market for the DVDs once he got back home. It shouldn't be too difficult to get rid of them. He'd done a bit of asking around and there were several supposedly legitimate newsagents and clubs as well as sex shops that might be interested.

Jenks wouldn't be too happy if he discovered this little sideline, but then if the boss hadn't decided to drop him, finding another source of income wouldn't have been necessary in the first place.

There were definite advantages working for Jenks. True it wasn't without its risks but, apart from letting the boss deal with negotiating with the heavies, it was considerably more lucrative than pedalling a few puny DVDs. Was there a chance of getting his old job back? If Jenks saw how reliable he could be, stepping in at the last minute when there was a crisis, perhaps he'd reconsider. Especially if he could get his partner to plead his case. That meant proving himself to him too, but surely that shouldn't be too difficult.

He gave a contented sigh and settled back in his seat. Today was going to be a good day; he could feel it in his bones.

Nineteen

With another guided tour around the diamond factory, it was proving to be an easy morning for Fiona. That didn't make it any easier for her to relax. Instead of listening to the explanation of the four Cs used to judge diamonds – colour, carat, clarity and cut – she found herself watching the men in the party. Foolish really. There was nothing to indicate that the Dutch contact had anything to do with a diamond factory, let alone this particular one. There must be many such factories scattered throughout the city and, according to all the guidebooks, at least five that gave guided tours of their operation.

Edward Collins was his usual grumpy self when he discovered that he would not be allowed to take photographs as they went through the various rooms. He stood at the back of the group muttering loud comments about petty officials and pointless regulations to anyone who would listen. Poor Joyce. She was such a pleasant woman. How had she managed to end up married to such a miserable old moaner?

As the group were led off into the first observation area, Edward hung back tailing behind the others. Whether it was out of pique or that little display of bad temper was simply a pretext for separating himself from the rest of the group, Fiona couldn't decide. Either way, she had no intention of letting him get left behind.

There were only four polishing wheels in the room but their guide had to shout to make himself heard above their noise. 'As you can see, the diamond is held in a metal clamp and the craftsman lowers it onto the polishing disc. Every few seconds, he examines the diamond through a magnifying glass.'

'I read somewhere that seventy percent of the world's diamonds are now polished in India.'

'Someone ought to gag that man.'

So Fiona wasn't the only one made to suffer his annoying distractions. Simon was quite prepared to interrupt the experts.

Not that their guide appeared at all put out. 'It is true that there are very few craftsmen left in the city but most of the really valuable stones are still cut in Europe in Antwerp and to a lesser extent here in Amsterdam. If there are no more questions, shall we move on?'

Edward Collins was not the only one who Fiona had to persuade to keep up. Felix Karpinski was far more intent on talking to the craftsmen than listening to the guide's explanation. He was deep in conversation with a man on one of the polishing wheels long after the majority of the party had gone through to the adjoining area. It was only when the next group of visitors came through that Fiona was able to persuade him to join the rest of the Super Sun party. It was understandable of course. As a jeweller, he would be fascinated by the various processes and the opportunity to talk to someone who spoke the same technical language was too good to pass up.

It wasn't until they were all in the last of the workshops that Fiona noticed Deirdre. Everyone else was in small clusters around each of the men avidly watching them performing their intricate work. Deirdre was flitting from group to group searching amongst the bowed heads. She tried to go back into the previous room but Fiona stood in the doorway.

'Andrew hasn't come through yet.'

'He must have done, Deirdre. I was the last.'

'I'll just go and check.'

Fiona held her ground. 'Mr Karpinski and I were the only two left and the next party are about to come in. Perhaps he's gone ahead.'

Deirdre stood on tiptoe in an attempt to peer over Fiona's head. Anger flashed in the pale, slightly bloodshot eyes. For a moment, Fiona wondered if the girl were about to hit her or at least push her out of the way. She had obviously decided that Fiona was part of some devious plot to keep her from Andrew, and after last night, who could blame her?

139

It was time for the group to move on again and, as the room began to empty, Fiona tried her best smile. 'Shall we go and see?'

Deirdre hesitated then turned, hurried the length of the room and pushed though the congestion in the doorway raising not a few indignant squawks of disapproval and irritation from those pushed aside.

So where had he got to? Escaping from Deirdre's clutches was providing an excellent excuse for absenting himself from the group if he had wanted to liaise with some Dutch contact. No point in speculation. Besides, the simplest explanation was that he had gone to find the toilets.

Andrew did not manage to escape from Deirdre's clutches for long. At the end of the tour, when they were all admiring the jewellery displays in the showroom, Fiona noticed Deirdre had the man pinned down. She didn't quite have her arm tucked into his, but she was standing so close, occasionally putting a hand on his arm to ensure his attention, there was no way she was going to let him out of her sight again. Fiona suppressed a giggle. Any minute now, she would march him over to the engagement rings.

Edward and Joyce were still talking with one of the salesmen. For all his faults, Fiona had to admit, meanness certainly wasn't one of them. He was always one of the first to buy a round at the bar and he certainly lavished money on Joyce. She had brought more jewellery on this trip alone than most women owned in a lifetime, and there was every indication they were about to buy more. Not that they were the only ones. From the radiant smile Iris was now bestowing on everyone, it looked as though Simon had decided to mark their coming anniversary with something more than a box of chocolates and a bunch of flowers.

The rest party were beginning to gather. Fiona went over to join them in time to hear Barbara Shuttleworth ask, 'You not tempted to treat yourself?'

'Certainly not,' came the sharp reply from Nesta Griffin. 'Have you any idea what a pittance the African miners receive for all their labour working in those appalling mines. Nobody seems to care that many of them are drowned or smothered under the mud walls when the mines collapse.'

Poor Barbara had only made a casual remark to include Nesta who had been standing on her own. But that did not stop Nesta who now had a captive audience and was not about to waste the opportunity to gain converts to her personal crusade.

'Their farmland has been turned into a barren waste, dug up in the search for diamonds. The ordinary people have been left with nothing while the dealers live in luxury. And all to satisfy the vanity of rich, spoilt women living in the developed world. It's an absolute disgrace.'

Eileen Finch put a restraining hand on Nesta's arm. 'Nesta feels passionately about third world exploitation, don't you, hun?'

'Well, yes. I didn't realize.' Poor Barbara was floundering for words. 'I always try to buy Fair Trade produce myself.'

The next item on the agenda was lunch. Once the coach had dropped them back in the city centre, Fiona confirmed that they all knew the meeting place for the afternoon's guided walking tour, pointed out the various places where they could get themselves something to eat and gave them the customary warnings.

'Do make sure you don't walk in the cycle lanes. There are as many bikes as cars in Amsterdam and they have right of way. And last but not least, you'll find there is a major difference between a coffee house and a coffee shop, where you might find yourself being offered something a little extra to go with your cup of coffee. So do check before you go in.'

When the laughter broke out, Nesta looked even more puzzled. 'Pardon?'

'Marijuana.' Simon cut in quickly before Fiona had time to explain.

'Amsterdam is a very liberal city. Selling soft drugs may be legal nowadays but buying them on the street is not; so be warned.'

She waited for the last of them to move off with a sense of relief. An hour and a half of peace.

There was a little cluster of people on the pavement and Fiona could hear Andrew inviting several others to join them for lunch. If he did have to spend it with Deirdre, he was making sure that the two of them would not be alone.

Before anyone could suggest that she join the growing party, Fiona turned and walked briskly away. She'd been involved in this little fiasco too much already and in any case, she fully intended to spend the time making a quick trot round this afternoon's route to familiarize herself with the various buildings and points of interest.

Once she'd turned the corner, Fiona saw that she was not the only one to make a quick getaway. Major Rawlins was already halfway down the street moving almost at a trot, he was going so quickly. Suddenly a man emerged from a doorway a few yards in front of the Major and turned to face him. Both men stopped and spoke to each other but Fiona was much too far away to hear what was said. Without warning, the Major turned and looked back before following the other man into the premises. If he recognized her presence, he gave no indication. There were at least a dozen pedestrians passing through so perhaps he hadn't noticed her. Fiona continued along the row of shops to the point where she thought the Major had disappeared. There was no way of telling which one he had gone in. None of the places looked that salubrious – a coffee shop where she saw a well-heeled but languid young man lounging back in his chair, his spliff elegantly poised between his fingers; a sex shop and a rather dark general store that sold everything from groceries to newspapers. There was no sign of the Major, but then it was impossible to see into the dim recesses of any of them. They were not the kind of places she wanted to be seen showing any interest in so, apart from a quick glance, she had no chance to investigate further even if she'd wanted to.

What the Major got up to was hardly any concern of hers, she told herself sharply and continued on to the end of the street. If it hadn't been for all this talk of smugglers, she probably would have thought nothing of it. It was impossible to stop herself glancing back as she turned the corner. Impossible to miss the Major coming back out onto the street. Had he looked in her direction, he could not fail to spot her this time. Tucking a small package into an inside pocket, he turned and, almost at a run, retraced his steps. Seconds later, the other man appeared. He was in no hurry and stood looking up and down the road. Fiona disappeared from his view – fast.

Her heart was pounding. What was in the package the man had handed over? She had diamonds and smuggling on the brain. Could the man she had just seen been the same one she'd seen talking to the Major at Keukenhof? Had they been arranging this meeting? She tried to picture the stranger on the bench but she couldn't remember anything about him. This was pointless. Should she phone Jane and let her know now and no doubt get a lecture on not playing detective, or wait until Jane called her in the evening?

There were not that many people wandering alongside the normally busy Keizersgracht. No doubt, most of the tourists were now enjoying lunch like the other members of the Super Sun party. Fiona stopped to take a breath and gaze across the water trying to enjoy a moment of quiet. She studied the map. Where was she exactly? If she carried on to the next canal, she should come across the Greenpeace Building. Looking back, she saw someone else doing much the same. Another lone tourist perhaps.

The next landmark was Anne Franks House on Prinsengracht. There was that man again. Nothing to start getting worried about, she told herself firmly. He was probably trying to do the same suggested walk that she was following. Just because he was a similar height and build to the man she'd seen with the Major earlier didn't mean she was being followed. If only there were a few more people around. Perhaps after all she should head back to Dam Square and the city centre. She quickened her step and did a sharp left turn before she reached the church. If he were a tourist, he would logically go straight on to the Westerkerk.

Straining her ears for the sound of footsteps behind, she strode the short passageway linking two of the main canals, but all she could hear was the sharp tap tap of her own heels. Perhaps she was safe after all. Her breathing became less rapid. She had almost reached the end when, on a sudden impulse, she stopped and spun round to give any possible pursuer no time to duck into a doorway.

There he was. Already half way down. How had he got here so quickly? No doubts now. He was definitely following her. The paralysing fear lasted only for a second. She turned and fled.

Twenty

The atmosphere in the small room was heavy. All three men seated around the table wore dark, sombre expressions. Even the Commander's normally inscrutable face showed signs of strain.

'The body will be taken back to Britain the day after tomorrow.' He had never been prone to levity but there was a marked solemnity in the voice.

'So there's been an official identification, sir?'

'The brother flew in this morning and asked to be taken straight to the mortuary. Not that there was ever any doubt.' He picked up the pencil lying on top of the papers in front of him and idly twirled it in his fingers. 'I take it there has been no progress on the murder weapon?'

'No, sir,' ventured the third man. 'We're still waiting to hear back from forensics about what's left of the bullet removed by the pathologist but the 9mm Luger cartridge shell found at the scene is definitely WWII issue.'

'What about finger prints?'

'Only partials. Not enough for a positive identification.'

'Pity.'

Further conversation was cut short by an urgent knocking at the door.

'Come in?' barked the Commander.

Jane stood in the doorway. 'Sir, we have a problem. Geritt has just phoned to say that his cover has been blown.'

'What?'

Jane reeled at the force of the expletive.

'He was full of apologies, sir, but he said he couldn't help it. He hung back as much as he could but there were so few people around that it was inevitable that he would be spotted eventually. It was either that or risk something happening to the person he was trailing.'

The cold grey eyes continued to bore into her but the jaw gradually relaxed. 'Give me the details.'

There were not many customers in the café considering that it was lunch time, although it was a little off the beaten track and somewhat dingy especially in the far recesses where Fiona was now sitting. Although there were more people by the tables nearer the windows, Fiona was happier sitting in a darker corner. Not that she was worried about any potential attacker any more, nothing could happen in a public place like this, but she wanted to recover her shattered nerves. Besides, she'd probably overreacted in any case.

She was sipping the brown liquid that masqueraded as a café latte when the unexpected ring of her mobile made her jump spilling the coffee onto the table. At least she hadn't got it all over her clothes.

'Fiona, it's Jane. Are you all right?'

There was a long pause as Fiona slowly wiped away the splashes with a paper napkin. Eventually she answered somewhat tentatively, 'Shouldn't I be?'

'Geritt was worried that he'd frightened you when you took off suddenly.'

Geritt?'

'Your minder. He was there to keep an eye on you.'

'I beg your pardon?'

'It's all right, he...'

'It's far from all right! Do you realize I've been frightened half out of my wits?' Fiona snapped off the phone and banged it down on plastic tabletop before she said something she'd regret later.

Her mobile rang before she had time to pick up her cup. She let it ring for some time before she answered. 'You should have told me,' she snapped before Jane had time to explain.

'Yes. I'm really sorry, but he is there for your protection.' And to make doubly sure I'm not the smuggler, Fiona thought. She let the silence hang between them until eventually Jane continued, 'What are you doing now?'

'Sitting in some rundown café.'

'Let's talk face to face. Where are you exactly?'

'No idea.'

'Geritt said he lost you near Westerkerk.'

Fiona sighed, pulled the plastic menu stand towards her and read out the name and address at the top.

'I can be there in five minutes.'

Fiona looked at her watch. The five minutes had already stretched to ten. She'd almost finished her coffee when she looked up to see a woman coming towards her. It was a moment or two before she recognized Jane smart business suit with her light brown hair scraped back in a formal pleat.

Jane was full of apologies and, now her anger was spent, Fiona found herself making light of her earlier terror.

'Put it down to an overactive imagination. If it hadn't been for the Major, I probably wouldn't have thought anything of it.' She explained about the earlier incident. 'I was convinced that the man the Major spoke to must have seen me watching and that he was the one following me.'

'I see. As you say, it was a probably just a chance meeting and nothing to worry about. I'll run a more detailed check on the Major just to be certain.'

'So, how's the investigation going?' Silly question, Jane was hardly likely to tell her, but she had to ask.

'Still chasing up on background info on your passengers. All the initial paperwork checks out, but that's only to be expected. It takes time and a lot of manpower to go round knocking on doors to confirm every detail.'

'So you're no further forward?'

'I wouldn't say that exactly.'

'You said before that there had been an anonymous tip-off. Did it mention the names of any of the smugglers?'

Jane licked her lips. Not a woman who liked lying. 'We've no definite information about the people we're looking for.'

The carefully worded response only added substance to the wild idea she'd had ever since the nightmare. 'Henry Unsworth's name wasn't mentioned by any chance?'

Jane's eyes widened. 'What makes you ask that?'

Cagey as ever, but Fiona had her answer.

Fiona shrugged her shoulders. There was no point in saying that if they'd been given a name but were still looking, it had to be someone who was now out of the picture.

'You never did tell me what happened to Tim? Where did he get to?'

'Chasing a lead, that's all. So how are things going with you?'

'So busy that he took all that time before he made contact with you again?' Fiona was not prepared to be fobbed off.

'Yes, well.' There was a long silence.

'He's dead, isn't he?' Fiona voiced the fears that had been growing at the back of her mind for some time now.

Jane flinched.

Fiona knew she had no right to ask but couldn't stop herself pressing further. 'So what happened?'

Jane looked down at her hands. 'He wasn't the easiest of colleagues to work with I have to admit, but he didn't deserve that.'

'So tell me. I assume it wasn't an accident?'

Jane gave a snort. 'Not unless you'd call a bullet in the chest an accident.'

'What!' Fiona stared wide-eyed.

Jane looked up quickly. 'I shouldn't have said that. I shouldn't have told you anything. The Commander will have me drummed out of the service.'

'Then don't tell him.' Fiona leant across the table and took Jane's hands in her own. 'What happened?'

'His body was dumped in one the wheelie bins at the back of a café.' Though she held back the tears, Jane couldn't keep the emotion from her voice. 'It wasn't found until the next morning. It must have happened soon after Barbara saw him from the windmill.'

'But,' Fiona protested, 'how come no one saw anything? It was crowded around the windmill when I went up there.'

'But not in that corner of park. You can't see much from ground level and the café was closed so presumably there was no reason for anyone else to go over there. It was only coincidence that Barbara happened to glance over and see Tim when she came out onto the viewing platform.'

'And no one heard the gunshot?'

Jane shrugged her shoulders. She had regained her composure and went on matter-of-factly, 'Perhaps the killer used a silencer. In any case it was very noisy what with the bell clock and everything.'

Fiona suddenly felt very cold. Her mind went numb. It was what she had suspected all along though, until now, she had refused to put it into words even in her own mind, pushing the idea away as too horrific to contemplate. She picked up the jug and stirred more cream into her coffee.

'Are you okay?'

Fiona looked up at Jane's guilty, worried expression. 'It is pretty disconcerting to realize you're living with a murderer in your party especially when you don't know who.'

'Not necessarily,' Jane said quickly. 'It could just as easily have been the Dutch contact. In fact that's much more likely.'

'Having a smuggler is bad enough. It doesn't help that there is only one unaccompanied man in the party plus Winston of course. If it is one of the others, surely the wife must know.'

'Who's to say?' Jane gave a small, noncommittal shrug. 'In any case, why assume it's a man. It could just as easily be a woman. I've arrested far more women smugglers than men.'

'Really?'

'I suppose that's hardy surprising because I don't do body searches on the men but, even so, there are far more women than men bringing in diamonds, especially in smallish amounts. More places to hide them.' Fiona's eyebrows raised in question. 'You'd be surprised. Hidden under wigs and in false boobs as well as wrapped in bandages around supposedly dodgy ankles and wrists. For really valuable gems they may even bring paste jewellery over here then get them reset with the real thing before going home.'

'I see, but surely this is a completely different situation. A woman couldn't lift a body up into a wheelie-bin.'

This time Jane did not protest and simply answered Fiona's question. 'Perhaps a fit, younger one might be able to. Tim wasn't exactly a big man was he? And the bin wasn't that high apparently. The Commander certainly hasn't ruled out any-body. You'd be surprised what people can do when they're desperate.'

'I suppose so.'

'We don't know what went on exactly, but I think it's fair to say that what happened to Tim wasn't planned. Someone panicked. In any case, our smuggler may not have been working alone. These people often work in pairs, maybe more, with one carrying the diamonds and the other acting as a backup, a sort of decoy if things get tough.'

'So it could be one of the married couples?'

'Possibly, but the wife may not be involved. Where money and maintaining their lifestyle is concerned, you'd be sur-prised how many women will turn a blind eye to their hus-band's activities when they bring in a bit extra on the side.'

Fiona looked unconvinced. 'It's more than that surely? You said these people were terrorists.'

'Organizing the deals yes, but we're talking about the little people. Our couriers don't handle the buying or selling. All they do is collect from Holland or Belgium and deliver it to someone back in Britain, usually in relatively small amounts. What we need to do is try to get to the big men. The buyers and sellers. If all we did was take out the odd courier, we wouldn't be any nearer to rooting out the problem.'

'So you and Tim were trying to identify him or her so who-ever it was could be followed when they got back to Britain.'

'Exactly that.'

'And you still have no idea who it might be?'

Jane smiled. 'We have a few leads, but you leave all that to us. As I said before, you just concentrate on keeping everyone happy. You're doing a grand job by the way.'

'Thanks.' It was obvious that Fiona was not going to learn any more. She glanced at her watch and gave a start. It was getting late. Her party would be waiting for her. With hurried goodbyes, she made her exit.

If Geritt was following her as she raced back, she didn't spot him. Not that she had time to keep slowing down to look over her shoulder for him besides he'd probably been replaced by someone else by now. No doubt, her minder was in for a rollicking for blowing his cover. Serve him right, frightening her like that. She wasn't sure how she felt about being kept under observation. Perhaps that waiter back at the hotel had been a plant after all. Was it really all for her protection or was it because, despite Jane's reassurances, she was still under suspicion?

It was only possible to maintain her frenetic pace for ten minutes although the increasing numbers of people nearer the centre meant she was forced to slow down in any case. Not that it was a problem. There was no absolute rule that said she had to be more than a quarter of an hour early at every meeting place. She could see several of her party on the far side of the canal heading towards Dam Square. The Smiths and the Dobsons were strolling along and further on she spotted Edward Collins still endlessly clicking away with his camera. Ought she to remind him of the time?

'Hi, Fiona.' She turned and saw Barbara and Gordon Shuttleworth coming out of one of the cafés looking out over the canal. 'At least we know we're not in danger of getting lost finding our way back.'

Fiona smiled. 'Did you have a nice lunch?'

As the three of them entered the square, Fiona could see a cluster of half a dozen of her party already waiting by the National Monument. A rather weary-looking Lavinia Rawlings was perched – not very comfortably – on the low steps up to the monument's towering obelisk.

'Are you all right?'

The Major's wife looked up and managed a smile. 'Just a bit of a headache and a sore throat, that's all.'

'Do you feel well enough to do the walk with us or would you like to go straight back to the hotel?'

'I'll be fine, dear. It's just a summer cold. You're not to worry about me. Cyril will look after me, won't you, dear?'

'Absolutely, old girl.'

The Major plonked himself down on the step beside his wife.

'I wouldn't want to miss out on anything and I'm so looking forward to the trip to Volendam later.'

The woman obviously didn't want a fuss so Fiona left them to it and went to see who was still missing. She was still counting heads when Edward crossed the square. She needed have worried after all. Only two more to come. There was still a couple of minutes to go so no point in getting anxious. Nesta and Eileen were never normally late and there was no reason to suppose that they would be today.

The walking tour proved to be far more problematic than Fiona could possibly have imagined, but not for the reasons she had anticipated.

'Here in the square is where the first dam was built on the River Amstel and from which the city gets its name.'

They moved across to stand in front of the Koninklijk Paleis. Fiona was trying to concentrate on her story about the former town hall's first royal occupant, Napoleon's incompetent and unpopular brother Louis, but Andrew's antics were making it difficult to concentrate. He had moved back from the group attempting to take photographs of the allegorical figures and sculptures on the high pediment, but every time he moved to a new spot, inevitably Deirdre trailed behind. He darted to the side then, before she had a chance to follow, he hurried round in front of the whole group, down on one knee. Best to ignore them, Fiona decided.

'And alongside to our right is the Nieuwe Kerk which is actually the coronation church.'

The party slowly trooped after Fiona to admire the profusion of Gothic style pinnacles and high slender gables. Fiona turned round for the next part of her spiel only to discover that half her party had wandered off to take photos.

'Watch out for the trams,' she called after Edward as he blithely crossed the square, oblivious of the traffic, in his efforts to get far enough away to fit in the vast sombre sandstone façade of the palace. She would just have to hope he found his way back to them in all the crowds.

The square was dotted with various living statues standing on their plinths elaborately dressed with painted faces and Edward's diversion had given several of the photographers the opportunity to get a quick picture of a roman gladiator, Neptune or a bronze cowboy. Yvonne Lee was glued to her phone again and her husband had wandered off to get a shot of one of the horse-drawn carriages waiting for custom.

Even though she had good reason to hurry her party on, perhaps she should give everyone a couple of minutes before continuing. Andrew and Deirdre now appeared to be having a heated discussion. Fiona watched as Andrew suddenly broke away and ran to join Edward presumably to take some long shots of the Palace incurring the wrath of several speeding cyclists as he did so. For a moment or two, it looked as though Deirdre might go after him, but she must have thought better of it and trudged back to join her mother and the rest of the party.

Some ten minutes later, as they were walking alongside one of the canals, Yvonne Lee, at the front of their disorderly procession, called out. 'Fiona, what are those hooks for up on the sides of the houses? Nearly all of them have got one.'

Everyone looked up to see what she was talking about.'

'Would you believe they use them to hoist up furniture?'

There were several shaking heads. 'You're joking.'

'Not at all. The houses are so tall and the staircases so narrow that the easiest way to get bulky goods up to the top floor is to pull them up the outside then in through the windows.'

Half of the party was still not quite ready to believe her. Fiona gave a mischievous laugh and glanced at her watch. With luck, the men would not yet have finished, but best not to make any promises, just in case.

'Follow me.' Fiona led the party across one of the small bridges and turned down a side street. Success. 'I should have taken bets from all you doubting Thomases.'

The chairs and the chest of drawers had disappeared but the job was not yet finished. She had noticed three men lining up all the furniture as she'd raced back from her meeting with Jane. At that stage, all the ropes were still lying on the ground so she had planned to come back this way in the hope that she would have something a little more out of the ordinary to show her group. Yvonne's question had been well timed.

Her audience was not disappointed. They crowded around to watch a single wardrobe being carefully manoeuvred sky-wards by the simple pulley system. Not until it had disappeared through an upper window did the clicking cameras stop.

It was a day for photo opportunities. The tree-lined canals were looking at their best in the pleasant spring sunshine and the colourful houseboats and the wide variety of architecture in the steep gabled houses meant the party made slow progress from then on as almost everyone stopped to take pictures.

As time wore on, several of the older members of the group were obviously getting tired and began to lag behind which made trying to keep everyone together amongst the general melee of tourists somewhat difficult. As they crossed one of the busy bridges over the Herengraat, the photographers lingered yet again and the party became even more strung out. Worried that she might lose sight of those at the front, Fiona hoisted her guide pole high in the air and marched on scanning the far bank for those ahead. From behind her came a sudden cry followed by an almighty splash.

Fiona wheeled round to see an apoplectic Edward, whom she had noticed moments before packing away his lenses, rendered speechless with rage.

'What happened?'

'Edward's dropped his camera bag into the canal.' Joyce tried to put a consoling hand on her husband's arm.

He brushed it aside and turned on her angrily. 'I didn't drop it! Someone pushed it out of my hands.' The sea of disbelieving faces around him did nothing to improve his temper. 'Someone did it deliberately, I tell you.' At the sound of his great bellow, all the tourists and general passers-by began melting away leaving only his fellow Super Sun Executive Travellers.

'There were an awful lot of people on the bridge, dear. Someone must have bumped against you.'

Edward gave a sharp intake of breath. His right hand balled into a fist. For a heart stopping moment, Fiona stood – powerless. Nobody moved. Nobody breathed. It was as though someone had pressed the pause button on a video. The first to move was Eileen Finch who stepped quickly between husband and wife. Edward came to his senses. His mouth opened and closed like a fish gasping for air. Slowly the face subsided from puce to an unpleasant shade of crimson. The bulging eyes still glared at Joyce.

'Somebody,' he thundered, separating each syllable as though talking to an idiot, 'deliberately pushed it from my hand.'

Fiona covered the short distance to his side. 'How dreadful for you, Edward. Can we can retrieve it?'

Just how she could go about such an impossible task, Fiona had no idea but the sound of her sympathetic, calming voice appeared to have the desired effect and Edward allowed himself to be ushered off the bridge.

'Luckily, it was insured…'

Before his wife could continue, Edward turned on her again. 'But I've lost all my pictures, you stupid woman!' His voice rose to a crescendo, 'I need a camera, now!'

'Now, now! Keep the toys in the pram.' From the little group gathered on the far bank, Andrew's stage whisper could clearly be heard.

Edward reeled round, his face contorted in pure venom. 'What did you say?'

Andrew gave a dismissive laugh. He knew he'd gone too far.

'It was you, wasn't it? You pushed...'

'No it wasn't!' Roused from the sulks that Andrew's earlier treatment had reduced her to for the past half hour, Deirdre rose to her beau's defence. 'Andrew was nowhere near you, you stupid man...'

Her protest was drowned by a sudden hubbub as half a dozen others joined in, eager to add their two-pennyworth.

'That's enough, all of you!' Fiona had lost her patience. There was a time for the diplomatic approach, but this was not it.

Edward swung round to Fiona but, catching her determined expression, immediately became suitably chastened. Andrew looked sheepish and slunk behind a rather frightened-looking Felix Karpinski. Only Deirdre remained defiant, standing hands on hips still glaring at Edward.

'Gordon, would you lead the way please,' Fiona said firmly. 'Straight on.'

Without a word, the whole group turned and followed the reliable Gordon Shuttleworth in a slow crocodile like a class of chastened schoolchildren reprimanded by their teacher.

The last stop was the Bloemenmarkt. Thankfully, the floating flower market didn't need any commentary which was good because, even if they had been in the mood to listen, Fiona was not in the right frame of mind to start extolling the praises of this part of the city and its history. Instead she sent them away saying she was giving them some time to themselves to have a wander round the stalls. No doubt most of them would seize it as yet another opportunity for spending money and would return laden with bulbs or general souvenirs but that was a problem for later.

A coffee. After that little altercation, Fiona needed to sit down and have five minutes to herself. She made her way over to a café not far from the clock tower which she had pointed out as their meeting place. Woe betided any of her charges who attempted to claim her attention for the next quarter of an hour. One more upset and she would leave the lot of them and they could find their own way back to the hotel.

Twenty-One

Stupid man. Why had he felt the need to cover his own care-lessness by making up such a ridiculous story? Edward Collins was probably many things, but, it had to be admitted, stupid he probably wasn't. Joyce may have exaggerated her husband's business acumen, but by all accounts, he had estab-lished and run a successful haulage business. They certainly weren't short of money. Edward had all the latest fancy cam-era gear and the earrings he had bought for Joyce that morn-ing had not come cheap. Why was he so insistent that some-one had deliberately pushed the camera bag off the railing? The police had been very interested in examining all the pho-tographs he had taken at Keukenhof; had he unknowingly captured something on camera that might incriminate their murdering diamond smuggler?

Which raised yet another question. If Tim had been shot, why hadn't everyone's luggage been searched for a gun? It was all very well to say that the killer would hardly be stupid enough to wrap it in a pair of dirty underpants and stuff it in the bottom of a suitcase, but it was decidedly strange that no attempt had been made to search the passengers' belongings. The most obvious explanation was that the gun had been abandoned and found. Yes, that must be it. But why hadn't they taken fingerprints? In their determination to capture eve-ryone involved in the racket including the top people, had the authorities allowed the killer to remain lose until he'd led them to the big guns? Surely not! No point in thinking the worst. It was very unlikely that Jane had told her the whole story.

It was hard to picture any of the group wandering around Keukenhof admiring the flowers with a gun in his pocket. As Jane had been at pains to point out, wasn't it far more likely to

157

have been the Dutch contact who had been responsible? Bringing a gun into Holland as a member of a touring coach party on the ferry might be a darn sight easier than trying to get it through airport or Eurostar security, but it was still risky. Spot searches were not unknown.

So why did she still have this pit of emptiness in her stomach? Why wasn't she convinced by her own argument?

Fiona spent so long trying to sort out the puzzle that she lost track of time. After her highhanded display less than half an hour ago, it would not look good if she were the last to arrive at the rendezvous point.

The sudden blare of the William Tell overture cut into the quiet lull that had descended on the coach. Only Yvonne Lee could have chosen such a ring tone for her mobile.

'Hi, sweetie. How's things?' Interspersed with brief lulls while she listened to her caller, Yvonne treated everyone on the coach to her daily news update. 'Kids okay?... Oh really?... We're on our way to Volendam at the moment... The weather's lovely... Yes, lots of shopping. I bought a huge box of mixed bulbs for you in the flower market and treated myself to an orchid... I wanted to but your father said no... Did I tell you yesterday, I've bought these cute little slippers for the girls shaped just like clogs?'

Fiona tried not to listen in, but Yvonne's excited chatter was difficult to ignore. It was as though the woman thought that because she was abroad she would have to shout to be heard back in Sidcup, or wherever her daughter lived, but then Yvonne didn't know how to talk normally at the best of times. Concentrate on something else, Fiona told herself firmly.

Inevitably, that led back to thoughts of her conversation with Jane. If frequent phone calls were anything to go by, Yvonne would be the prime suspect, Fiona thought with a touch of rancour. She shouldn't let the woman get to her. But what if the daily calls were not from her daughter at all but a way of keeping in touch with her contacts. That's why she had mentioned where they were now heading. She gave a girlish giggle at the absurdity of the thought. If she was the smuggler, where might Yvonne hide the diamonds? Certainly not under a wig. As she'd already decided, that garish orange-red colour had to be her own badly-dyed hair.

Fiona stared out of the window trying to distract her thoughts but Yvonne's droning voice was a constant reminder. So if not a wig, where else? In the orchid compost? Perhaps the slippers might be a better place. All she had to do was carefully unpick a few stitches, push the stones into the kapok stuffing, and sew them back up again. That was why she'd mentioned them. To tell her contact where she intended to hide the loot.

This time her chuckle caused Winston to ask her what was up.

'Just a silly thought,' she said dismissively.

The trouble was it was hardly a laughing matter. One of those people sitting behind her was not only a smuggler but possibly also a murderer. Until Jane had made the comment, Fiona had never considered one of the women as a possible culprit even though they made up almost two thirds of the party and four of them were unaccompanied. The idea of Margery Pettigrew or Vera Ellis as a ruthless killer seemed ludicrous; or even mousey Nesta Griffin come to that. Eileen Finch was a much stronger personality. Possibly even calculating. Definitely not the sort of person to miss much. One of life's observers. And she had been standing near to Edward on the bridge when his camera ended up in the canal.

The two younger women spent much of their time together, but apart from their age and the fact that they were both single, it was difficult to see what else they had in common. Striking up a friendship with someone for the duration of a holiday could hardly be compared with the more lasting relationships people made in their lives back home so it would be foolish to read anything more into it just because Jane had talked about pairs or groups of smugglers working hand in hand.

The coach turned off the main road skirting the edge of the huge inland sea that was Lake Ijsselmeer onto the narrow one-way approach that led to the little village of Volendam. Once a

159

thriving port on the shores of the old Zuider Zee, it now found its income from the steady stream of day-trippers. Time to stop her speculations and get back to work. Fiona pulled out her notes and picked up the microphone.

As luck would have it, they had arrived on a day when there was some kind of sailing race. Twenty to thirty schooners were tacking across the bay towards the harbour. That should keep the photographers amused for some time, thought Fiona as they turned off to the tiny parking area.

There were some anxious faces as Winston slowly backed the coach into the tight space until the rear of the coach overhung the cliff edge almost as far as the back wheels. Margery Pettigrew had her eyes tight shut and even Tricia Dobson looked quite grey and refused to look out of the window at the sheer drop below. Some of the men were laughing at their discomfort, but Fiona noticed that once the coach had stopped they were not slow in coming forward to get off.

It did not take long to wander along the narrow streets admiring the wooden houses and locals dressed in traditional costumes. And, though some of the group were happy to watch the single fishing boat unloading its crates in the tiny harbour for a while, most quickly disappeared into the shops or one of the numerous cafés no doubt tempted by the boards outside offering all sorts of edible delights.

Fiona chose one of the outside tables overlooking the entrance to the harbour. The fresh wind, though not cold, was still strong enough to whip the hair back from her face as she watched the crews of each of the boats furling the sails as they came through the breakwater.

It took awhile to catch the waitress's eye as she constantly bustled back and forth across the busy little road taking orders and bringing trays for the crowded café terrace. Once the bill was paid, Fiona glanced at her watch. There was still time for a short stroll further along the harbour front.

She had almost reached the end when she felt a sudden hand on her shoulder.

'Hi there.'

'Andrew! You nearly made me jump out of skin.'

'Sorry,' he laughed, in no way contrite.

Fiona looked around. 'So you managed to get away from Deirdre's clutches?'

The smile vanished and he gave a groan. 'I have tried. Honestly, short of being downright cruel, I don't know what to say to the girl to make her realize. It's only because this place is so jam-packed I was able to escape when she was looking in one of the shop windows.'

'You haven't left her on her own?'

'No, no. There's a little posse of them back there. I've learnt not to let her drag me off, just the two of us. But please let's not talk about that wretched girl. What are you up to? Did you see that barkentine, the big three-masted boat, coming in? Quite spectacular the way they took down all those sails in almost no time at all. Not an easy task I can assure you, as I know to my cost.'

It wasn't long before tales of his own disastrous yachting experiences had Fiona in fits of laughter. Suddenly she caught sight of a red-faced Deirdre, eyes blazing, standing a few feet away.

'Bitch!'

Before the girl had time to say another word, Andrew stepped forward, seized her arm and marched her further down the harbour.

With all the hustle and bustle going on around them, it was impossible to hear more than the odd word, but it was all too evident from their body language that a fierce argument was in progress.

Fiona stood helpless. There was nothing she could do. She realized that Mrs Oppenheimer was standing next to her, and glancing back, Fiona saw Margery and the Harvey sisters struggling through the crowds towards them.

Even though she was facing in the other direction, Deirdre's screech could be heard above the wind. She was becoming more and more hysterical. Whatever his arguments, it was evident that Andrew was making little headway in getting her to be more reasonable. Eventually he lifted his hands in despair and turned away from her.

'Don't you turn your back on me.' This time the words were clear.

For one dreadful moment, Deirdre raised clenched fists and it looked as though she was about to run after him and pound on his back. One push and he would be over into the water.

'Deirdre!'

In that half second of indecision caused by her mother's cry, Deirdre came to her senses. She stood stock still as though frozen in time; then broke down into loud, uncontrollable sobs.

Pretty though the little town was, Fiona was more than thankful when their visit to Volendam drew to a close. On her way back to the coach park, she passed Major Rawlings and his wife sitting with Yvonne and Gerald Lee at an outside table of one of the cafés at the top of the hill.

'Are you feeling any better?' she asked Lavinia.

'Yes thank you, Fiona. This all-in-one flu stuff Cyril managed to get for me at lunch time has worked wonders.' Lavinia certainly had more colour in her cheeks and she sounded much more like her old self.

'Had the devil of a job trying to find a chemist though,' commented the Major. 'Ended up in a little general store on one the side streets in the end. Paid through the nose for it of course, but it's in liquid form so the old girl could take a swig right away. Thought I might have a problem at first, trying to explain exactly what I wanted, but, say one thing for these Dutch Jonnies, most of them seem to understand English.'

So that's what the Major had been up to when she'd followed him earlier. Fiona had to bite her bottom lip to stop herself laughing aloud. She could hardly explain how she'd got it wrong so completely. The Major looked somewhat put out at her obvious suppressed fit of giggles.

'Well you have to admit, they are a damn funny lot. Found one chap in that park place we went to at the beginning of the week sat on a bench reading. Why spend all that money to come in to see all the flowers and then sit there with your nose buried in a newspaper? Pleasant enough fellow, asked me

162

where I'd come from, but got out of there a bit sharpish I can tell you.'

'Oh?'

'Just in case he tried to sell me dirty postcards or drugs or some such.'

The others began to chuckle and Fiona felt a mixture of relief and satisfaction now that all her suspicions of the man had been laid to rest. After raising the alarm unnecessarily she would have to get back in touch Jane but she could hardly ring now. It was difficult not to like the Major and his wife. For all their cut-glass accents, neither was pretentious or aloof and both were friendly with everyone. True the Major had a sharp wit and a dry humour and he was not above a sly dig, even the odd scathing rejoinder but, for the most part, only with those who fully deserved it. He had cut Simon down to size on several occasions, but he was essentially good-natured and thoughtful and always ready to help the older ladies down steps or carry their bags.

'If you'll all excuse me, it about time I wandered back to the coach. I like to be there early before everyone starts arriving, but there really is no reason for all of you to rush. Do sit and enjoy your coffees. It's far more pleasant sitting here looking out across the harbour for another quarter of an hour or so than cooped up on the coach.'

'I think you'll find some are already down there,' Yvonne piped up. 'That dreadful Simon and his wife have just gone past. My how that man loves the sound of his own voice!' Thankfully, she was still staring down the road at the retreating couple and missed the rolling eyes and smothered giggles. 'I do hope Iris hasn't been overdoing it.'

Everyone gave her a quizzical stare.

'The big C, you know,' she explained in hushed, dramatic tones.

Lavinia snorted. 'It's true she had a mastectomy a few months ago, but at the risk of sounding heartless, it can't have been that advanced because she didn't need any chemo or radiotherapy. Breast cancer is hardly the end of the world these days. One in nine of us women get it. And we don't feel the need to make a great song and dance about the fact. Statistically there are probably several other passengers on this trip who've had some form of cancer.'

There was little anyone could say in the face of Lavinia's revelation, but the embarrassed hiatus was quickly broken when they spotted the Karpinskis walking down on the far side of the steep road. Everyone waved. A good opportunity for Fiona to make a retreat.

'I'd better go before everyone gets there ahead of me,' she laughed.

Most people were back long before the coach was due to leave. Fiona kept a wary eye for Deirdre and her mother. Surely the girl wouldn't refuse to come back? She didn't like to ask Margery what had happened after she had made a tactful retreat and she certainly wasn't going to draw attention to herself by speaking to Andrew who had come back all smiles working his charm on Nesta. If she were in Deirdre's position, Fiona decided, she would want to slip onboard at the last moment too.

Many of the party, especially those who had seats at the back, had decided to wait outside rather than to sit in the coach over the drop which, though understandable, made it difficult for Fiona to work out who they were still waiting for. It was something of a relief when she spotted Deirdre – her sun hat pulled well down over her forehead no doubt to hide the blood-shot eyes – and her mother making their way across the car park. Fiona decided it was time to encourage everyone to take their places. However, her plan to depart as soon as the Oppenheimers got onboard was somewhat thwarted. One person was still missing.

After ten minutes, Eileen still hadn't arrived. It wasn't like her to be the last, let alone late. Fiona looked at her watch. Had there been a falling out with Nesta? If that were the case, it would hardy be tactful to ask if she knew where Eileen had got to. People were getting restless.

'Someone still AWOL?' called out Major Rawlings looking round the coach.

'Eileen's not back yet.' A worried-looking Nesta pointed out.

'Don't worry. We won't go without her. Anyone know where she could have got to?'

Nesta gave a quick, guilty glance across the aisle at Andrew. 'She said something about taking some shots of the old houses.'

'We saw her about an hour ago, didn't we Iris?' Simon's wife looked at him blankly but said nothing. 'We went for a stroll round some of the back streets. She was talking to one of the locals standing in his doorway.'

'I expect she'll be here soon. She's only a few minutes late.' Fiona smiled and turned back to her seat. A few days ago, she'd probably be starting to panic by now, but she had learnt that such things were par for the course and, in any case, in the scheme things this was no more than a minor hiccup. Unlike the comfortable relining seats behind her, Fiona's little pop-down effort did not allow for the possibility of stretching out, but, settling herself into as relaxed a position as she could manage, she put her head back and closed her eyes.

Almost immediately, she felt a gentle nudge from Winston. 'Here she comes now.'

'I'm so sorry everyone. I completely lost track of time.'

Twenty-Two

'Difficult day?' Winston asked as the last passengers disappeared into the hotel.

'No more than usual,' Fiona replied with a mock grimace before recounting the fiasco of Edward's camera and the latest episode in the Andrew and Deirdre saga. And, although she could not say so to Winston, she could console herself with the thought that at least no one had died today, although without Mrs Oppenheimer's timely intervention, Andrew might well now be lying in some hospital after a near drowning.

If only Winston could be crossed off the suspect list. There was no doubt in Fiona's mind of the man's innocence, but Jane had been so insistent that she confide in no one. It would have been so good to be able to pour out her earlier terrors of being followed to the big West Indian let alone talk through all her suspicions. His calm, measured view would be bound to help her put things in perspective and reign in the wild flights of fancy that beset her whenever one of her passengers did something unpredicted.

'Shall we go through tomorrow's programme now or is there something else you need to do?'

'Sounds good to me, sweetheart.'

Jane knocked tentatively on the Commander's door. She could tell this was going to be a difficult session from the way he barked at her to come in. He was standing by his desk. Jane had never seen him in shirtsleeves before. The dark pinstripe jacket was on the back of his chair. Even the knot of his tie was loosened revealing half of the top button. Never before had she seen him other than immaculately dressed. The normally imperturbable expression had given way to dark fury.

'What have I done that I am surrounded by incompetent operatives?'

Jane's heart sank. Had he found out that, thanks to her, Fiona now knew about Tim?

'All that patient work trailing the supplier and our man takes his eye off the ball at the last minute. All he had to do was observe the handover of the diamonds and now we have no idea if it even took place.'

'There was quite a commotion on the bridge when the camera was dropped into the canal.'

'What kind of justification is that? It was inevitable that there would be some kind of diversion at the critical moment. Our man should have been expecting it. His attention should have been focused solely on the supplier.'

Easy enough to say with hindsight, thought Jane though she would never dare to say as much to the Commander.

'Now we have to waste manpower trying to keep track of the whole party. Four men. That is all they have seen fit to give me. Four!'

His request for extra manpower had obviously been denied. The final blow that had shattered the fragile glass of his restraint.

'The group returns to England the day after tomorrow and still the bureaucrats are arguing over budgets. Heaven save me from trumped-up pen-pushers who are more interested in expense accounts than putting murderers and terrorists behind bars. This whole operation is turning into a complete and utter shambles.' He spun the chair round and threw himself into it.

Jane stood there. There was nothing she could say that would not unleash a further tirade.

'We have been stretched to the limit all week and tomorrow the whole Super Sun party will be let loose over the city. How exactly am I expected to keep track of twenty seven passengers plus a driver and the tour manager with only four men?' His fist banged down on the desk top with such force that the silver propelling pencil jumped a good half centimetre into the air. 'We are no farther forward than when we started.'

Surely he hadn't sent for her simply to rant and rave?

'We have to make a decision. Assuming we still need to protect Fiona Mason, keep an eye on the driver and the only unaccompanied man in the party, who else would you suggest?'

'Umm.' Her mind went blank.

'When you were speaking to Mrs Mason earlier did she mention anything else that might prove useful?'

'Only about Major Rawlings and I've asked for further checks on him.'

'And?'

'Nothing's come back yet.'

'The coach party will all be home before we get the results unless you chase them up.'

'I'll get on to it straightaway, sir.'

Before he could harangue her any further, the phone rang. As he snatched up the receiver, Jane made good her escape.

It was no surprise when Deirdre failed to make an appearance at dinner that evening. A grim-faced Mrs O came down late after everyone else had started eating, but Fiona was the last person who would be welcome if she were to go over and ask how Deirdre was feeling.

'Are you planning on going out this evening? I expect you've seen it all before.' Margery Pettigrew's question brought Fiona's attention back to the present. Margery wasn't really interested in an answer so Fiona just smiled.

Margery and the other ladies had far too much tact to refer to the unpleasant little scene they had witnessed that afternoon, but Fiona was pleased when the meal was over and they could all retire to the bar.

Few people wanted to linger over dinner that evening and some even decided miss coffee all together. The prospect of strolling around the cobbled streets to see the city lit up at night with its bright, bustling bars and illuminated bridges seemed to put a new lease of life into even the oldest members of the Super Sun party.

The Smiths and the Dobsons smiled and nodded at Fiona as they passed each other in the foyer. The four were almost at the large, glass front doors when a voice rang out, 'Off already? Can't wait to get to the Red Light District eh?'

Everyone turned to stare at the chortling Edward Collins emerging from the restaurant. Kevin Dobson glanced back over his shoulder with a look of distain before pulling open the heavy door for the women.

'Someone seems to have recovered his spirits.' Phyllis Harvey's disgust at Edward's bad taste was all too apparent in the sarcasm she injected into the seemingly uncritical statement.

'Odious little man,' muttered her usually timid sister.

Fiona tried to stifle a grin. Little, Edward Collins was not. Nothing about the man was on the small side. Big build, big ego and even bigger temper. But she was in no position to express such an opinion. 'Coffee,' she said with a bright smile and led the way to the bar lounge.

A good stiff G and T would be just the ticket right now but, as she had not had a drink all holiday, it might provoke questions if she started now. On second thoughts, what she would really like to do was go up to her room and lie back in a nice hot bath with lots of sweet-smelling bubbles and forget about the lot of them. One way and another, it had been an emotionally draining day. All in good time, she told herself. Margery and the Harvey sisters would probably be off soon and they might even manage to persuade Vera Ellis to go with them.

The self-service coffee table was more crowded than usual and, as people jostled to get cups and milk, the inevitable happened.

'I'm so sorry!' Margery had stepped back and knocked against someone's elbow.

'Not to worry.' Eileen Finch put down the spilt cup and saucer and wiped the coffee from the back of her hand with the paper serviette that Fiona held out to her.

'But it's all over your sleeve.'

'Only a splash. It'll soon wash out.'

'Let me get you another.' Suiting action to words, Margery tried to make amends. 'Do come and sit with us.'

Margery's invitation brooked no refusal and the two younger women came to join Fiona and the older ladies.

'It's Irene and Nesta isn't it?' Phyllis made room for the extra cups on the small table.

'Eileen.'

'But you are the German teacher?'

'That's right.'

'How clever of you. I do wish I was good at languages. Do you speak Dutch too?'

'Only a few very basic phrases, I'm afraid. It's not the easiest language to learn.'

'I know even the girls in the shops speak excellent English, but it must be wonderful to be able talk to the locals. Whenever I go abroad, I'm always worried about getting lost and not being able to ask for directions.'

The general chitchat required nothing from Fiona, but as she settled back in the comfortable easy chair, Edward Collins' strange antics attracted her attention. He was flitting from group to group asking questions. Surely he wasn't still intent on trying to pin the blame for losing his camera on someone else? Not that he was getting much joy from the Major who was shaking his head with a very grim expression on his face.

Eventually Edward arrived at their table. 'Sorry to interrupt you ladies. Mrs Finch?' He glanced round the little circle expectantly.

'That's me, although it's Ms not Mrs.'

'Jolly good. Someone was saying you're a member of a photography club.'

'Yes,' came the tentative response.

'So you've got a decent camera?'

There was a pause before she answered, 'A Nikon 70D.'

'The thing is, as you know, I've lost all my stuff, but I would like to have some decent pictures when I get back home. I wondered if there was any chance of getting copies of some of yours.' The silence went on for some time. 'I'm more than happy to pay for them,' he urged.

Eileen shook her head. 'That's not an issue. The thing is, when the police questioned us the other night, they asked if they could take my memory cards and make copies. I haven't had them back yet.'

'That's what the Major said. But they will return them,' he said eagerly. 'If I give you my address, you could send me copies when we get back home.'

Even the insensitive Edward couldn't miss Eileen's reluctance as she took the proffered business card he thrust at her. 'The reason I hesitate is that if I start handing out copies of my photos, I won't be able to enter them in the club competitions.'

'Fine, fine.' He put up his hands in meek acceptance. 'I understand exactly. But if you do change your mind, I would be very grateful.' With a pleasant smile, he turned away and went back to his wife.

'That was a surprise.'

'Him asking for my photos?'

'No.' Nesta smiled. 'I mean him meekly taking no for an answer. Not really in character is it? I half expected him to start browbeating you until you gave in.'

'There's still time. We've a couple more days to go yet. I suppose I'm being mean. Anyone else and I'd probably have said yes without a second's thought, but that man does have the uncanny knack of putting people's backs up. Anyway, have you finished your coffee? Amsterdam's nightlife awaits! Are we ready for the off.'

After Eileen and Nesta's departure, the others quickly followed suit and disappeared to collect jackets. Time for that bath, thought Fiona.

Fiona gave a sigh of relief. For a moment back then she had visions of yet another battle royal. Especially as things so often went in threes. What a day! Were Super Sun clients always this difficult, this demanding? A group of ASBO tearaways couldn't be more trouble than this lot. Perhaps she was handling them all wrong but, with the best will in the world, how else was she supposed to keep them from tearing each other's eyes out?

Wednesday, 2nd May

We have an early morning start to Aalsmeer to see the world's largest flower auction – The Blomemenveiling. Why not try your hand helping to churn the cheese on our visit to a farm that still makes cheese by the traditional Dutch method? In the afternoon, there is more time for you to discover the delights of Amsterdam at your leisure. Visit one of the many fascinating museums – The Rijksmuseum with its extensive collection of paintings by the Dutch masters; the Koninklijk Paleis, a former town hall still regularly used by Queen Beatrix on official occasions; the Joods Historisch Museum with its four adjoining synagogues or, if ships and maritime history are your thing why not visit the Nederlands Scheepvaart Museum. A visit to the world famous Anne Frankhuis where Anne and the rest of her family hid from the Nazis during World War II is surely a must.

Super Sun Executive Travel

Twenty-Three

Fiona felt a surge of apprehension when the lift doors opened and she saw a grim-faced Mrs Oppenheimer sitting in one of easy chairs by the entrance to the restaurant evidently waiting for her. Surely the woman wasn't about to start haranguing her in such a public place with dozens of people walking past?

'Good morning.' She could hardly ignore the woman.

Before Fiona could escape into breakfast, Mrs Oppenheimer was at her side, a hand under Fiona's elbow to steer her to a more secluded spot in the corner. 'I'd like a word. Let me tell you, what you've been doing has not gone unnoticed.'

That sounded ominous! 'How is Deirdre this morning?' Best to take the initiative.

'She's still pretty upset and says she's not coming down for breakfast, but I think I've gotten her to join us for the outings today.'

'That is good news. I'm so sorry she was hurt yesterday.'

'Better now than later, the silly girl.' Fiona stared at her like some startled rabbit caught in the headlights. It wasn't the response she had been expecting. 'I told her she was making a fool of herself throwing herself at the man and that it would all end in tears, but would she listen? As stubborn as her father. If you hadn't given Andrew the excuse to get away from her when you did, the situation would only have gotten worse.'

'Well, I...' What could she say?

'I just wanted to thank you and to apologize for what happened yesterday on her behalf. She was unforgivably rude to you with no good reason and you would have had every right to ask her to leave the holiday. However, she appreciates now that you weren't trying to steal Andrew from her and she's feeling very ashamed of herself.'

'You can assure her, it's all forgotten. She's probably a bit embarrassed about facing everyone, but do tell her not to worry. Most people were far too busy enjoying their holiday to notice and, those that did, have probably forgotten about it already. It would be such a shame to miss out on the flower market and the cheese factory.'

'That's very good of you. You're a good courier. You care about the people you're looking after and I shall be putting that on my form at the end of the trip.'

'Mrs Oppenheimer, I don't know what to say.'

'Do call me Miriam.' The woman actually smiled. A genuine smile, with her eyes as well as her lips. She disappeared into the restaurant leaving a stunned Fiona staring after her.

Despite the seven o'clock departure, everyone was on time and, once Fiona had explained the reason was because trading at the flower auction was all over by midmorning, the grumbles quickly died down.

When she saw the long flight of stairs up to the viewing platforms above all the action, Fiona wondered if the whinging might start again. As usual, Simon and Iris bounded on ahead and the more athletic Smiths and Dobsons quickly followed suit. As others clattered up the noisy iron steps, Fiona thought it best to hold back with some of the older members who might have more difficulty.

'My goodness. It's a long way up! I feel quite breathless already,' confided Phyllis Harvey to Fiona when they were only a third of the way up the steep, open-work stairway.

'It's the altitude that does it. The air gets thinner as you go up,' said the Major who was just behind them prompting smiles all round.

This was Fiona's first visit to Aalsmeer and the flower auction and, as they all moved out onto the overhead walkway, she was as overawed as everyone else at the sheer size of the place. Cartloads of flowers crammed tight against each other stretched as far as the eye could see, all waiting to be brought forward.

'Goodness. Does it ever end?' Even the normally uncommunicative Vera, standing next to her, was moved to words.'

'Impressive isn't it?' Fiona gave her a broad smile. 'The biggest single room in the world, so they say. One million square metres, or a hundred and fifty football pitches, although I must confess that means absolutely nothing to me.'

'Me neither.'

In the other direction, there were signs of activity and the party slowly edged along to take a closer look. The laden seven-foot tall carts were being pulled into place by what looked like bright red bumper cars. Most of the steel frame carts were two tiered although some of the shorter plants were stacked on three layers, each holding half a dozen containers.

It was only by shouting over the noise, that Fiona managed to get everyone's attention. 'Shall we go and watch the bidding?'

From the viewing gallery alongside one of the auction rooms everyone looked down at the lines of carts slowly moving round the circular track-way.

'You all know the principle of the Dutch auction?' A few heads nodded. 'Instead of selling to the highest bidder, the price starts high and is reduced until someone is prepared to buy. You see the nearest big white dial up at the top? Once the growers name comes up on the central information board, you can see the red light start to count down from a hundred until someone is willing to pay that sum.'

'So how do they make their bids?' asked Phyllis Harvey.

'If you look at the buyers sitting in those rows of desks, once they've registered on the keypads in front of them, they simply press a button when the figure drops to a price they're prepared to pay and then they tap in the number of crates they want. They may buy the lot or perhaps just one container. The remainder are then put up for bid until all containers on the cart are sold. If you watch those figures in the middle of the dials, you can see the way each lot is divided up. The whole system is amazingly fast and efficient.'

All that time she spent looking things up on the internet back home had not been wasted, she thought. Everyone seemed to be finding it all as fascinating as she had done.

'So how do the people collect their flowers?'

'Once they are sold, the individual containers are split off and loaded onto other carts belonging to the buyers. From there, most of them will be taken to the airport and sent all over Europe and even America.'

'Really?'

'The bidders could be buyers for major florist chains right down to the owner of a local flower shop or even a stall on Amsterdam's floating market.'

'Minimum paper work as well. Some of our businesses could learn a lot from the speed and efficiency here.' Gerald Lee's rueful observation was met with several nods of agreement.

'Right, folks, I'm sorry to rush you but we must be moving on or we'll be late for our next stop. Back on the coach in half an hour.'

Fiona still had difficulty rounding up everyone outside. They had to weave their way through all the pantechnicans, lorries and vans, not mention the odd cyclist with his trailer laden with boxes of blooms, back to the coach.

'Is that everyone?'

'Just the two lovebirds,' laughed Barbara Shuttleworth. 'Here they are now. Did you know it's their wedding anniversary today?'

'I think everyone does. Including the hotel staff so there might just be a little surprise tonight.'

'Oh how lovely!'

Fiona put a finger to her lips and turned back to watch Simon and Iris sauntering hand in hand towards the coach. As he mounted the coach steps, Simon gave her a beaming smile. 'That was great, Fiona. We really enjoyed that.'

Simon had been too busy fussing over Iris all morning to keep up his usual barrage of interruptions. Not once had he held forth. Everyone seemed happy and the day was definitely going well. This was exactly as the job was supposed to be. Fiona gave a contended sigh.

'Someone in a good mood.' Winston's rumbling chuckle brought her back to the matter in hand. 'I is ready for the off if you are, boss.'

'Then make it so, Mr Taylor. Make it so,' she said in her best Captain Picard imitation sweeping her arm forward and pointing to the road ahead.

The cheese farm was not far away and as soon as the coach pulled into the yard, their guide, a smiling woman in white coat and cap emerged from one of the buildings ready to show them around.

'We have sixty cows on the farm and our day starts with the early morning milking. Stainless steel pipes carry about 900 litres of milk into a large vat, which we will go and see first.'

Over in the dairy, the farmer, introduced by their guide as Willem, invited them to gather round the large, wooden, steel-lined tub. There was a fair amount of shuffling until everyone had a chance to peer over the edge to see the creamy milk being churned. Willem proceeded to shovel the curds into a round, plastic mould letting the watery liquid drain out at the bottom.

After a second demonstration, Willem reached for another mould and invited someone to have a try. Iris, who always managed to muscle her way through to the front, was the first to volunteer. She donned the enormous, white apron and for once managed a broad smile as she posed holding the white bowl over the large vat as Simon snapped away happily.

'Go on, Gerald,' urged Yvonne waving her mobile as Iris stepped down. 'I'll take a picture to send to Stephanie.'

Fiona was pleased to see Deirdre had cheered up considerably as the day had progressed and was now taking a keen interest in what was going on. 'How about you, Deirdre? Why don't you have a try?'

Gerald held out a fresh mould and, encouraged by the older ladies, she was soon persuaded. Cameras flashed as Deirdre enthusiastically scooped up the contents of the great vat helped by the farmer.

'From here, the moulds are taken to the cheese presses where the last of the whey will be squeezed out.'

More volunteers were requested to try their hand squeezing down the lids on top of the moulds and putting them under the presses. Almost half the party had been involved in one or other of the tasks and it was some time before they eventually filed out into the next room to see the large round cheeses stored on the shelves.

'Now we go and taste some of the special cheeses that have been made on the farm. We have many, many flavours.' Their guide led the way to the final room.

'Do try this, Fiona. Would you believe it? It's flavoured with stinging nettle. It's really nice! Not a bit as I expected,' Yvonne called out enthusiastically. 'We'll definitely have one of these, Gerald.'

'I can't make up my mind. They're all so tasty,' pronounced Barbara Shuttleworth.

To judge from the number of parcels quite a few of them were holding, that seemed to be a common problem. Perhaps, Fiona decided, she had better remind them not to leave their purchases on the coach overnight or the smell would be overpowering on the way back home tomorrow.

Time to start gathering the group together. She turned to see Margery busy showing Deirdre the pictures she'd just taken. There was quite a crowd gathered around looking at each other's digital photos. Fiona smiled. It was good to see people rallying round Deirdre and it must be a great consolation to both her and her mother that the poor girl was not an object of derision.

'That is a good one!' Even Edward was there being surprisingly sociable and magnanimous. 'Why don't you show us the ones you took, Andrew?'

Andrew's face darkened. 'I'm afraid the lighting was really bad. They were much too dark so I've deleted them all I'm afraid.'

'That's a shame. Still I expect you got some great shots this morning at the flower market, eh?' Edward persisted.

Andrew gave a weak smile and made his way through the door out into the yard. Not to be deterred, Edward followed.

Fiona was filled with a sense of foreboding. It was obvious that Andrew did not intend to let Edward see his photos so why wouldn't the man just let it go. She could hear raised voices before she got to the door. Andrew and Edward were someway across the yard but their argument was beginning to attract attention.

'What on earth is going on?'

They both turned to face her as she marched over.

'All I did was ask to look at the pictures on his bloody camera.' Edward stomped off and went back into the parlour.

'That man!' Andrew snarled, 'He's nothing but a bully.'

'Did you have to react like a kid in the playground? What was so dreadful about letting him see a few photos? What have you got on there you don't want him to see?'

'That's just what he said.' The handsome face was distorted in a bitter grimace. 'Started trying to make out I'd taken mucky shots in the Red Light District. And he's still accusing me of pushing his camera into the canal. I was nowhere near as everyone else has told him, but…'

'I don't want to hear it, Andrew. Just grow up and stop making such an exhibition of yourself.'

She left him open-mouthed. Not the way a tour manager was supposed to behave to a client, but her patience was being pushed to the limit. An anxious-looking Cynthia Harvey was hovering by the door. Fiona forced a smile. 'Time for us all to get back on the coach, everyone.'

If anyone referred to the fracas between Andrew and Edward on the journey back to Amsterdam, Fiona did not overhear. Andrew threw himself down in his seat and sat arms folded staring out of the window. Every time she glanced up in her mirror, Edward was still sitting in a sulky silence. Poor Joyce. Not that she seemed bothered; presumably, she was used to his moroseness.

'We're going to make a couple of drop-off stops when we get to Amsterdam. The first will be in the museum quarter by the Rijksmuseum for those of you who'd like to go and see Rembrandt's masterpiece, "The Night Watch". And it's only a short walk from there to the Van Gogh Museum. For the rest of you, we will drop off where we did yesterday outside the hotel by the top of the Damrak opposite the railway station. I hope you all still have your city maps. All the major sites are clearly marked, but if you have any questions let me know.'

'Which is the best stop for Anne Franks' house?' It wasn't only Mrs Oppenheimer who was trying to work that out.

'The second, by the hotel. I know a lot of you are planning to go there, but don't forget, as I said before, there will be long queues outside so do be prepared to wait.'

Fiona moved slowly down the aisle answering questions and pointing out the various places on the map.

It was a relief to wave the last of them on their way.

'You comin' back to the hotel, sweetheart?'

'Thanks, Winston, but I think I'll stay. I'd like to see some of the sites myself. And what are you going to do with yourself all afternoon?'

'First a bite to eat then most like take a look around the town. Some places we go, our hotels and coach parks are so far out, not much to do but readin'. You be amazed how many books I get through on some trips.'

Fiona couldn't quite picture Winston as a reader somehow. So what sort of books took his fancy, she wondered as the coach pulled away. Fast paced thrillers or perhaps SF. For all she knew he could have a passion for real life stories or some hobby that he liked to read up on. To her shame, she realized she knew very little about the man apart from the fact that he still lived with his mother because he spent so much time on the road that it wasn't worth getting his own place. It wasn't that he was secretive or evasive; she just hadn't bothered to find out. Apart from his mother, she had no idea about his family, his background or how he spent his free time. This smuggling business had put a barrier between them, but that was no excuse.

Rapid footsteps came up behind him and suddenly his arm was seized in a vice-like grip.

'Not so fast, sunshine!'

Curly swung round and stared into the angry face.

'What's up, old boy?'

'I want them back. Now.'

'What are you talking about?'

'You know bloody well! Give me back the diamonds.'

'But that's not the arrangement. They're always split in two lots to minimize the risk getting them back through Customs. You know that.'

'Not this time. Not when you've been kicked off the team they aren't. I thought there was something odd from that first night when you sidled over and said there were going to be three of us on the job. You failed to mention that Unsworth was your replacement not an addition to the team.'

Curly's mind was working overtime. Was the man guessing or had he rung London to find out? 'That's rubbish, old boy. You're putting two and two together and making enough numbers to play bingo.'

His poor attempt at humour only served to infuriate the man more.

'I have the proof right here.' He pulled a piece of hotel writing paper from his pocket and waved it under Curly's nose. 'This was pushed under my door at lunch time and it's signed Mavis Jenks. I've been trying to track you down ever since. Seems she suspected both of us were trying to do a double cross when you suddenly turned up and Unsworth conveniently disappeared off the radar. She knew her brother had booted you out, but when she realized that I was still playing it by the book, she thought it was time I knew what's what.'

Curly's world suddenly collapsed around him. A black mist clouded his vision. What was he to do?

The man took a step towards him.

Twenty-Four

When she came out of the Historisch Museum, there wasn't enough time to visit any of the other museums so Fiona decided to take a stroll through the backstreets heading for one of the parks. Apart from the upset at the cheese farm, the day had gone surprisingly well. It had helped that she had encountered none of her charges all afternoon. At long last, she had even managed to find a something suitable to send to Adam Junior. She had solved her granddaughter, Becky's present on the first day in The Hague: a dressing up outfit complete with cap and cloth overshoes with turned up toes like clogs, but finding something for eighteen month old that wouldn't cost the earth to send all the way to Canada had proved more tricky.

Perhaps on the short stop in Belgium on the way home she should get some boxes of chocolates for friends. It would be nice to get something for Caroline. If it hadn't been for her, she would never have applied for this job in the first place. Her mind still occupied with a quick run through of other people for whom she ought to take back a small gift, Fiona didn't see the woman hurrying round the corner until she almost bumped into her.

'Vera!'

A startled expression flashed across the woman's face as recognition dawned.

Vera Ellis seized hold of Fiona's forearm and held it in a vicelike grip. Her chest began to heave and, though the lips opened and closed, no words came out. She was struggling for breath. Perhaps she was having an asthma attack.

'It's all right. Try to breathe normally. Do you have your inhaler with you?' Vera shook her head and waved her hand dismissively to indicate that wasn't the problem. She was still clutching her chest. Could it be something more serious? Swallowing her own panic, Fiona rummaged in her bag for her mobile. 'Try to stay calm. I'm going to ring for an ambulance.'

'No!' The single strangled cry was as much as Vera could manage. She leant back against the wall until her breathing became easier.

As Fiona waited for Vera to recover, a commotion attracted her attention. Fiona could hear shouting and there were people running past the top of the short stretch of road.

'Something seems to be happening back there? Did you see anything?'

'A body,' she eventually gasped, relaxing her grip on Fiona's arm. 'In the canal.'

Fiona eye's widened. If that were true, no wonder the poor woman was in such a state. But she must have made a mistake. 'Are you sure?'

Once again, Vera flapped a hand in frustration. Gradually her breathing returned to normal. 'I was coming for help.'

As they made their way, Fiona offered to take Vera's bag but, frail as she was, the woman was fiercely independent. At least now, she was able to walk.

They reached the corner and turned to see that a small crowd had already begun to gather. Fiona saw a couple of men kneeling down peering over the canal side. The body lay spread-eagled in the water. The face was turned away but blood was seeping from a great gash across the back of the head; a slowing increasing pool of red reluctant to mix with the murky water. Fiona recoiled but found herself unable to look away. There was something familiar about the figure.

The man who had been trying to reach the body muttered something in Dutch then stood up and pulled off his shoes before lowering himself gently down into the water. In two strokes, he had hold of the body and expertly rolled it over keeping one hand under the head. For the first time Fiona saw the face.

'Oh no, no, no, no!'

In the general melee of people who had gathered seemingly from nowhere, no one heard Fiona's low moan. Several pairs of hands lifted out the limp body and laid it on ground. Water ran from the mouth and nose as he was turned on his side. Someone started to give him artificial respiration.

Every instinct told Fiona to rush to his side, but her feet were fixed to the spot. Transfixed, fist to her mouth. Every thing had stopped. Even the noise of all the activity around her seemed to have faded to a distant murmur. The strident wail of a siren pulled her back to reality. The ambulance was on its way.

There was a sudden tug on her arm. 'Can we go now? I need to sit down.' Vera's voice was hardly above a whisper.

Fiona pulled herself together sharply. The woman needed her help. She was probably suffering from shock. Besides there was nothing she could do for Andrew. He appeared to be in capable hands.

'We can't. Not yet. It's Andrew.'

Vera's expression registered nothing. The name probably meant little to her. 'Mr Killigan. One of the people on the coach with us. Did you see what happened?'

'Oh no! Not at all,' Vera protested quickly. 'I heard a great splash behind me and when I looked saw something floating in the water. As soon as I realized what it was, I knew there was nothing I could do so I ran to fetch more help. That's when I met you.'

She was becoming agitated again. Fiona led her over to a low wall where she could sit and rest. 'Wait there. I won't be a moment, but I must go and tell them who he is and find out where they're going to take him. Then I'll get a taxi and see you back to the hotel. I won't be long, I promise.'

By the time they arrived back at the Black Tulip, Vera seemed much more like her old self and having something positive to do had helped Fiona to calm her own fraught nerves. She contemplated dropping Vera at the entrance and taking the taxi straight on to the hospital, but decided that, after that nasty shock, the least she could do was see that the poor woman was safely settled back inside.

'Are you sure you wouldn't like me to get you a doctor?'

'No thank you, dear. I'm much better now.'

'Then let me take you up to your room? If you give me your number, I'll collect your key for you.'

'Actually dear, if you don't mind, I think I'd rather go to lounge and order myself some tea.'

'That sounds like a good idea.'

They walked over together and, as luck would have it, the Harvey sisters were already there sitting in a couple of easy chairs by the window, sipping their cappuccinos looking out over the rear gardens.

'Come and join us. Cynthia was a bit tired. We've been on our feet all day so we decided to come back early.'

Fiona left Vera to tell the other two what had been happening and was able to hurry away with a clear conscience. At least that was one worry off her mind. She pulled the Amsterdam map out of her bag. There were three hospitals in the city but the only one with a casualty unit was located alongside Oosterpark, to the east of the city, not far from the hotel.

It wasn't only her fears for Andrew that sent a shiver down Fiona's spine as she walked into what she hoped was the Emergency Unit. She had spent too many interminable hours waiting with Bill in various hospital departments over the last few years to willingly step into one ever again. When only last month, the vicar's wife had suggested Fiona consider becoming a hospital visitor, it had taken all Fiona's effort to bite back the stinging retort and give her a polite refusal. For a woman in her position she had shown a marked lack of sensitivity.

Like all the Dutch Fiona had encountered on their holiday so far, the girl on the reception desk spoke excellent English. However, it took sometime to discover if Andrew had been admitted.

'If he was brought in such a short time ago, it is possible his details have not been entered into the system.'

'I'm not sure you have any personal details, not unless he's regained consciousness. He came in with the paramedics on his own.'

Fiona explained how she had been at the scene and the receptionist took down details of the hotel and Andrew's address.

'If you take a seat over there, I will see what I can find out for you.'

There was a steady stream of people, staff as well as new patients, demanding the receptionist's attention so Fiona decided she was in for a long wait. There were some magazines and papers lying around but, as they were all in Dutch, they weren't much use. If she'd given it any thought before she'd left the hotel, she could have fetched her book. The only one she'd brought on holiday still had the bookmark tucked into the first page. By the time she crawled into bed most nights, she was either too tired to concentrate or her mind was so busy with the day's events that, after only a couple of paragraphs, she had given up the effort and had put out the light.

Not that she was exactly in the mood for reading now. Poor Andrew. Best to look on the bright side. He couldn't have been in the water for long. The men who'd pulled him out seemed to know what they were doing and the paramedics were there within minutes. Amazingly quickly, now she came to think about it. But there had been so much blood. Not that it needed much. She tried to console herself with that thought. Even a teaspoonful of blood could spread a remarkably long way, making a tiny cut seem like a major gash, as she had learnt often enough when the boys were small, let alone from her days as a nurse.

So what can have happened? Surely, a blow on the back of the head like that was no accident? If Andrew were walking along the edge of the canal, there was nowhere for anything to fall from. If he'd tripped and fallen into the water, how come he'd hit the back of his head and then ended up lying on his front? A much more likely explanation would seem to be that he'd been hit over the head from behind. But if that were the case, surely Vera would have seen the culprit? Assuming she

186

turned round as soon as she heard the splash, even at that distance, she would have noticed someone running away. Perhaps she was too busy trying to work out what it was in the water.

No doubt, the police would find out soon enough. They already appeared to be on the case. They had arrived at the scene almost at the same time as the ambulance. Amsterdam's emergency services certainly could not be faulted. Surprising when there had been no evidence of police on the streets all week.

They were even here in the hospital right now. She could just see two officers at the end of the corridor. That didn't mean they were investigating what had happened to Andrew of course. It could be to do with another incident entirely. They were talking to a man who was vaguely familiar although she couldn't see his face. Hardly likely, she didn't know anyone in The Netherlands.

Before she could give the matter more thought, she saw the receptionist pointing her out to one of the nurses who was holding a large plastic carrier bag. Fiona got to her feet, but the nurse came over and motioned her to sit down again.

'Mr Killigan still in emergency. The doctors look at him. He go up to a ward very soon.' Again the English, though far from perfect, was good although the accent was more marked that that of the receptionist.

'Can I see him?'

'Is not possible. He not awake. He ... How you say?' She jabbed her upper arm with one extended finger.

'Sedated?'

'Yes, yes.' The nurse smiled.

'So do you know how he is?'

'I not able to tell you. The specialist must see him. But you not worry.' She patted Fiona's arm. 'He stay in hospital. He sleep for a long time. You go back now. If it pleases you, I give you number and you ring hospital later.'

Fiona didn't have much choice.

Twenty-Five

Back at the hotel, it was no surprise to discover that the news had spread and there was quite a reception party in the foyer waiting for her return. The moment she stepped through the doors, Fiona was bombarded with questions.

She tried to reassure everyone by repeating what the nurse had told her.

'You look as though you've just been shopping rather than coming from the hospital.' Yvonne indicated the large bag Fiona was holding.

'Andrew's things. The hospital asked me to bring them back to the hotel.'

'That's standard practice these days. When Gerald went in for his op they only kept him in overnight, but I had to bring all his clothes home and take them back next day. Something to do with security. A lot of stuff gets pinched in hospitals and understandably the staff don't want the added responsibility.'

As everyone began to discuss their experiences and air their views on the lawless state of modern society, Fiona was able to make her escape. First she would have to go to reception and explain about Andrew and collect a passkey so that she could put his things in his room.

For all that show of concern downstairs, none of them was really interested in Andrew, she thought as she let herself in, some ten minutes later. They just wanted the vicarious thrill of an eyewitness account to take back home and regale their friends and relations for weeks to come. Ghouls the lot of them. No doubt, already Yvonne had been on that mobile of hers passing on the lurid details.

She felt so irritated that she almost threw the bag onto the bed banging against the bedside table.

'Blast!' One of the small batteries had rolled off the top onto the floor. Grovelling on all fours to retrieve it from under the bed did nothing to improve her temper.

Much as she wanted to get back to her own room and stand under a nice hot shower, she couldn't leave Andrew's things just dumped on the bed. She should at least put his trousers on a hanger rather than leaving them folded up in the bag to be creased. Andrew clearly wasn't going to be back anytime soon. From what she'd been told at the hospital, it was highly unlikely that he would be out in time to travel back with them in the morning. The wardrobe door groaned on its runners as she slid it open and it occurred to her that instead of putting his things away she should be packing everything into his suitcase. It wasn't a pleasant thought. She caught sight of the bedside clock and sighed; if she didn't go now there would be no time for that shower.

The rest of his things could stay on the bed, but it probably wasn't a good idea to leave Andrew's camera sitting there in full view. Best to put it out of sight.

The phone rang almost as soon as she stepped into the shower. Her heart sank. She was tempted to ignore it, but too many people had seen her come up. Perhaps she could plead that she hadn't heard it over the noise in the shower. Her conscience got the better of her and, wrapping herself in the less-than-adequately-sized hotel towel, she padded across to the phone by her bedside.

'Fiona Mason.'

'This is the reception desk. A Sergeant Viljoen from the Amsterdam police is asking for you. He is down here in the foyer.'

'Tell him I'll be there in ten minutes.'

She hurried back to the bathroom and started to towel herself dry. No. She still felt hot and sticky. The man could wait. After the afternoon she'd had, she deserved a decent shower at least.

Sergeant Viljoen was sitting on one of the easy chairs in the foyer talking to someone with his back to her. As she walked across, both men got to their feet and turned to face her.

'Mrs Mason? Thank you for coming down.' She shook the hand the sergeant held out to her. 'And I believe you two have already met.'

'Mr Montgomery-Jones. Yes indeed. Although at our last meeting, I hadn't appreciated you were actually based here in Amsterdam.'

His brow furrowed. 'What makes you think that?'

'I thought I recognised you in the hospital earlier this afternoon. No more than half an hour or so after Andrew Killigan was taken there. I know Holland's motorways are good and don't have speed limits, but you would have had to have driven pretty recklessly to make it from The Hague in that short a time.' It was good to feel she had him on the hop. The man had made her feel so inadequate at their last encounter. 'How is Mr Killigan by the way? Do you have any news, sergeant?'

It was Montgomery-Jones who answered. 'Last we heard, he was still unconscious, but stable.'

'As I am sure you realize it is about him that we are here. I understand you witnessed the accident?' The sergeant continued with his questions.

So that's what they were still calling it. This wasn't really the time or place to question the sergeant's choice of words.

'No, I didn't actually; though I did arrive soon after.'

The sergeant tried to take back the initiative. 'I hope you do not mind answering a few questions.'

'I'd be happy to help, but will this take long? Dinner will be in twenty minutes and though I have no objections to missing my meal, I do need to see to my passengers.'

'We will not keep you. The hotel has kindly set aside a room for us. Shall we?'

He led the way along the corridor behind the reception desk, opened the first door on the left and waved her inside. The men took the two easy chairs and she walked round the other side of the low table and perched on the edge of the settee opposite them.

Once they were settled, it was Montgomery-Jones who took out a silver ballpoint pen and small notepad from an inside pocket and laid it on the arm of his chair. The questions began. Fiona ran through the sequence of events from her meeting with Vera to the time they left in the taxi. They listened without interruption, watching her intently as she spoke, before Montgomery-Jones began making notes in a small neat copperplate. Though impossible to read the words upside down, she sat mesmerized. Even in her day, schools didn't teach handwriting like that anymore, but then no doubt he'd been sent to one of the better preparatory schools. He was probably wearing an Eton or Harrow tie even now, not that she would recognize it.

When she'd finished, Peter Montgomery-Jones asked several questions about what she'd noticed; the number of people at the scene, her conversations with Vera and if she recognized anyone else who was there. At last, they seemed content.

'We will obviously need to speak to Miss Ellis,' said the sergeant.

'What can you tell us about Andrew Killigan? Has he made any particular friends amongst the other passengers?' asked Montgomery-Jones before she could get to her feet.

Why should he ask that? It must mean that she was not the only one to suspect foul play. How much should she tell them?

'I think he gets on with most people. He's a very amiable, outgoing man.'

'Has there been any tension between him and anyone else?'

Much more tricky! It was not in her nature to lie, but there was a fine line between truth and discretion. He must have been aware of her reticence because he made some remark about asking the other passengers. Better to hear it from her than a lurid account from some of the more imaginative gossipers such as Yvonne Lee. Briefly, Fiona explained about Andrew's problems with Edward Collins and Deidre Oppenheimer

'Then perhaps,' he glanced at his watch, 'after dinner we should have a word with both of them after we've spoken to Miss Ellis.'

'You may have some time to wait, I'm afraid. As it's the last night, a group of people have booked the optional dinner cruise, and that includes both the Collinses and the Oppenheimers. They will all have left by now.'

There were no more questions, but something had been troubling her all through the interview. It was obvious why the sergeant had come, but what exactly was Montgomery-Jones's involvement in all of this? Even if she asked, the man was hardly likely to give her a truthful answer.

It was a relief to get away. There had been no implication that she had been responsible for what had happened to Andrew, but the interview had made her feel ill at ease – at a disadvantage. Perhaps it was simply because she reacted badly to authority figures. So many of those she'd had to deal with in the last few years had taken the attitude that to be official they needed to be officious, although she could hardly claim that was true of the sergeant or, on this occasion, of Peter Montgomery-Jones.

People were already coming down to dinner. They were gathered in small clusters outside the door to the restaurant talking animatedly. For the second time that evening, she found herself besieged by questions on all sides. In the space of the last hour, rumours had escalated; Andrew had been involved in a fight, set upon by muggers, stabbed and thrown in the canal. Scotching the stories as best she could, Fiona ushered them all into the restaurant to take their seats.

She stood in the doorway scanning the Super Sun tables. Vera Ellis still hadn't come down. Perhaps she should go up to her room and see how she was. Seeing a body floating in the water like that had been a considerable shock to the system for her, let alone someone as frail as Vera. Finding out that it was one of their own party hadn't made matters any easier. No doubt, the other passengers had bombarded the unfortunate woman with questions when they had returned just as they had done to Fiona. It would be no surprise if Vera had opted to have something up in her room.

Still undecided as to whether to leave her post and go back upstairs or ring Vera's room from reception, the decision was suddenly made for her when the lift doors opened and Vera emerged.

'How are you feeling?'

'Much better now, thank you, dear.' Vera patted Fiona's arm. She still looked very pale. 'I'm so sorry I was such a nuisance earlier.'

'You weren't at all.'

'And how is poor Mr Killigan? Are they keeping him in hospital?'

'Oh yes. I'm afraid he'll be there for a few days yet.' No need to go into detail.

'Oh dear. That is a shame, but I must confess when I saw him in the water like that, I was convinced he was already dead so we must be grateful for that.'

'If someone hadn't pulled him out as quickly as they did, I think there is every chance that we would have lost him.'

'Has he recovered consciousness?'

'All the hospital would tell me is that he is stable.'

'Have they discovered how the accident happened?'

'The police are still investigating. Actually they're here in the hotel now and they would like to speak to you after dinner.'

'But I didn't see anything.' She shrank back clutching her hands to her chest.

'It's nothing to get worried about. Just a few simple questions. They need to speak to everyone in the immediate area. They've already spoken to me.'

Before she could reassure Vera further, a piercing cry rang out from across the foyer. 'Fiona!' Yvonne Lee came rushing up quickly followed by a gaggle of others.

'Is there any more news?'

Everyone was talking at once. Fiona wanted to scream at them to go away.

'Yvonne was telling us you two witnessed the whole thing,' Barbara said to Vera.

'Oh no! Not at all.' Protested Vera. 'We weren't there. Not till much later. There was a crowd of people round him by the time we arrived. We only saw the ambulance. That's all.'

Forcing her lips into the semblance of a smile, Fiona said, 'Andrew is still in hospital, I'm afraid but more than that I can't really tell you.' Not exactly a lie, but she had no intention of pandering to them.

In response to yet another stream of questions, Fiona held up her hand. 'Shall we go into dinner? We're keeping the staff waiting.' Her arm firmly round Vera, Fiona guided her towards the door. To her immense relief there was a spare space at the table were Margery and the Harvey sisters were sitting.

'Thank you, dear. I shall be fine now.'

Fiona stayed talking to them for a few moments until she was certain that Yvonne and her cronies had come in and seated themselves. Now she could go back to her post by the door.

Surely everyone was down by now. She took a last look around the foyer. It was only then that she noticed Iris Wick staring anxiously out of the main entrance into the street outside. Not more problems? Suppressing a sigh, Fiona made her way over to the agitated woman.

'Iris, is something wrong?'

'It's Simon. He's not back yet. We were supposed to meet here ages ago.'

Not again! Fiona tried to sound reassuring, 'I expect he's just forgotten the time.'

Everyone else was sitting down and had been served their soup before Fiona managed to persuade Iris to come into the restaurant with her. Now that the numbers of her party were dwindling on an almost daily basis, together with the half dozen or so who had chosen to go out for the evening, there were plenty of spare places available.

'We'll sit here nearest to the door so you'll be bound to see him as soon as he gets here.'

It was difficult to keep up a flow of polite non-committal banter in the face of the uncomfortable silences brought about by Iris's obvious distress, not to mention Fiona's own disquiet over Andrew. That wasn't helped when, at the next table, Yvonne Lee began to speculate to the Major and Lavinia Rawlings who might have been responsible for pushing Andrew into the canal. Although it was said jokingly, with Edward and Deirdre as the obvious main contenders, Fiona felt distinctly uncomfortable especially after her recent conversation with Sergeant Viljoen and Peter Montgomery-Jones. Not that they were the only ones to come up with the idea. With both the Collinses and Oppenheimers absent, no one felt the need to keep their voices down.

Fiona turned to Eileen Finch and Nesta Griffin, the only other occupants of their table and asked, 'So where did you two get to this afternoon?' Not exactly the most original question, but it was the only thing she could think of on the spur of the moment. Anything to break the pained silence and to blot out the thoughtless chatter around them.

'Nesta went to the Rijksmuseum and I went to the Van Gogh.'

'Oh!' Silly really, she thought, just because she was so used to seeing them together was no reason to assume that they were joined at the hip, especially after what had happened in Volendam.

Seeing the surprise registered on Fiona face, Nesta gave a little chuckle. 'We did have lunch together, but then we went our separate ways. Vermeer is one of my favourite artists and I particularly wanted to see his "Kitchen Maid" in the flesh so to speak.'

'That's the girl pouring milk into a bowl isn't it? Did it meet your expectations?'

'Oh yes! I love the way the light from the window falls across the figure and the fantastic contrast of light and dark with the yellow and blues. Absolutely marvellous.'

Eileen gave a gentle laugh. 'Not one for half measures about her passions is our Nesta.'

'Sorry. I know I do go on sometimes about the things that matter to me.'

'And so you should. What's wrong with that?' Fiona turned to Eileen. 'And were you similarly excited by the paintings you went to see.'

'It was very enjoyable although I must confess I didn't go round every floor. A huge building devoted to just one artist can be a bit too much of a good thing after awhile.'

'But I thought there were lots of works by some of his contemporaries. Gauguin, Monet and Lautrec?' What was she thinking of pulling up one of the paying clients? So much for diplomatic discretion! 'I'm so sorry; that was rude.'

'Not at all!' Eileen gave a genuine trill of laughter. 'You've caught me out. I am glad I went, but I didn't ever intend to spend all afternoon there. Having come to Amsterdam, I didn't want go back home without seeing the Red Light District. I didn't think Nesta would approve so I wasn't going to say anything.'

'I admit it's not somewhere I'd like to have been seen, but some of the architecture is supposed to be impressive. You'll have to show me your photographs.'

'No can do, I'm afraid. All photography in that area is strictly banned. A definite no-no. Although, to be honest, it wasn't exactly the architecture that I went to look at.' Eileen's pleasant deep-throated chuckle made even her straight-laced friend's face break out in a momentary smile. 'But I can tell you, all those ladies, with their alluring cleavages and skirts far wider than they are long, really do sit in their windows making lascivious glances at every male that passes.'

Nesta looked decided uncomfortable and with flushed cheeks said in a barely audible voice, 'Eileen.'

Fiona smiled, but her mind was working overtime. It was quite a hike from the museum quarter of the city in the south all the way up to the Red Light District. Now she was being silly. Eileen could just have easily caught a tram or a taxi.

Twenty-Six

Simon still hadn't arrived by the end of dinner. Fiona guided a weepy Iris across to the lounge area and sat her down in a quiet corner with a cup of coffee. Now there was no option. It was time to report him missing. Leaving Iris in Marjory's capable care, Fiona went into the foyer.

If Simon had rung the hotel to leave a message, someone would have informed them, but it wouldn't hurt to check at reception. Fiona was about to ask if she could use the phone – it might be as well to check the hospitals, just in case – when she noticed a couple, a man and a woman, in navy uniforms standing at the far end of the desk. Police. Even if they were not able to help, they would at least be able to tell her to whom she should pass on the information and ask advice.

Her task accomplished, she left everything in their hands and hurried back to Iris.

Ten minutes later Fiona was still sitting with a distraught Iris Wick when a shadow fell across them. Looking up she saw Sergeant Viljoen and Peter Montgomery-Jones.

'Mrs Wick? May we have a word?'

Iris threw Fiona a beseeching look.

'Can't it wait, Sergeant? Her husband still hasn't come back yet and she's very upset.'

'It is about Mr Wick that we wish to talk.'

'You're going to look for him?' A look of relief swept over the tearstained face.

'We are already, madam. Would you come with us please?'

The worried frown returned. 'Can Fiona come with me?'

The man hesitated then glanced at Montgomery-Jones who gave a barely perceptible nod. Perhaps she'd imagined it. Why should a Dutch policeman seek the approval of a British Embassy official? Fiona's heart sank. Were they about to give the poor woman some dire news? The same thought must have gone through Iris's mind to judge from the look of desperate appeal she threw at Fiona and from the way she tottered across the foyer needing support with each step. She kept a tight hold on Fiona's arm as they followed the sergeant along the corridor.

Once inside the room, the officer motioned the two women to the settee and, once again, he and Montgomery-Jones took the chairs opposite.

'You don't mind if we record this interview do you?' He gestured towards the large official-looking black box on the small table between them. Fiona couldn't remember it being there earlier and there had been no mention of a recording then. What on earth was going on?

Iris turned wide questioning eyes on Fiona

'It is standard practice now. Part of the Human Rights Protection Procedures. We thought you would prefer to be interviewed here in the hotel rather than asking you to come down to the station,' he continued. He leant forward, picked up a couple of tapes, and slowly peeled off their cellophane wrappers. 'You will be given a copy.'

Iris licked her lips.

'Can you tell us what you and your husband did this afternoon?'

Before answering, Iris pulled a soggy handkerchief from her pocket and began twisting it nervously between her fingers. 'I wanted to see Anne Frank's House, but Simon said he didn't want to wait in the queue for half the afternoon. He's not really the most patient of people. He said he'd much rather go and look round that old sailing ship we saw in the harbour. Ships aren't my sort of thing so it made sense for us to go our separate ways.'

'At what time was that?'

'I'm not sure exactly. About half two, I suppose.'

'And you have not seen him since?'

She shook her head.

'For the tape, madam.'

'No.' The voice was barely audible.

'The museum closes at five o'clock. You have no idea where he might have gone after that?'

She shook her head. 'He didn't say he was going anywhere else.'

'Do you often do things separately like that?' asked Montgomery-Jones gently.

'Sometimes.'

'On this trip?'

'Once or twice.'

'Which is it?' The sergeant was harshly insistent.

Iris's bottom lip trembled.

'He likes taking photos so he goes off most times when we've been out. But not for long. Half an hour at most.'

'How well do you both know the Netherlands?'

Confused by the sergeant's sudden change of subject, Iris's bottom lip quivered. 'Simon used to come here quite often with his first wife and we had booked a holiday for last autumn, but I had to have an operation in the September and didn't feel up to it.'

'Did your husband come on his own?'

'Oh no. It was cancelled.'

'So you both stayed home?'

Surely this was harassment. Fiona bit back her protest. She was hardly a trained solicitor and if she did intervene, she might well make the situation worse by antagonizing the policeman or sending her from the room.

'Yes. Although a job came up and Simon had to go away in any case.'

'Does he often go on business trips?'

'Fairly often. Part of his job is to install computer software systems.'

'That must be quite lonely for you.' Montgomery-Jones gave her an encouraging smile. Perhaps he too thought the policeman was being too harsh.

Iris shrugged. 'You get used to it. It's usually only for four or five days. Sometimes a week. Though most of the time he works from home over the internet.'

'What is the name of the company he works for?' Presumably, Sergeant Viljoen had a reason for all these seemingly irrelevant questions. The fact that Montgomery-Jones was here with him gave every indication that they must suspect that Simon was involved in the smuggling racket in some way.

Iris shook her head. 'He's a consultant so he does things for lots of different companies.'

'In the Netherlands or only in Britain?'

'He did have a contract in Belgium last summer and one in France, almost three years ago it must have been. Not long after we were married.'

'Do you know if he has friends over here? People he gets in touch with when he comes?'

'He's never mentioned anyone.'

There was a long pause while the two men contemplated what she had said or possibly, Fiona wondered, trying to tempt Iris to say something more to break the silence.

When nothing else was forthcoming, the Sergeant said reluctantly, 'That will be all for now.' Making a note of the time, he then leant forward and switched off the recorder. He took out both tapes and slipped them back into their plastic boxes.

As he filled in the details on the covers, he said casually, 'It will be necessary to make a search of your room, Mrs Wick.'

Iris, already looking pale and wan, lost any colour she'd had. She turned a bewildered glance on Fiona. 'Is that really necessary?'

'The police need to see if they can find any clues as to where your husband might have gone,' said Montgomery-Jones, not unkindly. 'If you would like to go with the sergeant; it would be best if he does this with you present.'

Before Iris had a chance to make a plea for Fiona to with them, she was forestalled. 'It will not take long and in the meantime there are one or two things I would like to ask Mrs Mason. There is a WPC outside. She will go with you.'

As soon as the door closed, Fiona turned to Montgomery-Jones. 'That was unforgivable,' she snapped.

'I beg your pardon.'

'Bullying the poor woman when she's worried sick about her missing husband.' He raised an imperious eyebrow but she refused to be intimidated. 'From all those questions, anyone would think that her husband is a common criminal on the run.'

'At this stage, we are not able to rule out that possibility.'

She stared at him in disbelief but he held her gaze steadily. It was impossible to prove him wrong but there was no way she was letting the man off the hook. 'You're not from the Embassy at all, are you? You're Jane's boss, the man she calls the Commander.'

A faint sardonic smile flickered over his lips. The fact that he did not deny it was confirmation enough. Before she could ask anything more, he asked pleasantly, 'Can you give me your thoughts on Simon Wick?'

Fiona hesitated. She was tempted to ignore his question and storm out of the room but that might lead to even more trouble. Even at his best, Simon was not the most likeable of people and as Montgomery-Jones could, and probably would, ask the whole group, it was best he heard her less emotive account first. When she'd finished, he looked at her for several moments in silence.

'Sounds like a real pain in the backside.'

Fiona found herself laughing out loud at the comment so in contrast with this aloof, aristocratic man. Which, she though ruefully, had probably been exactly his intention. A way of breaking the ice between them; trying to win her over.

'Would you have said that he is the violent type?'

'From the limited knowledge I have of the man, I wouldn't have said so. I've never seen him lose his temper. Rather a timid person really. The sort to back down in any confrontation.'

'Excitable? Panicky?'

She shrugged her shoulders. 'Not that I noticed. Why do you ask?'

Before he could say anything, there was a knock at the door and Sergeant Viljoen entered carrying a plastic carrier bag which he placed on the table. 'We found this in the safe.'

Montgomery-Jones looked in. 'Interesting.'

For a moment, Fiona thought she was not about to learn what the two men appeared so pleased to have discovered, but then Montgomery-Jones took his handkerchief from his top pocket, shook it out, then used it to pull out a DVD. 'Our Mr Wick has evidently been doing a little business on his own account.' He lifted out a few more, replacing each one carefully back into the bag.

Fiona couldn't see their covers but decided to curb the impulse to ask. The two men were so absorbed in their task, it was probably best not to remind them of her presence by drawing attention to herself.

'So what does his wife have to say?'

'She claims she knows nothing about them and has no idea what he keeps in the safe. He did not give her the combination. It was necessary to use the hotel's override code. She is still up in the room with a woman police officer.'

'Was there anything else in the safe?'

The man shook his head. 'That was all, apart from a few Euros. No diamonds, sir.'

'So where are they, I wonder?' Montgomery-Jones sat back, tugging on his ear lobe, deep in thought. We need another word with Mrs Wick. And I suppose it had better be down here where we can record it on tape.'

Twenty-Seven

Fiona did not intend to let the vulnerable woman face these two again on her own. Determined that Iris should have at least one person present with her interests at heart, Fiona, remained sitting where she was. If they wanted her gone, she would put up a fight. Whatever Simon may have done, there was no proof that Iris was involved.

In the event, Iris was not subjected to the ferocious questioning that Fiona had feared. It was obvious to everyone that Iris was totally distraught, hardly able to string a sentence together before breaking down into hiccupping sobs. Either she knew nothing or was giving a performance for which even Dame Judi Dench would receive resounding acclaim from the critics. It was difficult enough to get her to repeat the statements she had made up in her room.

'We do appreciate how distressing all this has been for you, Mrs Wick.' There was nothing perfunctory or hollow about Montgomery-Jones's concern. 'I am sure you will feel better after a good night's sleep. Perhaps the doctor could give you a sedative.'

Iris made to get to her feet and just as Fiona was about to offer to take her up to her room, Montgomery-Jones forestalled them with another question, 'What kind of relationship did your husband have with Andrew Killigan?'

The sudden change of tack, clearly bemused Iris and she dabbed her eyes before replying, 'I don't think he had much to do with him. We tend to keep ourselves to ourselves mostly.'

'But they did know each other. They had met before on previous tours.' They were not questions but statements of fact.

Iris shrugged her shoulders, 'If they did, Simon didn't say.'

Montgomery-Jones gave her one his charming smiles and said, 'The woman police officer will help you up to your room and she can stay with you until the doctor arrives.'

Fiona hesitated. She knew Iris would prefer her company to that of the policewoman, but there was a question she needed to ask. Sergeant Viljoen handed Iris a copy of the tape and took her arm, guiding the dazed and forlorn-looking woman to the door.

Once the two of them had disappeared, Fiona turned to Montgomery-Jones before he too had a chance to get away. 'What you were saying to Iris just now...'

'Yes?' he said, as she paused uncertain how to phrase her question.

'Are you suggesting that Simon was responsible for what happened to Andrew?'

After a long pause, he said guardedly, 'We cannot rule that out.'

'So what makes you so certain?' When no answer was forthcoming she continued, her voice hard, 'Don't you think I deserve to know? It's me who has been pushed right onto the front line all week and I've been kept in the dark at every stage.'

'We deemed it would be safer that way.'

'Safer for your interests or mine?'

'Both.'

'Rubbish,' she snapped. 'I would never have been told anything about your operation after Tim's death if you hadn't checked me out thoroughly in the first place so you knew I wasn't the smuggler. Is it any wonder I feel like a pawn in your little games? I've spent a week on the edge of my nerves trusting no one and analysing every petty remark made by my passengers whilst, at the same time, trying to protect each and every one of them from falling foul of a murderer in their midst. Have you any idea of how that feels? Torn in two directions at the same time.'

'I am sorry you feel like that.'

'I didn't ask to be involved in all this. That was your department's choice. But once I was pulled in, it would have been nice to have had some support.'

'We have had people looking out for you and your party the whole time.'

'Really! So where were they when someone tried to kill Andrew?' His only response was a stony glare. 'Don't tell me,' she snorted. 'The other side of the canal. That's how you know it was Simon.'

There was a long pause before he eventually said, 'I am not your enemy you know.'

But you are certainly not my friend. Perhaps it would be more politic not to voice such thoughts aloud. 'That is not an answer.'

Another silence. 'Yes. It was Wick.'

'And is he a suspect for Tim's murder?'

'In the light of information recently received, that now looks a distinct possibility,' he admitted reluctantly.

'But your surveillance was so good, he managed to shoot one man and damn near drown another! How many more of my passengers does he have to kill before you arrest him? Don't give me any excuses about needing him free until you catch the big boys. Risking the lives of innocent bystanders cannot be morally justified. It makes you no better than the criminals you're supposed to be after.'

'I can assure you, it was not like that at all,' he snapped. 'Brooke was one of my best men and I would never deliberately sacrifice anyone either in the service or among the general public. To my great regret, I have to admit that we did not fully identify the risk until it was too late.'

'Really! What a surprise!'

Perhaps she had gone over the top, but she wasn't about to back down now. Fiona stared at him defiantly waiting for the clever remark intended to cut her down to size.

When it came, his response took her by surprise. 'I admit I should have given more weight to Brooke's instinct and demanded an autopsy straight away. Then we might have known what we were up against much earlier.'

'Surely you didn't need an autopsy to tell you he'd been shot?'

He frowned and gave her a fleeting glance. When she got no answer, she pressed him further. 'If it's not Tim Brooke's death we're talking about here, whose do you mean?' The silence continued to hang in the air. 'The only other person was the man who had a heart attack. Henry Unsworth. Are you saying that he was murdered?'

Peter Montgomery-Jones let out a long sigh. 'Yes. We had to wait until Monday for the autopsy and only then did we learn that he had been poisoned.'

'But what reason would anyone have to murder him?'

'Ah. So you failed to wheedle that little snippet out of Jane.' He gave her an ironic half smile. 'I assumed that she had told you. Hence my indiscretion. According to some information we received, anonymously of course, Unsworth was our smuggler. That was the justification for setting up this whole operation.'

'And you think that was Simon was responsible for his death too?'

'Possibly. Though as yet, we have no idea of his motive. We are still trying to piece together exactly what happened. Even after Unsworth, Brooke's death came as a complete surprise. In our experience, whatever their masters might do, couriers do not usually resort to guns let alone murder.'

'So what is Simon saying? Has he admitted shooting Tim?'

Her only answer was silence.

Her eyes narrowed. 'He got away didn't he? You had a man watching him, who saw him attack Andrew, and he still walks away? Are you people totally incompetent?'

'Our man was not following Wick.'

'You were tailing Andrew!' She was incredulous. 'You were following the wrong man!'

He gave a snort. 'You think?'

'So what happened?' Across the table, he threw her a look of pure sardonic distain that roused every rebellious fibre in her body. 'I have no intention of leaving here until I get an

206

answer. And I should warn you I am not prepared to be fobbed off.'

The look on his face indicated that Peter Montgomery-Jones was not a man used to being challenged. She refused to back down and sat glowering at him. Eventually, after a long pause as though weighing up just how much he should say, he answered. 'There was definitely some kind of altercation between him and Killigan by the canal this afternoon. Killigan turned his back and when he started to walk away, Wick lunged at him with his camera and then fled. Killigan was knocked unconscious and my man was kept busy having to pull him out of the water instead of giving chase.'

She had her answer and could hardly protest at the man's decision. The anger seeped out of her as quickly as it had risen.

'Is that why you were asking me about Simon earlier?' He nodded. Time now for her to be more reasonable. 'All I can say is that I never noticed anything to suggest he might react like that. His constant interruptions, spouting out spurious details no one was interested in, got up everyone's nose. People were downright rude to him, telling him to shut up, but he never ever retaliated by word or look. He seemed quite impervious to it all.'

Montgomery-Jones looked thoughtful. 'That sort of annoying behaviour might stop everyone else in the party from having much to do with him.'

'You think it could all have been an act?'

'As a smuggler, he might not want to strike up any friendships. He would need to keep his distance so he could get away on his own when he needed to.'

'Perhaps he was provoked.'

'Meaning?'

'It wouldn't surprise me if Andrew hadn't said or done something to cause Simon to flip.'

A smile played at the corners of his mouth. 'I thought you liked Killigan.'

'I did. I do. Beneath that well-practiced little-boy smile and ingratiating bonhomie there is a certain appeal. But, thinking about it, there was definitely something between him and Simon.'

'What makes you think that?'

'Intangible things really. As I said, Andrew had a considerable charisma. He turned the charm on everyone, but he would go out of his way to avoid Simon. Never sat at the same table, never stood near him when we were out. There wasn't a great deal of love lost between Andrew and Edward Collins, but most of the time those two managed to speak civilly to each other, but Andrew seemed to want to have nothing to do with Simon. He disliked the man intensely, even said as much to me once.'

'Could Wick have something on him?'

Fiona furrowed her brow in thought. 'Possibly, but somehow I doubt it. Simon's attitude to Andrew was too deferential, as though he was seeking his approval all the time.'

Any further discussion was cut short by the insistent buzz of Montgomery-Jones's mobile.

'Forgive me.' Fiona watched his face as he listened but his expression remained impassive. Eventually he said, 'I see.'

Fiona's heart gave a jump. Could it be news of Andrew? He was on the critical list. She sat on tenterhooks, waiting for the call to finish.

'If you will excuse me, I must go.' He got to his feet.

'Was that about Andrew?'

'No. Still no news on that front. I doubt that we will hear anything soon.' His voice softened. 'His condition is not very good you know. I promise if I hear of any change, I will let you know straight away.'

'You think he was Simon's partner don't you? You said earlier, the two of them had been on previous trips together. Could the argument have been a falling out of thieves?'

He didn't answer straight away. 'That could be a possible explanation.'

'That's why you turned up at the hospital. You needed to go through Andrew's things before they were given to me. Which means if you didn't find the diamonds – and you must have searched his room as well – then you don't have any proof that Andrew was involved.'

'We will know more when we talk to Wick himself. That phone call just now, was about him. Wick has been arrested. I owe you that at least.' He looked at her for a moment, as though making a decision before continuing, 'A man came under suspicion during an earlier investigation when the diamonds were recovered. After a report that came through this afternoon, we now strongly suspect that man to be Wick. Since then, he has shaved off the beard, got rid of the spectacles and acquired a passport in a new name. I know it is little consolation, but if that information had arrived earlier, I assure you, he would have been in custody long before now.'

'Do you still think Andrew is one of smugglers?'

He looked at her for a moment then sat down again. 'I have to say we have no other suspects.'

'Does that mean you have recovered the diamonds?'

He gave a deep sigh. 'Not yet.'

For some reason she felt close to tears. He put out a hand and laid it gently on her arm. 'Would it help if I said that Killigan is not a suspect for Brooke's murder? Several members of the party were able to vouch for his whereabouts throughout the afternoon. It seems he teamed up with several of the ladies including Mrs Oppenheimer and her daughter. He seems to have made quite an impression on them all.'

Fiona chuckled. 'He always does. Thank you for telling me. I'd hate to think I was tricked into liking a cold-blooded killer.' She took out a handkerchief and blew her nose. 'I thought you were in a hurry to be off.' The smile softened the rebuke in her words.

'True. The interview cannot begin without me.' He still sat there. 'The point is, now this whole affair is over. There are still a few loose ends to tie up, that is true, but, once we have spoken with Wick, we will be able to close the case. There really is no need for you to worry any more. I do appreciate that this has been a very difficult situation for you. Thank you for all your help. It really has been appreciated.'

He stood up. It was now or never. 'I know I shouldn't ask but, after everything that's happened, I don't think I could bear not knowing the final outcome. If you do learn anything significant from the interview with Wick, will you let me know? After all,' she looked at him from under her lashes, 'if you are going to charge him, Iris is going to need my support. I promise none of this will go any further.'

His impassive stare broke into slow smile. 'That might be possible. And now I really must go.'

At the door, he turned. There was a gleam in his eye as he gave her a parting shot. 'You would make an excellent member of my team.'

'I don't think so,' she laughed. 'You can have too much excitement.'

Twenty-Eight

Even though Iris had not been left alone, she would no doubt welcome a familiar face. Wearily, Fiona got to her feet and headed up to the third floor. As she passed her own door on the way to Room 322, at the end of the corridor, Fiona was tempted to abandon the idea and sneak back into her own room. To be alone. To have time to put the jumble of assorted information that had come to light into some sort of order so that she could make sense of it all. But duty called.

Iris was perched on the edge of the bed, her whole body taut. The soggy handkerchief had been replaced by a box of tissues beside her, but she could not keep her hands still and was twisting her wedding ring round and round her finger.

'I tried to get her to lie down,' the policewoman confided in a low voice.

'I'm not seeing some foreign doctor in my nightie.' Iris was evidently not so distracted that she had not heard.

'I'll stay with her until the doctor comes, if you like.' Fiona ushered the policewoman to the door. 'She'll probably feel better with someone she knows.'

There was little that Fiona could say to comfort Iris who was now rocking back and forth. Her husband was missing, he had hidden pornographic DVDs in their room and she might even be aware that he was suspected of even worse crimes. Fiona could hardy tell the woman not to worry or that it would be all right. The only thing she could do was to sit next to Iris and hold her hand.

'What's going to happen? Are they going to arrest me?' Iris turned to her with pleading wide eyes. '*I* didn't do anything.'

'No of course not.' Fiona put an arm around her.

'But they won't be able to keep me here, will they? I don't know anything. It's nothing to do with me. You will tell them that, won't you? I had no idea what he was up to.'

'I'm sure they realize that.' The rocking began again. 'Everything is going to be all right.' So much for all her resolution!

'You won't let them stop me coming back with you all tomorrow, will you?'

There was no answer to that. All Fiona could do was smile and put her arms around the woman cradling her like a child until the noisy sobs subsided.

'Why don't we get you ready for bed? When the doctor comes, he'll be able to give you something to make you sleep. This has all been a terrible shock. Everything will seem so much better in the morning when you're properly rested.' Hardly the most original comment and probably a long way from the truth.

Things were going from bad to absolute bloody disaster. It all began with the argument over the diamonds. Not that he could remember the details. He'd thought the man was going to punch his lights out when he took a step towards him with that look on his face, but after that things got very hazy. At some point, he must have hit out himself because he could picture the man doubling over from a blow to the stomach followed by a great smack on the side of his head that knocked him off his feet and into the water. That was when he bolted. The next thing he remembered was sitting in one of the booths at the back of some seedy coffee shop vaguely aware of three or four other single men sprawled in their own recesses dreamily smoking their hash or skunk or whatever it was called.

He'd thought about going back to the hotel and trying to brazen it out. Andrew was hardly going to report him to the police. But, assuming the man was telling the truth, Mavis must be somewhere about keeping a beady eye and god knows what she'd do next. Had she booked into the hotel as another guest or was she actually on the tour as one of the party? He had no idea what she looked like or even how old she was.

As if all that weren't catastrophic enough, now he'd been arrested. Strictly speaking they'd asked him to accompany them to the station to answer some questions. They wouldn't tell him what it was all about when he'd asked but it wasn't until they took his fingerprints that what little bravado he had left finally got knocked out of him.

What a mess. He put his head in his hands and tried to pull himself together and organize the barrage of disordered thoughts flitting about in his mind.

He looked up when the door opened and two men came into the airless interview room. Perhaps this wasn't going to be so bad after all. One of them was that posh chap from the Embassy who'd come with the local police back in The Hague a few days ago. Presumably the man was here to protect his interests as a British subject. With luck they'd let him off with just a caution for brawling in the street. What was it they called it, causing an affray? He gave the grey man a tentative smile but there was no response in the man's steady gaze.

The two newcomers sat down on the far side of the table and the Dutchman put down the brown folder he'd brought with him and took out a pen from the inside pocket of his jacket. He settled himself in his chair and asked, 'Will you give me your name, sir.'

No point in antagonizing the man by refusing to answer. He licked his lips but his voice still came out a strangulated whine. 'Simon Christopher Wick.'

'Your home address.'

The man wrote it down as Simon dictated and then sat back.

'So, Mr Wick, would you tell us about the argument you had with Mr Killigan this afternoon.'

He knew this was coming but he still didn't have an answer.

'Just a stupid misunderstanding,' he blustered. 'It got a bit out of hand that's all.'

'What was it about?'

'Not really sure myself. Andrew was very upset about something, but to tell the truth, he wasn't making much sense.' He attempted a wry smile but he knew it must look more of a grimace.

'Let me make it a little easier for you, Mr Wick. We know about the diamonds and the role you and Mr Killigan have in the smuggling syndicate.'

His heart dropped like a lead weight to the pit of his stomach.

'I don't know what you're talking about?'

Andrew must have coughed to the lot. And Jenks had called him flaky! But it was bloody Golden Boy Killigan who couldn't take the heat not him. He threw a beseeching glance at the grey man who remained stubbornly silent. No help was coming from that quarter.

'So tell us where the diamonds are now.'

'I don't know what you're talking about,' he repeated.

'Do you really want to add obstruction to the other charges?' the Dutchman asked conversationally. Somehow, the bland manner made it more terrifying than if he'd used the hard man tactics seen on television cop shows. 'A little co-operation on your part might go a long way to helping your case.'

What could he say? 'No idea. You'll have to ask Killigan.'

It wasn't quite an admission but he would need to keep his wits about him.

'So you are saying that Andrew Killigan is the mastermind here? You are only a small cog in the machinery so to speak.'

'I'm not saying anything.'

The Dutchman smiled. 'Perhaps we should ask your wife? I assume she really is your wife and not simply a convenient piece of window dressing to act as a cover for you. Even if like you, she denies all knowledge of the diamonds, the DVDs were found in her possession.'

'You leave Iris out of this!' He was up and out of his seat. 'She's got nothing to do with any of it. She's a sick woman. She mustn't be upset.'

'I am sorry to tell you, Mr Wick that she is already.' The grey man spoke for the first time. 'Your failure to return to the hotel for dinner has caused her considerable distress.'

'Sit down, Mr Wick,' said the Dutchman. 'Perhaps for her sake you should reconsider your position.'

'If I give you the name of the man who runs the whole show will you promise to leave her alone?'

'We have no desire to cause Mrs Wick any further stress.'

The Dutchman took a blank sheet of paper from his folder, laid his pen on top and slid them both across the table.

After a momentary pause, Simon picked up the pen and scribbled down Jenks's details. Not that there was much he could give them. Jenks was too fly ever to meet him anywhere else than the back room of The Nag's Head. When he'd finished, he looked across at the grey man.

'Can I go now?'

'I am afraid not,' the other man said sharply. 'Apart from your smuggling exploits, there is still the matter of the murders of Tim Brooke and Henry Unsworth to discuss.'

A black mist descended and he collapsed.

Much to Fiona's relief, they did not have long to wait for the arrival of the doctor and, in the knowledge that Iris would soon be sleeping soundly, she was able to slip away. After all the trauma of the last few hours, Fiona felt in need of a mild sedative herself. Especially when she thought of the rest of her charges all waiting for her in the lounge, eager for any juicy titbit of news. A good stiff brandy would go down very well.

The dinner cruise people still had not yet returned and, as usual, the Dobsons and the Smiths were off out somewhere, which meant that only a dozen or so of the Super Sun party were left in the lounge. They were so few that the chairs had been arranged in a large circle to include them all.

'What would you like to drink?' Gordon Shuttleworth was the first on his feet. The Major and Gerald Lee were ready to manoeuvre another armchair into the fold and, like it or not, Fiona was ensconced in their midst, a fresh cup of coffee in front of her.

'Have you heard from the hospital? Have you any idea how long they'll be keeping Andrew in?' asked Lavinia Rawlings.

'Not yet, but I'm afraid he won't be well enough to travel back with us tomorrow.'

'So what about all his things?' Any moment now, Fiona thought and Yvonne would be volunteering to pack them up for her.

'I've popped the clothes they gave me at the hospital in his room, but things have been a bit hectic since then. I'll see to everything in the morning.'

'Yes of course. We saw you and Iris with the police.' Avid for gossip, Yvonne seized the opportunity. 'So is there any news on poor Simon? Have they found him yet?'

Poor Simon indeed! Yvonne hadn't had a good word to say for the man throughout the trip. She was the most vociferous when it came to carping about his constant interjections.

'The police are still investigating.'

'How's Iris?' There was genuine concern in Margery's voice.

'Naturally she's very upset, but the doctor has given her a sedative and I've just left her tucked up in bed. She should sleep soundly until morning.'

'Plays havoc with the nerves, something like that,' interposed Major Rawlins. 'The wife went to pieces when our son didn't come home on time one evening. Turned out okay of course, these things always do, but it took two dry sherries and a whole box of liquorice allsorts to calm her down.'

The ring of worried frowns turned into smiles and titters. Bless the man. The mood of doom and gloom had been oppressive.

Iris wasn't the only one who'd had a nasty shock that day. Fiona glanced round the circle searching for Vera Ellis. She looked relaxed enough now tucked between Barbara Shuttleworth and Phyllis Harvey. It was a surprise to find the old dear still up. Fiona expected that she would have opted for an early night. Still it was good to know she was fully recovered and not suffering any ill effects after her ordeal. That at least was one less worry off her shoulders.

Fiona would not have minded an early night herself, but no one seemed interested in going up. Whether that was because they thought they might miss out on something or simply because it was their last night and, with a late start next morning, they could lie in, there was no way of knowing.

Her eyelids felt heavy and her whole body was leaden. She massaged away the dull ache beginning to throb gently at her temples. It was no good, she would have to give her apologies and make a move.

Before she could get to her feet, the Karpinskis and the Collinses came into the lounge.

'Did you have a good time?'

'Excellent, thank you, Fiona.' Joyce enthused. 'It really was quite magical seeing the lights all round the bridges and the reflections shimmering on the water as we glided past. Quite romantic, wasn't it Edward?'

'Well, at least you can't see all the muck and grime in the dark.' Her husband was clearly not a man with a sensitive soul.

'And did you enjoy the meal?' asked Margery as more chairs were pulled into the circle. Fiona was tempted to offer her

217

own seat, but it might seem rude if she hurried away just as the others arrived.

'Oh yes, very much. A really unusual starter with potato, smoked salmon and chopped onion with a sour cream dressing, then I had the chicken and Eddie chose the salmon. And to finish there was a gorgeous, chocolate truffle cake with caramel sauce which was so rich I couldn't eat all mine and Edward had to finish it off for me.'

'It certainly took you long enough to get through it,' said Gerald with a laugh.

'We all went for a walk after that,' she paused dramatically. 'Through the Red Light District.'

'Really?' Cynthia Harvey looked quite shocked but most of the others were laughing.

'We were talking to Tricia Dobson and her husband earlier and they said it was fascinating and well worth a visit. Apparently it's best to go at night when it's all lit up.'

'So what was it like?'

'Full of red neon lights everywhere,' she gave a girlish giggle. 'Actually it was fun, not a bit as I expected, and the place was crowded with tourists just like us, wandering around.'

'And did you see the alluring, scantily clad ladies displaying their wares in the windows?' asked the Major with a twinkle in his eye.

'Oh yes. But actually there weren't that many pretty ones were there?' She turned to Rozalia Karpinska who shook her head and pulled a face. 'In fact most of them were downright ugly, lots of really fat ones. It was an experience as they say. But we all enjoyed it didn't we?'

Edward snorted at his wife's enthusiasm. 'Could have got some lovely shots, if some idiot hadn't pushed my camera in the drink.'

There was an embarrassed lull. No doubt, like Fiona, the others would have fingers crossed that the man wouldn't go into yet another rant. Men and their toys! A sudden thought struck her. Edward had not been the only one to make a fuss about a camera.

'So what have you done with the Oppenheimers?' Surely not more problems, Fiona thought.

'Miriam's feet were hurting with all the walking so they've just popped up so she can change her shoes. Here they come now.'

Orders were taken for another round of drinks and Fiona went to help bring them over as their little circle was extended. She was about to pick up the first tray when a great shriek went up that brought the whole room to a sudden standstill. Everyone turned to look. Deirdre, now on her feet again, was staring at Yvonne Lee with a look of horror on her face.

It hadn't taken long for that poisonous woman to tell the poor girl about Andrew.

Pushing her way in a blind panic past those unfortunate enough to be sitting next to her, Deirdre rushed over to Fiona, crying out at the top of her voice, 'Is it true? Tell me it's not true.'

The only sound in the crowded room was the girl's penetrating, hysterical sobs. Wrapping an arm around the distraught girl, Fiona led her out into the foyer to a quiet corner where they would not be so public.

With Mrs Oppenheimer's help, Fiona managed to get Deirdre seated on a settee sandwiched between the two of them until the din began to subside.

'It's all my fault,' Deirdre stammered before the ear-piercing wail resumed.

A shock wave went through Fiona. Surely not! 'How do you mean, your fault?'

Between gulps, Deirdre spluttered in disjointed snatches, 'If I hadn't... If the two of us had still been friends... We would have been together and it wouldn't have happened.'

Deirdre bit her lip and large tears cascaded down her cheeks. Fiona made consoling noises, but it was evident her words went unheard.

'I must go and see him. We'll call a cab straight away.'

'No.' Fiona put a restraining hand firmly on the girl's arm. 'It's much too late for that now.'

There was another eruption of noisy, hiccupping sobs. Mrs Oppenheimer produced a travel pack of tissues from her bag, pulled out a couple and thrust them at her daughter. Eventually the noisy wail subsidised. Clearly, any resentment she might have felt at Andrew's rejection in Volendam was now entirely forgotten.

'Why don't the two of us go downtown first thing in the morning and find a get-well-soon card and perhaps a nice little gift; flowers or chocolates or something,' suggested her mother.

'What a good idea!' said Fiona with an enthusiasm she did not feel. 'I'm going to be really busy tomorrow and it will be difficult for me to get out, so would you do me a big favour and get a card that we could send from the rest us as well? And a big basket of fruit.' She pulled her purse from her bag. 'I doubt he'll be allowed visitors in any case but, after we've all had a chance to sign the card, I'll ask the hotel to send someone over to the hospital and make sure he gets everything. I'm sure it would make him feel better to know we were all thinking about him.'

The last thing she wanted was the Oppenheimers turning up at the hospital and discovering exactly how severe Andrew's condition really was.

Fiona was up in her room already half-undressed when the call came.

'Montgomery-Jones here. I trust you were not asleep? You did ask me to get back to you. Wick denied everything at first but he did eventually admit to the smuggling.'

'What about Tim Brooke? Did he confess to shooting him?'

'He denies knowing anything about that so we are going to have to rely on forensic evidence.'

'But at least you have the diamonds.'

'He claims they are still in Killigan's possession, so for the time being we have drawn a blank.'

'Does that mean you have to question Iris again?' When he failed to answer, she continued. 'I don't think you'll get much more out of her.'

'No,' he agreed. 'Although we would like to know if Wick ever talked about a Jenks or mentioned any of his contacts.'

'Would she tell you if he had?'

'I doubt it.' There was a pause.

That explained it. Montgomery-Jones was being extraordinarily communicative and she suspected he must have some ulterior motive. 'You want me to see if I can wheedle it out of her?'

'She is much more likely to talk to you,' he admitted.

Fiona hesitated. 'I won't if it's a trap.'

'Nothing like that. Wick was quite adamant that his wife knew nothing about the smuggling. It was only when we talked about charging her for possession of the DVDs that he agreed to give us the name of his contact back in Britain. He has agreed to testify against Jenks and Killigan in exchange for her being looked after while he is in prison. According to him, it will be difficult for her to manage without him, both financially and emotionally. She is not a well woman, which is why he became involved with smuggling in the first place. He needed the money to buy her some new cancer treatment.'

'Do you believe him?'

'Is there any reason not to?'

'She definitely has had a mastectomy; I helped her get ready for bed.' Fiona admitted doubtfully. 'Still, as far as Customs and Revenue is concerned it's a positive result I suppose. You can at least close down the British end of the operation.'

'Unfortunately, unless we find the diamonds, we still don't have a strong case against Jenks and the rest of his associates even with Wick's testimony.'

'Surely Andrew must know where they are?'

There was a pause before he said, 'Possibly.'

'He's not still unconscious?' It was impossible to keep the concern from her voice.

'He is still on life support,' he replied gently. 'If there is any news, I will let you know.'

'I'd appreciate that.'

It was stupid to be so upset. She hardly knew the man and he was a criminal working with evil business partners, but that was no reason to wish him dead.

When she climbed wearily into bed ten minutes later, she consoled herself with the thought that at least now, as far as she was concerned, the case was closed. She could dismiss all thought about smugglers or murderers. The rest of her party were safe. There was nothing to worry about any more. Nothing to keep her awake.

Thursday, 3rd May

Sadly, today we must bid farewell to Holland. Driving back through Belgium, we will make a short stop in the medieval town of Bruges, 'Venice of the North', in time for lunch. There will also be an opportunity to buy lace or some mouth-watering, hand-made chocolates for which the town is famous.

At the Eurotunnel terminal in Calais, we say goodbye to our fellow passengers and transfer to the return coaches for home.

Super Sun Executive Travel

Twenty-Nine

Something woke her. She was instantly alert; lifting her head from the pillow; straining to catch the slightest noise. A thump. It sounded as though there was someone moving around in the room next to hers. Andrew's room!

She had to be imagining things. The room was empty. She turned to look at the illuminated figures on her bedside clock – 03.27. Far too early for cleaners. No one would be padding around in there at this time in the morning. She lay back down again. All the keyed up stress and tension of the last week was making her hear things.

Another creak. Louder this time.

Probably the pipe work. She tried to shut out the sounds and drift back to sleep. It was the sneeze that made her start up again. That had not been her imagination. Feeling like some schoolgirl detective, one of Enid Blyton's Famous Five or Secret Seven, she slowly eased herself up the bed and put an ear against the dividing wall.

Those rustlings were definitely not the natural noises of the night; someone was in there. As if in confirmation, there was a sudden scrapping sound. Harsh and rasping. Someone was sliding back the wardrobe door just the other side of the thin wall between them. Or closing it. Perhaps it was the noise of it being opened that had roused her from sleep in the first place.

Footsteps – then the familiar click of the heavy bedroom door.

She threw back the covers, tiptoed to her own door, and looked out.

Nothing. No sign of anyone in either direction. All was still and silent. In those ten short seconds, the trespasser had disappeared.

Seven thirty. He might not thank her for ringing so early, especially if he decided her story was nothing but wild imaginings. She had managed to get on the wrong side of the man at almost every encounter and yesterday, the more she thought about it, she had to admit that her outburst had been far from justified. It had been the sergeant, not Montgomery-Jones, who had subjected Iris to the Gestapo treatment. He was far too proper – too civilized – to slam the phone down on her, but there was every chance the man would give very little credence to anything she had to say.

'Montgomery-Jones.' If he were surprised at a call at such an hour, his voice did not indicate it. And he didn't sound annoyed. Not yet.

As briefly and unemotionally as possible, she related last night's incident.

He was instantly on the alert. 'Do you know if anything has been taken?'

Fiona hesitated. 'I'm not sure. Probably not. But a couple of things have been moved.'

'Such as?'

Rather than answering his question immediately, she asked one of her own. 'When you went through Andrew's things at the hospital, did you take a good look at his camera?'

'We thought his latest photographs might give us a lead but there was something wrong with the camera. It was probably damaged during the attack.'

'You didn't check the batteries?'

'The catch was jammed. I took out the memory card to check it over but it was blank. I assumed he had recently put in a new one. What did you mean when you said something had been returned?'

Fiona was hesitant. 'Just an idea I had. I could be way off beam.'

There was a long pause at the other end. 'I am coming over. I will be there in half an hour.'

The sense of relief that he hadn't dismissed her story as an hysterical overreaction, was quickly replaced by a growing apprehension. She hadn't expected him to rush straight over especially as she had no solid evidence of any intruder to offer. He would be none too pleased if his journey turned out to be a wild goose chase.

So who could the intruder be? With Simon in custody and Andrew still in hospital who else would even know about the diamonds? At least she had some time to mull over a few more ideas before he arrived. And on the bright side, last night's little escapade had considerably narrowed down the number of suspects.

Fiona went into the restaurant. Not that she was particularly interested in food – she was too much on the qui vive to think about eating – but there were a few questions she needed to ask before Montgomery-Jones arrived.

She glanced around the room. It was surprisingly busy for so early in the morning but perhaps folk were planning on a last look round the city before the coach left. The Smiths and the Dobsons were over by the window, the Kapinskis by themselves, no doubt jabbering away in their native Polish, and the Shuttleworths were sitting with the Collinses. There were several people helping themselves at the buffet including Eileen Finch who was investigating the contents of the hot trays. The last thing Fiona fancied was a fried breakfast; perhaps she could get away with half a spoonful of scrabbled egg on a piece of toast.

'Good morning.'

'Oh hello, Fiona.' Eileen turned to her and frowned.

'Problem?'

'No, no.' Eileen smiled. 'It was just seeing you in your Super Sun uniform underlines the fact that we're heading home today.' She gave a rueful grimace.

'I hope that means you've enjoyed your holiday.'

Armed with their plates, they made their way over to an empty table in the corner.

'Very much so. The week has simply flown by. I was hoping to get more time to try out my Dutch. The only real chance I had was in Volendam when I went exploring on my own. That was why I was late back to the coach.'

'But I thought this was your first visit to Holland?'

'That's right.'

'But you speak Dutch?'

'Good heavens no! Whenever I go to a new country, I try to get a basic grasp of the language before I come. Enough to get by – ordering a meal, asking directions, that sort of thing – but the opportunities to practice have been few and far between. I only managed to sneak away then because Andrew came over to join us in one of the cafés. Nesta was so taken with him that I thought she'd like him all to herself for half an hour.'

Fiona smiled. Did she really believe Eileen's story?

'Then yesterday when we went our separate ways, all the people wandering around Amsterdam seemed to be foreign tourists. Still, it's a good excuse to come back another time, but that will probably be under my own steam.'

'So you've had your fill of coach holidays?'

'It's not my usual sort of thing I admit. A last minute decision. After the term I've had, one member of my department off for months with stress and an Ofsted inspection to cap it off, I needed to get away. And, despite my initial reservations, it has worked out well. At one stage, after some of the snide comments from the staff back at the college, I confess I did begin to have second thoughts. But, as I say, it's been great.'

It was difficult to imagine Eileen being concerned about what other people thought. 'I'm glad you didn't change your mind. So what did they have against coach tours?'

'You know the sort of thing. Must be feeling my age to choose a holiday designed for the Blue Rinse Brigade and did I really want to spend my evenings playing bingo with the wrinklies?'

Fiona smiled. 'Not quite the Super Sun style. So you've never done anything like this before?'

'As Head of Languages, for my sins, as well as the German A' level students, I'm expected to bring the Year 9s over for their exchange visits every summer so believe me I get my fill of cramped, stuffy coach journeys. I fancied seeing the bulb fields and a taster of the rest of the country without the hassle of having to sort out all the arrangements for myself. But I was determined to do it in style on a luxury coach with proper air conditioning and staying in decent four star hotels.'

'And have you managed to get some good photographs?'

'I can't really tell until I get them back home and look at them properly, but I hope so. Far more of the picture post card variety than I usually take.'

'Oh?' Fiona raised an eyebrow.

'I'm more into the moody shots – scruffy streets, dingy doorways. Playing with light and shade and what have you. Something different for competitions rather than the chocolate box, run-of-the-mill stuff. Obviously not the sort of thing that would interest most people which is why I don't generally show them around.'

That explained a lot. Her reaction to Edward's request for copies of her pictures plus her reluctance to show even Nesta.

A shadow fell across the table. 'Is there any news this morning?'

Yvonne was there at Fiona's elbow. She set down a bowl of cereal in the place next to Fiona and pulled out a chair. Fiona glanced up and met the apologetic gaze of Gerald who had followed reluctantly in her wake.

'I have just rung the hospital and they say Andrew spent a comfortable night.'

What the ward sister had actually said was that there was no change in his condition and he was still unconscious, but she had given up trying not to tell an out-and-out lie. It was too much like hard work constantly finding the words which implied things were better than they were without revealing information which might hamper the investigation.

'That's a relief.'

Before Yvonne could park herself down beside them, Gerald interrupted. 'Really Yvonne! You can't just sit yourself down uninvited.'

'No please. It's not a problem. Do join us both of you.' What else could she say?

'You see?' Yvonne turned on her shamefaced husband. 'Fiona knows that it's only because I'm concerned about Andrew.' She spun back to Fiona. 'And of course there's Simon?

228

What about him? Has he turned up? His poor wife must be in a dreadful state. Have you seen Iris this morning?'

'Not yet. I thought it best not to disturb her too early.'

If she was honest, after last's night's excitement, Iris had not exactly been on the top of her list of priorities, she thought guiltily.

'One way and another, this whole trip has been a series of disasters hasn't it?' Yvonne said with relish. 'First Tim Brooke running out on his wife, then poor Andrew's accident and now Simon going missing. And of course, there was that poor man who was taken ill at the ferry terminal and couldn't even join us. You know I had a premonition as soon as we got on the coach that there were going to be problems. I have a sixth sense about these things don't I, Gerald?' Her poor husband looked nonplussed. 'Take Gloria Walker. She's on the committee of our Ladies Fellowship Group...'

As Yvonne began to elaborate on examples of what she called her natural empathy, Fiona glanced across at Eileen who was having great difficulty in keeping a straight face. Gerald, on the other hand, looked as though he would willingly have the ground open up and swallow him.

'How's the scrambled egg this morning?' Yvonne's sudden change of subject brought Fiona's concentration sharply back to the conversation. 'It was a little watery I thought yesterday. Perhaps I'd be better off with a fried egg.'

Waiting until Yvonne and Gerald were out of earshot at the buffet table, Eileen exploded in a fit of giggles. 'That woman takes the biscuit. How do you stop yourself telling the nosey old biddy to mind her own business? I have to hand it to you, Fiona. You need the patience of a saint for your job. I wouldn't last ten minutes having to be mega polite to everyone all the time even when they're being a real pain.'

'Don't start giving me a halo. Apart from anything else, it would play havoc with my hairdo. Besides, I'd have thought you needed a great deal of patience to be a teacher.'

'That's different. At least you have some sort of control.'

'Aah, but I have the advantage of knowing that once we reach Calais and change back to the feeder coaches, my job's done. At six o'clock this evening I shall be saying goodbye to Yvonne for good. Although you didn't hear me say that.'

Eileen chuckled. 'Indeed not. And I bet there are one or two others you won't be sorry to see the back of either. I know I won't.'

'Such as?'

'Edward "Victor Meldrew" Collins for a start.'

'He can be difficult at times and for one horrible moment, when his camera went into the drink, I thought he was about to hit Joyce. It was a good job you were there to stop him. Did you see what really happened?'

'No. It was all over so quickly.' Eileen gave a mischievous grin. 'Mind you, the way the man behaves, it wouldn't surprise me if someone did give it a shove just like he said?'

Playing along as though it was all a game, Fiona asked, 'So who else was there? Who could have done the deed?'

'Unless you are going to accuse one of the old ladies, I think Nesta and I were the only ones close enough. Simon and his wife were around at one point but I think they'd just moved on. Now there's another one I won't miss in a hurry. Mind you, I must be hard to please because, just between the two of us, I shan't be sorry to say goodbye to almost all of them.'

'Even Nesta?'

Eileen turned sharply to look at Fiona and there was an edge to her voice as she asked, 'What makes you say that?'

'I have noticed you've been doing a lot less together these last few days.'

There was a short pause. 'She has become rather clingy to be honest. Don't get me wrong; Nesta is a nice person, but it's hard work finding things to say after a few days when you have such different interests and opinions. We're chalk and cheese when it comes to politics. And our tastes in art and literature, if it comes to that. Nesta can get a bit earnest about her passions as you know and, to be perfectly frank, there are only so many times I can put up with her jumping up on her soapbox and banging on about the need for conservation and the exploitation of natural resources.'

Before Fiona could press her further, the Lees arrived back with fully laden plates. Damn. Just as she was beginning to get somewhere.

'My goodness,' joked Eileen eying the mountains of food. 'You two eating for England?'

'Well you never know when we'll get another chance to find somewhere. I know there's a stop in Bruges, but going back through the tunnel, it's not like the ferry where you can buy a proper meal.'

Fiona glanced at her watch. 'Good heavens! Where does the time go? If you'll forgive me folks, I must get on. I've still got Andrew's things to see to and I'd like to look in on Iris.'

No point in waiting. She could hardly continue probing with the others listening in. In any case, Fiona consoled herself as she got up from the table, she'd already learnt what she really wanted to know. Not that she had the solution to the mystery but things were definitely beginning to fall into place.

Thirty

Peter Montgomery-Jones was walking through the glass entrance doors as Fiona came out of the restaurant.

'That was well timed,' she said as they shook hands. 'I still have the pass key so we can go straight up to Andrew's room.'

At the door, she paused before inserting the card key into its slot. 'I wonder how he got in. Presumably a smuggler wouldn't have much difficulty picking an old fashioned lock but a set of skeleton keys wouldn't be much use for these electronic types.'

'There must be a great many pass keys around. Perhaps he stole one from a cleaner or tried the old sliding a credit card down the gap trick.'

Montgomery-Jones stood in the centre of the small room and slowly looked around scanning every surface. 'Superficially at least, everything looks exactly as we left it yesterday evening. So what is it that you think is missing?'

'I'm not certain that they are. When I brought Andrew's things back from the hospital I didn't exactly take an inventory. There may have been papers but I didn't go through them. The safe is still locked. I imagine our burglar would have a problem getting in without the combination. Presumably you can check that.'

Montgomery-Jones walked over to wardrobe alongside the bed, pushed back the heavy sliding door to reveal the room safe. Removing a pencil from his pocket, he proceeded to use the end to tap in a number on the keypad.

'His passport and a few Euros. The same as yesterday. It would appear that nothing has been touched. So why break in? You said something had been moved?'

Fiona walked over to join Montgomery-Jones at the wardrobe and pointed to the camera sitting on a high shelf above the safe.

'I put there last night but it's not as I left it.'

'Are you sure?'

'Oh yes. The strap was on the other side. I remember distinctly because it fell down as I lifted up the camera and, being left-handed, I flicked it over that way. And I put it much further back, as far as I could reach and, as you can see, it's virtually perched on the edge of the shelf. But I haven't touched it today, in case of fingerprints. Not that our burglar is likely to be foolish enough to leave them on the outside but you might like to take a look at the batteries.'

A puzzled frown furrowed his forehead.

'She gave a rueful laugh. 'If you switch the camera on now, I think you'll find it will work.'

Montgomery-Jones stared at her for a moment or two then picked up his brief case, laid it on the bed beside Fiona and took out a pair of latex gloves. He walked back to the wardrobe and carefully lifted down the camera and switched it on. Even from where she was now sitting, Fiona could see the flickering red light.

'It's working!' He shook his head and turned to Fiona.

He turned it upside down. 'This catch has been forced. There is a gouge across it that certainly was not there when I looked at it yesterday.

'I didn't do it.'

He walked over to join her then slipped open the flap and four AA batteries fell onto the bed.

'Bingo,' she said with a smile. 'I thought that's where they might be.'

He looked at her quizzically.

'Last night those batteries were sitting on this bedside table, but they weren't here this morning.'

'What am I missing? No one breaks into a room to replace batteries in a camera.'

'Isn't the significant question, why weren't they in the camera in the first place?'

His eyes narrowed in concentration, then realization dawned. 'You think it was because Killigan took them out so as to hide the diamonds inside the camera.'

'He could well have done. And then glued it shut just in case he was searched at customs. He could claim that he dropped it and the camera was damaged which is exactly what you thought at the hospital.'

'That certainly makes sense. But how would our burglar know that? Assuming Wick was telling the truth, which I appreciate could well be wide of the mark, Killigan refused to tell Wick where the diamonds were hidden. In which case he would hardly have been likely to tell some mystery third man.'

'Perhaps he worked it out the same way I did. There had to be a reason why Andrew made such a fuss when Edward Collins asked to see his pictures. It was quite unlike him to go way over the top like that and I suspect it was because he didn't want Edward to know that he hadn't taken any photos all day because his camera wasn't working.'

'Because by then, Killigan had already hidden the diamonds in the camera.'

'Exactly. Our mystery man's problem was getting hold of the camera. If he hadn't tried to be so clever and left the batteries where they were, I would never have made the connection.'

Fiona couldn't stop herself from glancing into the briefcase beside her as Montgomery-Jones flipped back the lid. Not exactly what you'd expect to find in a case belonging to someone in a three-piece Savile Row suit, but, as she was now well aware, despite all appearances, Montgomery-Jones was no career diplomat. But then no one on this trip was turning out to be quite what they seemed, she thought ruefully. From the assortment of boxes, packets, clear plastic pouches and canisters, he pulled out what she assumed from watching television police dramas was an evidence bag into which he dropped each battery. The camera then received the same careful treatment before he pulled off the gloves and stuffed them in his pocket.

Only when he'd closed the lid, did he give her his attention again. 'Next question. Who is our mystery man? Can we pool ideas? After your discussion with Jane, we doubled checked Major Rawlings and Edward Collins, but we have discovered nothing to incriminate either of them.'

'I think we can eliminate those two anyway. They're both on the floor below. As are the Dobsons, the Smiths, the Shuttleworths and the Oppenheimers. I checked all the room numbers with reception this morning. Whoever broke into the room had disappeared before I looked out. There wasn't time for him to walk the length of the corridor; I would have spotted him. And anyway I heard another door close just before I pulled mine open. He had to be in a room on this floor.'

'There is a fire escape at the far end of the corridor? Could it have been that?'

'Definitely not. It's the sort that makes an almighty clang when you push the bar to open it.'

He appeared to accept her judgement and took a folded sheet of paper from an inside jacket pocket. There was no table in the room, only a small shelf area under the mirror dominated by an oversized television, so he spread the copy of passenger list she'd given him in The Hague on the top of his briefcase. Removing his pen, he put a line through the names she had just given him.

'Which leaves us with these. It might help to draw up a room plan.' He turned the paper over and held out his pen to Fiona.

'There are twelve rooms altogether; seven singles on this side and five doubles on the other.' Fiona sketched them out as she spoke. 'This is Andrew's room, 317, next to mine roughly half way down the corridor opposite the Lees.'

'So who has the room next to Killigan?'

Fiona pulled out the room list she'd collected from reception before breakfast. 'Winston Taylor.'

'I doubt that it was him.'

Fiona smiled. She enjoyed working with Winston. The two of them made a good team and it was a relief to know that her colleague was not high on the suspect list.

235

'The driver was the first person we checked out and there has been a man on his tail ever since Sunday.'

As Fiona went through the rest of the names, Montgomery-Jones wrote them down in his precise copperplate in each of the numbered boxes.

'That door shutting for a second time; were you able to tell from which end of the corridor it came?'

'No, but it was much fainter. I did hear footsteps and I'm fairly certain they didn't pass my door, but I couldn't swear to it.'

'Let us assume for the moment that you are right. That would rule out the Kapinskis, the Harveys, plus Mrs Pettigrew and Miss Griffin at the lift end of the corridor. Any thoughts about the rest?'

Fiona sat staring at the room plan. Her nerves were on a knife-edge. The tension was getting to her. Dare she voice the ideas that had been running through her head all night? Eventually she asked, 'Is there any way you can find out just how ill Iris really is?'

'I would think so. Why?' When he got no answer, he went on, 'Surely you are not telling me that you suspect Iris?'

Out of the corner of her eye, Fiona caught the look he gave her, half surprise and half amusement.

'I know,' she said crossly. 'Perhaps I did go over the top a bit yesterday, but at the time I felt both you and Sergeant Viljoen were far too hard on her. Since then, being with Iris last night and after your phone call, I've had a chance to think and a couple of things just don't add up. Before he gave her the sedative, the doctor asked if she'd been prescribed any other medication and she mentioned tamoxifen. That's the standard National Health medication following a mastectomy which means she wasn't on one of the new expensive drugs which Simon would need to have to pay for privately.'

He gave a slight shrug of his shoulders. 'I will have to take your word for that.'

'I have a friend,' she said dismissively. 'At my age you get to know several women who've had breast cancer. For someone who is supposed to be as ill as Simon claims, she seems remarkably fit to me. She's always at the front when out walking with the group and when we climbed all those steps the other day, not only was she one of the few not to have to rest half way up, she wasn't even breathless at the top.'

'I need to get hold of her medical records.' He took out his mobile and put through a call.

When he'd finished, Fiona continued, 'Both Simon and Iris may have painted this picture of the utterly devoted couple, but I'm beginning to have my doubts.'

Montgomery-Jones looked surprised then shook his head. 'Wick would only to testify in exchange for a deal to look after his wife.'

'I suppose they really are married?' It was more a thinking out loud than a real question.

'Oh yes. After the incident with Killigan, every record was pulled and checks made on his home and background.

'So why, on their wedding anniversary of all days, weren't they together yesterday afternoon instead of going their separate ways? Does that sound logical to you? If their marriage really meant so much wouldn't Simon have been prepared to indulge her wishes, or she his?'

'The obvious answer is that he had a meeting with Killigan that he did not want her to know about?'

'That's possible I suppose, but whatever Simon claims to feel about her, Iris has no qualms about leaving him behind. If she were really so devoted, so much in love with him, wouldn't she have protested his innocence? She was worried enough when he didn't come back for dinner, that much I will concede, but once you started those interviews, never once did she ask what was going to happen to him. Doesn't that strike you as odd?'

'Perhaps she was just frightened for herself. People react to shock in different ways.'

Fiona was not so sure. 'Without a confession, do you have enough evidence to prove Simon murdered Tim and Henry Unsworth?'

Montgomery-Jones sighed. 'Although we are sure he is responsible, we have nothing to connect Wick with Unsworth's death. Brooke's possibly. It depends on whether the PPS consider the fingerprint evidence is strong enough to stand up in court.'

'You said that Simon confessed to the smuggling, but is there any way that he could get off on some kind of technicality? You haven't found the diamonds so all you have is the DVDs. What if he were to plead that he thought he was buying ordinary movies and didn't know that they contained pornography until after the handover?'

'These things are always a possibility.'

'What if the reason Simon made that deal with you, were so that Iris could go back home with his share? Which would explain why Iris didn't make a fuss and refuse to leave him.'

Montgomery-Jones didn't look convinced. 'Are you saying he was deliberately misleading us?'

'What if Simon knew where the diamonds were all along and told Iris? He wanted to make sure that she remained free so that she could collect them and complete the job,' Fiona said excitedly. 'She is our mystery third man!'

Before he could reply, Fiona's phone rang.

'Sorry about this,' she said before giving all her attention to her caller. 'No... I'll try her room straight away.' She snapped off the mobile then turned to Montgomery-Jones, alarm written on her face. 'That was Winston. He said that Iris hasn't put her case out. He's rung her room but there's no answer.

Montgomery-Jones swore softly under his breath as they both leapt to their feet and rushed down the corridor to the end room. The Do-Not-Disturb notice hung from the handle. Fiona hammered on the door. 'Iris, Iris.'

There was no answer. Fiona's fingers fumbled with the passkey. Stubbornly the light flashed red three times before Montgomery-Jones took the card from her and calmly slid it in correctly. In four long strides, he covered the passageway alongside the en suite and stopped looking into the main part of the room. Beyond his tall frame, Fiona could see little except the assortment of clutter on the dressing table facing the bed. If she'd made a quick exit in the night, why hadn't she taken her things with her? Fearful of what she mind find Fiona took a tentative step forward.

Iris lay on her back on the far side of the bed, still in her night things, her eyes half closed staring up at the ceiling. Montgomery-Jones leant across the width of the double bed and reached for her wrist lying on the pillow. Then he put his fingers to the side of the neck. He turned to Fiona and shook his head.

'She is cold already. She has been dead some time.'

Fiona walked round the end of the bed taking in the empty tablet bottle lying in the palm of the hand stretched over the covers.

'How could I have got it so badly wrong?' Tears began to flow down Fiona's cheeks. 'She must have been beside herself with grief.'

Fiona sank down on the bed beside the dead woman and reached to pick up the bottle.

'No!' Montgomery-Jones launched himself across the divide between them and seized her wrist. When she turned startled eyes upon him, he said softly. 'Things may not be what they appear to be. There is something not quite right about all this.'

He let go, pushed himself upright and pulled out his mobile.

'I want a forensic team to the Black Tulip hotel, Room 322, straightaway.'

The rest of the barked order went over her head. As she waited for him to finish, she got to her feet again holding her forearm to her chest looking pensive.

'I apologize. Did I hurt you?'

'Not at all. It reminded me of something that was all.' This was no time to puzzle over trivial things. There were far more important things to sort out. 'You think Iris was murdered?'

'Let us say that I have yet to be convinced that she took her own life. Where did she get the pills for a start? Given the circumstances and the state she was in, the doctor would not have left her with enough medication to do this.' He glanced at the pillow on the floor by the bed. 'I suspect that she may have been smothered.'

'But why?'

'That is exactly what we need to work out. You were here last night. Did you leave before or after the doctor?'

'Almost immediately after. Iris lay down when he went, I said goodnight and switched off the light. It must have been around nine thirty, perhaps a quarter to ten.'

'Is there anything different about the room?'

Fiona looked around. 'To be honest, I didn't really take a lot of notice.'

He pulled the latex gloves from his pocket and slipped them back on. Moving over to the dressing table, he opened both drawers then went across to the wardrobe and slid the door aside. 'Either the Wicks were a very untidy couple or someone has been rummaging through their things.'

'Everyone knew Iris had been given a sedative, I mentioned it when I went back down, so our intruder probably banked on her staying asleep. Perhaps she woke up while he was still searching the room.'

'He tried to cover up as best he could. He only needed a few hours. There was every chance that her death would be regarded as a suicide and by the time the autopsy had been conducted, the coach could well have left the country.'

'So presumably when he found nothing here, he realized Andrew must have the diamonds. Or did he?' She was hesitant. Would Montgomery-Jones think her idea too far fetched? 'Jane said that the smugglers were supposed to be taking back a big haul this time. I don't know much about diamonds and their value, but four AA batteries don't take up that much space. What if Simon were lying and he did have half of the diamonds.'

'But where could he have hidden them? The room was thoroughly searched and Wick had nothing on him.'

'Did you search Iris?'

'The policewoman would have checked her handbag and her pockets.'

Fiona looked around the room. She got to her feet and walked over to a mauve fabric-covered box lying on top of the dressing table.

She put out a hand but before she could unzip it, his voice rang out, 'Stop!'

He was by her side in an instant. She stared at him apprehensively.

'Sorry about that but a crime has been committed. We do need to preserve the scene. Besides the whole room was thoroughly searched yesterday.'

'Maybe. But the box would have been empty then.'

'I beg your pardon.'

She looked up at him with a smug grin. 'Open it.'

'A cosmetics bag?'

She shook her head. 'It's not for make-up.'

He stared at her for a moment before reluctantly un-zipping the lid. 'What on earth...?' He lifted the fabric-covered shape from its foam bed.

'It's a breast prosthesis. Iris would have been wearing it at the time the room was searched. Take off the cover.'

He slipped off the soft cotton envelop and cradled the pink pliable form on his gloved palm, a look of intense discomfort on his face that almost made her laugh out loud.

'Turn it over,' she urged.

Gingerly he did so and revealed a small strip of tape in the centre of the flat back. 'Good heavens,' he muttered as he pulled it off revealing a deep inch long slit. He slid a finger in the cavity. 'This has definitely been cut deliberately and a hollow excavated deep inside. Are you sure you were not a smuggler in an earlier life?' he said with a smile.

In spite of herself, Fiona could not resist a smirk of satisfaction at the rare, if somewhat backhanded, compliment.

'However,' he said as he put it back in its box, all trace of humour now gone from his voice. 'We still have a killer on the loose. 'Unless he or she is found in the next couple of hours I am very much afraid that your party will be going nowhere.'

Fiona's spirits came crashing down to earth. Would this nightmare never end? Montgomery-Jones was on his mobile again issuing orders, as he paced back and forth along the passageway. She sank down into the armchair in the corner by the window. Nine o'clock in the morning and she was already exhausted. She dropped her head into her hands, closed her eyes and gently massaged her temples.

The phone calls seemed to be going on forever. Eventually there was silence and he was standing before her.

'My men are already in the hotel and there will be more arriving soon. I am not happy with the idea of leaving you and your party, but it is imperative that I speak to Wick myself and it is probably best if I break the news about his wife to him personally.' He was interrupted by a sharp rap at the door. 'That will be them now. Your fingerprints will have to be taken.'

He moved swiftly to the door and stood back to allow two men clad in white paper suits and carrying large incident holdalls into the room.

'Shall we leave them to it?' Polite though it was, it was an order, not a request.

As she stepped outside, Fiona was surprised to see that the end section of the corridor, from Iris's room across to the now open fire escape door opposite, was partitioned off by large concertina screens. A woman dressed as a chambermaid, who was obviously anything but, was waiting for them. Checking through the narrow gap by the far wall that the corridor was empty, she eased back the end of the screen and led Montgomery-Jones and Fiona through before taking up a position by a trolley laden with sheets and towels and trays of small packets of soap and individual shampoo bottles. How long she would have to stand on guard making sure that no nosy guests tried to peep through was anyone's guess.

Montgomery-Jones turned to Fiona and put a reassuring hand on her shoulder. 'I will be back as soon as I can.'

'What do you want me to tell the rest of the party?'

'Nothing.'

'They are bound to ask about Iris.'

'True. Tell them she has been taken ill. As far as they are all concerned, the coach will be leaving as arranged. It is essential that everything continue as normal. And, Mrs Mason,' steely-grey eyes looked down uncompromisingly into hers and he finished emphasising each word, 'your sole responsibility is to keep your passengers happy. Leave the rest to us.'

The impersonal, bureaucratic manner was back. There was a job to be done. He had reached the end of the corridor and turned the corner before she had covered half the distance.

Thirty-One

Montgomery-Jones's warning to carry on as though nothing had happened was all well and good but the knowledge that they still had a smuggler in their midst who would clearly stop at nothing was a chilling thought and hardly one she was going to forget about in a hurry.

Both she and Montgomery-Jones had assumed that the man had broken into Wick's room first, but what if it were the other way round. If that were so, then the door she heard closing was someone going into to the end room, not returning their own. Which meant it could be any of the passengers. The culprit didn't even have to be on this floor let alone in this section.

Less than half an hour ago, she had been convinced that they'd narrowed the list of suspects down to a mere handful. Now it had shot up again and the whole party was back in the frame. Even if that were now the case, she told herself firmly, it really wasn't her problem. Not any more. Any time now and the hotel would be flooded with even more police and security people. Leave it all to them.

It was only after her fingerprints had been taken that another thought struck her. Assuming Andrew's room had been searched first, if she had done something there and then when she heard someone in there, Iris might never have been murdered. It was little consolation to tell herself she could hardly have started banging on doors at that time in the morning to find the intruder.

The next few hours were going to be far too busy to waste in pointless recrimination, she told herself firmly. Or in futile speculation, come to that. She had more pressing matters to attend to. For a start, she still hadn't spoken to Winston. It must be a good twenty minutes since his call. Should she tell him that in all probability they would not be leaving on time? Heaven only knew when they would be allowed to go. Not until the killer was caught presumably. Hours possibly, or even days?

Down in the foyer, a dozen or so cases with bright yellow Super Sun labels were still lined up by the entrance doors, but there was no sign of Winston. Presumably he was in the parking area at the rear of the hotel already loading up the coach. She could do with a breath of fresh air anyway.

'Hi, Winston.' The bent figure, half-hidden under one of the large flaps, backed out and stood up giving her his usual beaming smile. 'Sorry I've taken so long to get back to you. It was a good job you called me. Poor Iris is in no fit state to travel I'm afraid.'

'Her man still not back then?' Fiona shook her head. 'Poor woman.'

Best to let him think Iris was still waiting for him. She couldn't face long explanations at the moment.

'Did everyone else managed to get their cases out in time?'

He nodded. 'Just loadin' them up now.' He picked up a garish-patterned, fabric grip and squashed it gently into a gap.

That was a relief. At least the killer hadn't made off. But then he probably thought he'd got away with it; no doubt banking on Iris's "suicide" being hushed up so as not to upset the other passengers. As far as he knew, he was in clear and there was no reason to draw attention to himself by disappearing at this stage.

'And you are sure you have everyone's?'

He frowned. 'Check 'em all off myself. And you're the second one to ask me that in as many minutes.'

'Oh?'

'He was pretty insistent too. That Embassy chap. The one we saw before. He's left now. You know he was in the hotel?'

'Yes. I've just been speaking to him.'

'Get around, don't he?'

'Umm. Did he say anything else?'

Winston pulled a face. 'He tell me they brought out some new regulation about road worthiness and vehicle safety.

245

Doing some kind of random spot checks or something. I tell him we got all the certificates but the authorities say our coach got to be inspected. Someone coming in a quarter of hour to take it away for testing and do a thorough engine check. Be back in time for when we leave he say, but to load all the luggage now and save time later.'

'That's not a problem is it?' she said brightly.

'I just polished her up and cleaned all the windows so there'd better not be a mark on her when she gets back. You know what I'm sayin' ?' It was the first time she'd heard the placid Winston sound even vaguely bothered.

'You're obviously busy so don't let me hold you up. I'll leave you to finish and go and see if any of the passengers need my help. Someone is bound to have a problem of some kind.'

'I think you find most of them have gone for a last look round the town,' he said disappearing back under one of the luggage flaps with two very large hard shell suitcases.

Montgomery-Jones had been busy. That was one way of making sure every piece of luggage was thoroughly searched. No doubt, Winston would be even more unhappy if he knew that his coach, his pride and joy, was about be taken apart. Nothing would be left to chance.

Winston's prediction proved to be accurate. There was no one lingering in the foyer waiting to pounce. She glanced into the restaurant. Those who had decided not to bother with last minute shopping might well be having a late breakfast. Though there were still a few occupants dotted around the sizable room, the area set aside for the Super Sun party was empty and most of the tables had already been cleared. Even the lounge area was deserted, although it was still a little early for coffee.

She could go up to her room, pack her last few bits and bobs and get on with some of the final paperwork. Perhaps she ought to let them know on the reception desk where she would be just in case one of the group wanted to get hold of her.

The receptionist was still busy with a couple of the hotel's other patrons who were checking out and had a query over some item on their bill. Not wishing to give the impression she was listening in, Fiona wandered back into the main part of the foyer and perched on the edge of the padded circular bench that ran around the outside of the large display of assorted greenery that formed the central feature.

She was still staring vacantly out of the entrance doors lost in thought when a taxi drew up outside. Fiona paid it little attention until she realized that the elderly lady struggling to keep hold of a very large plant and find her purse at the same time was Vera Ellis. Fiona got her feet, pushed through the heavy plate-glass doors and hurried down the steps.

'Let me hold that for you.'

'Oh please, if you would, dear. Having managed to get this far, I'd hate it to get damaged now.'

Fiona took the cellophane wrapped orchid and stood back giving Vera room to sort herself out.

'It really is beautiful,' said Fiona as the taxi drew away.

'Isn't it lovely? Rather bigger than I'd intended, but that deep mauvey-pink is so unusual. I wanted to get myself one when we were in Keukenhof but I wasn't sure how I'd get it home. Then when I saw that other people had managed, I really regretted not getting one. I was talking with Joyce last night about it and when she said she and her husband were getting a taxi to the Flower Market first thing and offered me a lift, I couldn't refuse. She and Edward are still shopping of course, but this is all I wanted so I came straight back.'

'Let me help you upstairs with it.'

'I'm sure I'll be able to manage.'

'I'm going up to my room now anyway, and it will give you a free hand to unlock your door.'

Thirty-Two

Once Andrew's things had been packed and his case taken into storage until needed, Fiona was able to hide away in her room sorting out the paperwork and ticking off the final checklists. It was taking far longer than it should because her concentration was elsewhere and she found herself rereading the same instructions in the company guidelines several times over.

Pushing the last sheet of paper back into her folder, she glanced at her watch. Half ten. Time to go downstairs and see if the party had begun to gather. She would just have to hope and pray that they did not start asking awkward questions. It would help if the coach were back, but somehow she doubted that, despite all Peter Montgomery-Jones's promises to Winston.

Outside in the corridor, she was surprised to see the partitions screening off Iris's room had been removed. There was no sign either of the chambermaid who had been going back and forth to her trolley when Fiona had come up with Vera. The door to Room 322 was now slightly ajar. Sheer curiosity got the better of her. She listened at the door, but there was no sound from inside. Gingerly she pushed it open further. She could see nothing from the doorway and guilty tiptoed along the passageway. The room was empty, the bed had been stripped and there was no sign of Iris's belongings. It looked like any other vacated hotel room. Totally depersonalized. Ready for the next visitor. It was as though Iris had never been there. The forensic team had worked fast to process the scene in so short a time. It would take a great deal longer than that to wipe the memory from Fiona's mind.

She stood by the bed picturing the scene only a few hours ago. Who could have done such a dreadful thing? She blinked back the tears. This wasn't accomplishing anything. Time to go.

Fiona turned and walked slowly back the way she'd come. She was so preoccupied with her own thoughts that she didn't notice a door opening and someone backing out struggling with hand luggage. She'd almost careered into them before she managed to stop herself, putting out her hands to catch hold of the woman by the upper arms.

'Vera! I'm so sorry. Are you all right?'

The tiny figure spun round knocking Fiona completely off balance. With a grunt of pain and surprise, Fiona started to fall. A hand shot out to steady her but not before she'd crashed heavily against the wall.

'Oh dear! I think it should be me asking you that, dear. You gave me such a fright.'

Fiona took a few moments as much to collect her thoughts as to rub her throbbing knee.

'Not to worry. It'll be fine.' She hobbled forward a couple of steps clenching her teeth against the pain.

'Obviously not. Come and sit down for a moment.' Taking Fiona by the arm, Vera led her into her room. 'You make yourself comfortably on the bed while I get my bags.'

As Vera retrieved the bags she'd dropped in the corridor, Fiona's mind was still working overtime. The firm grip that Vera had used to stop Fiona crashing to the ground had retrieved the illusive memory she'd tried to recall at Iris's bedside.

Fiona looked around the almost empty room. The orchid stood on the floor by the wardrobe. Its protective cellophane wrapping was badly crumpled and flakes of coarse, wood chip fibre had fallen down the sides of the brimming pot forming a dark ring at its base. She was still looking at the trail of dark fibre dust marking the pale grey carpet when she became aware that Vera was standing by the door staring at her intently.

'A small accident I'm afraid. I knocked over with my case. I was lucky not to break the stem.'

'Yes of course,' Fiona commented a little too quickly. Mustering a smile, Fiona pushed herself to her feet. 'I'd best be off. I'm feeling much better now. It was just the shock and I do have things to do.'

Vera's usually dreamy eyes were staring at her with steely calculation and the vague expression had become cold and calculating.

'Not just yet, dear.' With amazing speed, Vera advanced to the bed and pushed Fiona back down.

'Is there something wrong?' Best to pretend she had no idea of what was going on.

The silence seemed to last an age, but was probably no more than a few seconds. 'Your knee, dear. I think we ought to put a cold compress on it before it starts to swell. We don't want it giving you problems on that long drive back, now do we?'

'No need, honestly.'

'I insist. I have something in my holdall that will do the trick.'

I bet you have, Fiona thought, and odds on it isn't a bandage. Time for some quick thinking. In the brief moment Vera looked away to find her bag, Fiona slipped her hand in her pocket. Her fingers closed around her mobile. Not that it would be much use. The chances of being able to summon help were absolutely zero.

'Some ice might help,' Fiona said brightly. 'There's a machine at the bottom of the corridor by the lift.' One look at Vera's expression told her that the woman was not going to fall for that. 'Or perhaps a cold flannel?'

Vera remained motionless. They were both playing games and the other knew it; but the pretence had to be maintained while each planned the next step. There was no way Vera would let Fiona walk out of this room. Vera had killed at least once. She would not hesitate to do so again. Fiona realized that the only reprieve she had was while Vera worked out how to get rid of her. Unlike Iris, she was no weak, half-drugged victim although if Vera were responsible for Tim's death then she must have a gun. In which case, staying put was probably Fiona's safest option. Vera could hardly shoot her here. Even if Vera were to disappear straight away, in the next hour or so the chambermaid would be in to clean the room ready for the next guest and the search would be on.

'Let me help you to the bathroom.'

Fiona pushed herself to her feet and took a tentative step before groaning loudly and sinking back onto the bed. 'Perhaps you could fetch it for me?'

After a moment or two, Vera decided to go along with the farce. Talking loudly so as to let Vera know she was still sitting on the bed and not attempting to run out of the door – not that she could run anywhere at the moment – Fiona took out her mobile. She had only time to text the single word, HELP, before she heard the tap being turned off and Vera came out of the bathroom.

'That's beginning to feel so much better already.' Fiona tried to keep up the flow of inconsequential banter, not an easy task when her mind was racing on totally different lines. The longer she kept up the pretence, the more chance she had of rescue; but would it be enough? Even if Montgomery-Jones had received her message, he would have no idea where to send his men to come to her aid.

'Perhaps it's time we went down. Everyone will begin to wonder where the two of us have got to.'

Before Vera could reply, Fiona's phone started bleeping. 'I expect that's Winston now.' She pulled her mobile from her pocket, but before she could press the button, Vera had seized it from her.

'I don't think so.' Stepping back swiftly, out of Fiona's reach, Vera switched off the phone and dropped it onto the dressing table. The pretence was over. What now? Fiona had no delusions the woman was dangerous. Best to show no fear. She inched forward ready to stand but Vera produced a small pistol from her shoulder bag which she levelled at Fiona.

'Sit down!' The tiny, frail hunched figure had suddenly become alert and upright. The voice, stronger and much younger. 'A pity you had to see the orchid.'

'That only confirmed my suspicions.'

Vera raised an eyebrow. 'So what gave it away?'

'You drop out of character too often. Frail old ladies don't have a vice-like grip plus the fact that only you or one of the Harvey sisters were near enough to push Edward's camera into the canal.'

Vera chuckled. 'Well done, Miss Clever Clogs.'

'What happened? Did he take a photo that might have given you away?' Keep the woman talking.

Vera shook her head. 'It was that idiot Wick's fault. The diamonds were about to be handed over and he was making the whole thing far too obvious. I had to create a diversion before anyone else spotted it. I knew there must be an under-cover agent in the party but I have to admit you were good. I only realized it was you when I saw the look on your face in the corridor just now.'

Now it was Fiona's turn to laugh. It was probably best not to enlighten her. The longer Vera thought the authorities were on to her the better. Keep stalling.

'Was it really necessary to smother poor Iris?' Fiona's voice sounded indignant with no trace of the fear that gripped every fibre of her being.

There was a bitter laugh. 'So you've worked that out too have you, Miss Clever Clogs? Well, you could say that was your fault. You said she'd been given knockout drops, but she woke up. I didn't have any choice.'

'And what about Tim? What reason did you have to shoot him?'

Vera's lips twisted into a sneer. 'Not down to me that one. Most likely that idiot Wick. Killigan would have had more sense than to bring a gun through customs.'

'You did.'

'I don't take risks. You could say,' her lips twisted in an un-pleasant sneer, 'You were the one who got the gun for me.'

Fiona frowned.

'I'd arranged to collect it on the ferry, but there were too many people about for that to happen; including you playing Miss Goody Twoshoes fussing all over me. Couldn't have someone from the Super Sun lot remembering something or start asking awkward questions, so I had to make alternative arrangements.'

'That's why you left your bag behind. So someone could put it in there when you'd gone without arousing suspicion.'

'Clever girl!' The gun waved menacingly. 'Not that I won't use this if I have to. Time now for a short walk in the direction of the fire escape I think. Up you get.'

'No can do, I'm afraid. I can't walk on this knee and that is definitely down to you.'

'Stop trying to be funny and shift yourself or I'll shoot you here and now.'

Fiona laughed. 'Somehow I don't think the man standing behind you would let you get away with that.'

Vera shook her head. 'That pathetic cliché only works in very old movies.'

'Unless it happens to be true.' Never had Fiona been so grateful to hear the aristocratic baritone.

Vera's hand was seized from behind and yanked upwards. She kicked and screamed abuse, but the conclusion was never in any doubt.

Suddenly the tiny room was filled with people. Montgomery-Jones took Vera's bag from her shoulder and handed it to one of the men. 'You better search the rest of her hand luggage as well.'

'If it's the diamonds you're looking for, I should try the orchid, if I were you,' Fiona said with a smug smile.

The protective cellophane was ripped apart and the exotic plant unceremoniously pulled up and cast aside. Someone brought a towel from the bathroom and laid it on the floor. The pot was upended spilling out its contents. Montgomery-Jones lent down and picked up a plastic bag shaking away the clinging compost.

'Vera Ellis, or should I say, Mavis Jenks, you will be charged with the possession of contraband diamonds and the murder of Iris Wick. Take her away.'

When the two men, a handcuffed Vera between them, had left the room, Peter Montgomery-Jones turned back to Fiona.

But instead of the reassuring smile she was anticipating, his face was hooded with anger.

'What in God's name did you think you were playing at?'

Fiona reeled back from the outburst, her eyes wide.

'You should never have tackled her yourself. You could have got yourself killed, woman! If I had not arrived when I did, your body would now be draped down the stone steps halfway down that fire escape.'

Pointless to explain that she had not been the one to initiate the showdown. He was in no mood to listen. She let him rant on for a minute or two, biting back the temptation to retaliate by demanding to know why she had been kept in the dark. If he knew that Vera Ellis was not who she said she was then he had broken any trust they had built between them.

When the tirade had died down she said, 'Thank you for coming when you did. It was a relief when I saw you come through the door. How did you know where I was?'

'I was about to get into the lift when I received your text message. When you were not in your own room, this was the next logical place.' Looking as weary as she felt, he sank down on the bed next to her. It was a relief not to have him towering over her anymore. 'You should have told me that you suspected Vera.'

'But I didn't, not until ten minutes ago. Then everything fell into place. Up until then, I'd more or less convinced myself that it must be Eileen.'

'Why her?'

'She's intelligent, shrewd and a bit of a dark horse. Unlike the others, she's never volunteered much about herself. After five minutes with most of them, you know all about their children, their previous holidays, all sorts. But not Eileen. I couldn't work out why she was so secretive about her photographs and she would disappear off talking to strangers. But then, when I thought about Andrew's camera, I realised she's too tall.'

'I am not sure that I follow.'

'Because it was perched on the very edge of the shelf, the person who moved it had to be shorter than me and as I'm only 5'3" in my stocking feet, that doesn't leave a lot of options. That set me thinking and then other things began to fall into place. Small, inconsequential things, but they all added up. You remember when you took hold of my arm in Vera's room? It jolted my memory. When I almost bumped into Vera yesterday just after Andrew's accident, she seized my wrist in the same way. There was something odd about that, but I was so busy worrying about her and then Andrew that, at the time, I thought no more about it. For a frail old lady, she has a grip as strong as yours. She was deliberately holding me back. All that wheezing was an attempt to stop me going any further. Perhaps she hoped that I would bring her straight back to the hotel. And why was she going for help when there were already people in the street? Then she told everyone here that she'd been nowhere near when the accident happened after she'd told me that she'd heard the splash and gone to see what it was. I just put it down to her being confused and not wanting to have to answer more questions.'

'When we spoke to her, she told us she arrived at the scene just as Killigan was being lifted from the water. It was quite a difficult interview because we had to keep repeating the questions.'

'That's another thing. For someone who made a great play of being deaf, why didn't she wear a hearing aid? She managed to hear things when she wanted to and I wasn't the only one to notice that. Despite all the noise at the flower auction, she caught the Major's joke from way up at the top of the steps and, if she were where she said she was when Andrew fell into the canal, how come she heard the splash? My guess is that she saw what happened and ran away before she was seen and identified.'

Fiona caught the sceptical look on his face. 'All very tenuous I know, but it was the orchid that was the real clincher. She told me she wished she'd bought one at Keukenhof so why not get it when we were all at the flower market on Tuesday or even yesterday afternoon? And why buy such an enormous one? When I carried it up to her room for her earlier, I noticed that there was a good inch and a half gap between the compost and the top of the pot. Ten minutes ago, when I came back in back in here after bashing my knee, it was brim to the top.'

'That is when you should have left and got in touch with me.'

'Oh I tried to leave, believe me. The last thing on my mind was to deliberately face down a murderer.'

He looked at her shrewdly then his lips parted in a slow half smile. 'I believe you.'

'So what do you know about this Mavis Jenks?' Try as she could, she failed to keep the accusation from her voice.

'Sister of the man behind the British operation. Once Wick had given us the man's name, we began to make enquiries into Jenks's background and they sent over pictures of known associates. It was Jane who picked it up. She double checked with the passport details and rang me when I was on my way here.'

'I thought you said that all the passengers had been checked out.'

'There is a real Vera Ellis. A seventy-five year old living in Wapping. The passport is quite genuine. The photograph is poor but with her hair in the same style the two women are sufficiently alike for Mavis to get away with it.'

'And did Simon know who she was?'

Montgomery-Jones shook his head. 'I doubt it. Apparently Jenks suspected a double cross and it's likely that she came to keep an eye on what was going. I think we can assume that she is the one who sent the anonymous note to Killigan about Wick being dropped.'

'Which is what caused the argument.'

'So it would appear. When I told Wick about Iris, he broke down completely. He maintained his wife was an innocent victim who knew nothing about what he was up to. Not even that he had hidden the diamonds in her prosthesis. He was so distraught about Iris that he was barely coherent, but he was only too willing to get his revenge for her death by giving us every detail of Jenks's operations that he knew. Some of it quite different from the information he gave last night. That is why it took me so long.'

'I presume the rest of us are now free to go back to Britain?' Fiona eased herself forward to the edge of the bed to plant both feet firmly on the ground before standing up.

'Indeed you are, but how is the knee?'

'Much better than I let Vera – Mavis – believe. It hurt like the devil at the time, but actually that compress, apart from saving my life, has done my knee a lot of good as well.'

Fiona took a few tentative steps.

'At least now you can relax. It is well and truly over. A pity it took so long. I am only sorry that your first tour has turned out to be so difficult. Quite a steep learning curve for you.'

Fiona gave a low chuckle. 'If I've learnt anything this week, it's not to take people at face value. Having spent a lifetime spreading the gospel of trusting people, I've turned into a suspicious old biddy convinced that everything anyone says needs to be taken with a very large dose of salt. People turn out to be not quite what they seem.' She looked at him pointedly, but all she got was a wry smile. 'Including me, if I'm honest.'

'Meaning?'

'What have I been doing all week if not playing a role? Trying to kid a coach load of people that I'm an experienced guide who knows Holland like the back of my hand – behaving like some demented comedienne warming up the audience before the real show started – hiding my total sense of inadequacy under a bravado of bonhomie that was about as genuine as a Dutch mountain.'

He gave a low chuckle and said, 'I find that very difficult to believe.'

'It's true!' she protested. 'Or at least it was. After the week I've had, I think I'm going to be bloody good at this job; ready for whatever's thrown at me. The problem is, going back with only half my passengers; I can't see Super Sun Tours having quite the same confidence in my ability.'

'Oh I doubt that. I doubt that very much!' he said laughing. 'But seriously, without your help, we would never have caught the culprits so quickly and a great many more innocent people could well have been harmed and, rest assured, that will be made very clear to your head office.'

'Thank you.'

'If they do decide to part with you or if ever you decide that being a tour manager is proving to be too humdrum for your tastes, remember what I said yesterday, there will always be a place for you on my team.'

Thirty-Three

The last traces of Fiona's euphoria that all her problems were now over quickly dissolved as she made her way to the foyer ready for their departure some five minutes later. She felt a definite knot of apprehension tightening in her stomach as she tried to work out exactly what she was going to say to the remaining members of her party.

Much to Fiona's surprise and relief, they all appeared to accept her story that Simon had been taken ill on his way back to the hotel, and Iris had gone to the hospital to see him and that Vera had elected to go with her. In all the hustle and bustle of getting on the coach and finding room for all the vast proliferation of hand luggage, it was quite likely that many of them had not even noticed their absence in any case.

Before anyone had time to start asking awkward questions, Fiona slipped another DVD into the player. Old episodes of "Open all Hours" wouldn't stop one or two from discussing her story amongst themselves, but it might divert their attention long enough for them to reach Bruges where, with luck, the prospect of looking round the charming little town and yet more food might be sufficient to make them forget about the absentees altogether. At least no one had seen Vera being escorted out to a waiting police car. Presumably, Montgomery-Jones had urged his men to be discreet and she had been bundled down the back stairs and out of the staff entrance.

Fiona baulked at telling even Winston the full story. It was only right that he should know about the smuggling, he knew something was up when he noticed that the cases had been put back in different places after the coach had been returned, but there was no need for him to know about the killings. It was enough that all three smugglers were now in custody. If Winston bore any resentment that she had not told him earlier about Tim and Jane being customs officers, he gave no indication.

Bathed in the full glare of the sunlight streaming in through the window, Fiona was beginning to feel drowsy when the soft bleep of her mobile dragged her back to full consciousness.

'Hi, Mum.'

'Adam?' It was the last person she was expecting.

'Just a quick buzz to check that all went well on your trip.'

'Yes thank you, darling.' What else could she say? 'The bulb fields were spectacular and we saw some wonderful places.'

'Great. I'll admit I wasn't sure you weren't taking on too much at first, but it sounds as though you've got yourself a cushy number there with this new little job of yours. Anyway, I've got some good news. The company is sending me over to England for a week's course and Kristy and I thought we'd make a break of it especially as we can save on my airfare. That's if you don't mind having us.'

'Of course not! It will be wonderful.'

'Are you sure you'll be able to manage. The kids do get a bit boisterous; we were a little worried that they might be too much for you.'

It was tempting to say that after pandering to the whims of a coach load of frequently demanding people, not to mention facing down a cold-blooded killer, one five-year-old and a toddler would be a doddle, but he'd probably think she was getting senile. 'I'm not going to deign to even answer that. I'm not in my dotage yet, young man and don't you forget it.'

He laughed. 'Glad to hear it, Ma. Anyway, it's great to know you enjoyed your holiday. You must tell us all about it when we see you. Bye now. Take care.'

'Bye, darling. Give my love to Kristy and the children.'

He'd already rung off.

She settled back into the seat with a contented sigh. There would be lots to tell them. The glorious blooms at Keukenhof, the magnificent Renaissance tomb of William of Orange in the Nieuwe Kerk in Delft and the canal cruise, but the really exciting stuff was probably best kept to herself. If ever Adam or Martin came to hear about her adventures into the world of crime, they would never let her near a coach again. And there was no way she was ready to give up on her new job. If the resounding cheers she had been given when she'd said goodbye to the last of her passengers at Calais were anything to go by, there was every reason to believe she would make a success of it. Without exception, everyone had ticked the excellent box on the evaluation forms and several people, including Mrs Oppenheimer, had been effusive in their praise about her contribution in the written comments at the bottom of the page. Even Deirdre had given her a hug.

With a sudden pang of guilt, Fiona realized that in all the rollercoaster turmoil of her day, not once had she thought of Bill. After all the upset last evening, she had been exhausted and must have dropped off to sleep as soon as she lay down. Even first thing this morning, she had been so intent on finding out what had been happening in Andrew's room that all thoughts of Bill had been pushed aside. But that had been the reason she'd taken a job in the first place. Bill wouldn't want her to spend every minute of her day reliving past memories of their lives together. She had to pick up the pieces and move on.

A slow smile spread over her face. Bill would have been proud of her today. Not that there hadn't been more than one sticky moment, but she hadn't disgraced herself. Even Peter Montgomery-Jones had seemed to value her contribution. Now there was an enigmatic man if ever there was one. And not only in his personality. Surely customs officers, even senior ones, didn't take charge of crime investigations especially in a foreign country. Now she would never know. The chances of their paths ever crossing again were very remote. A shame really. She would have liked to get to know him better. He had promised to let her know the outcome of the case but that probably meant a formal letter from someone in his department. It would be foolish to expect the man to pick up a phone and speak to her personally.

Montgomery-Jones had been right. In so many ways, this trip had turned out to be something of a major learning experience and she would be the first to admit that she was no longer the woman she had been this time last week. For too many years now she had been somebody's wife, somebody's mother, somebody's carer but there was no way she was going to spend the rest of her days being somebody's widow. Time for Fiona Mason to be her own person. The next trip wouldn't be the same of course. No doubt, it would have its problems, but difficult clients, changed itineraries, bluffing her way through talks on places she had never been to before; she could now take it all in her stride. There was no reason not to accept another assignment. As the coach pulled onto the M25, she drifted off to sleep happily contemplating what interesting places Super Sun Tours would line up for her to tackle next.